CHASING a BRIGHTER BLUE

Gerri Hill

Bella
BOOKS
2015

Bella Books, Inc.
P.O. Box 10543
Tallahassee, FL 32302

First Bella Books Edition 2015

Editor: Medora MacDougall
Cover Designer: Linda Callaghan

ISBN: 9-781-59493-469-8

Other Bella Books by Gerri Hill

Angel Fire
Artist's Dream
At Seventeen
Behind the Pine Curtain
The Cottage
Coyote Sky
Dawn of Change
Devil's Rock
Gulf Breeze
Hell's Highway
Hunter's Way
In the Name of the Father
Keepers of the Cave
The Killing Room
Love Waits
The Midnight Moon
No Strings
One Summer Night
Partners
Pelican's Landing
The Rainbow Cedar
The Scorpion
Sierra City
Snow Falls
Storms
The Target
Weeping Walls

About the Author

Gerri Hill has twenty-eight published works, including the 2014 GCLS winner *The Midnight Moon*, 2011, 2012 and 2013 GCLS winners *Devil's Rock*, *Hell's Highway* and *Snow Falls*, and the 2009 GCLS winner *Partners*, the last book in the popular Hunter Series, as well as the 2013 Lambda finalist *At Seventeen*. Hill's love of nature and of being outdoors usually makes its way into her stories as her characters often find themselves in beautiful natural settings. When she isn't writing, Gerri and her longtime partner, Diane, keep busy at their log cabin in East Texas tending to their two vegetable gardens, orchard and five acres of piney woods. They share their lives with two Australian shepherds and an assortment of furry felines.

CHAPTER ONE

"Isn't Christmas the most wonderful time of the year?"

Shelby Sutton slipped out of her coat and shook the snow from her hair. "Yes, it is. Only I wouldn't have picked it for a wedding," she said as she sat down at the bar. "There's a freakin' blizzard going on."

"It's not a blizzard. They said we won't get much more than an inch or two. Denver's getting slammed though. Aren't you glad we're not still there?"

"Well, there's that," she said dryly. "But it's winter, Steph. It's cold. Not wedding weather."

"Josh and I met at a Christmas party two years ago," her sister reminded her. "And he proposed last Christmas."

"Right. So get married in July like normal people do."

Stephanie stared at her with a quick shake of her head. "You love the snow, Shelby. Quit complaining."

"I love to ski. I don't love to drive in it." Shelby held her hand up, signaling Zach, the bartender. He was there in an instant. One of the perks of the family owning the hotel was getting prompt service. "Gin and tonic," she said. She glanced at Steph. "You?"

"Wine. Red. A merlot is fine. And you should have flown up with us yesterday before the storm hit."

"You know I don't like flying with Dad in that little tin can he calls a plane," she said.

"That's an excuse," Stephanie said. "I know you had a date. What was her name?"

Shelby slowly shook her head as she recalled her dinner date last night. "Jenna. And it was a disaster."

"Blind date again?"

"Yes. I can't understand why Brooke thought we would hit it off. We had nothing in common and struggled most of the night to keep the conversation going." She nodded her thanks at the bartender. "To top it off, she wanted to sleep with me. Can you believe that?"

"They always want to sleep with you. Who could blame her? You're gorgeous. Blond hair and blue eyes, I'm sure you're every lesbian's dream. You're also apparently every *man's* dream. You get hit on more than I do."

"Well, if I'm every lesbian's dream then, why am I still single at thirty?"

"Because you're looking for perfection and you're not going to find it. Besides, you're too suspicious. You think they're only after the family money."

Shelby nodded. "You're right on both counts." She held her glass up in a toast and touched it to Stephanie's wineglass. "To my baby sister. May you and Josh be blissfully happy."

"Thank you. This is going to be a wonderful two weeks. I'm so glad you're sharing it with me."

Shelby poked the lime wedge down with the tiny straw. Yes, nearly two weeks at the family hotel in Estes Park, Colorado. Nearly two weeks of wedding planning, parties and Christmas activities. Stephanie had always loved Christmas, loved the lights and decorations, loved gaudy trees and lots of gifts. Shelby was usually indifferent to the holiday, even today. She rarely bothered to put up a tree. If she wanted to soak in the Christmas spirit, she could always go to Stephanie's house, where every room was adorned with something. It was as if a slew of Christmas elves had invaded the place and redecorated at will.

"So a Christmas wedding and a beach honeymoon. Hardly seems fair to the rest of us who have to stay behind," she said.

"You're not going to Hawaii with us," Stephanie said with a laugh. "You have to stay in Denver and run the office."

"Don't remind me."

It was a late Tuesday afternoon, eleven days before Christmas, and the bar was filling with people and laughter. Shelby recognized one of her cousins whom she hadn't seen in years.

"Is that Holly? You invited *everyone* for the whole two weeks?"

"It was Mother's idea. And not everyone. Just family. Most of them aren't coming until next week though. Even *they* aren't crazy enough to spend two weeks here."

"Mother only wants to show off the hotel and gloat that she married money," she said. "You'd think she'd be over that by now."

"I know. Her excuse is that it'll be a big family Christmas party, even though we hardly ever see our cousins. Oh, and Josh's sister is supposed to come for the whole two weeks too," Stephanie said. "And about her. We need a favor."

"What kind of favor?"

Stephanie leaned closer. "Something's happened and Josh doesn't know what. Her name is Reagan. She's a photojournalist. She's not here in the States much. Most recently in Afghanistan. Before that, I think she spent a whole year in Colombia."

"Who does she work for?"

"I think she freelances. But Josh says she's really talented." Stephanie smiled. "Of course, he could be biased. Anyway, she showed up about two weeks ago, out of the blue."

"Where?"

"At her parents' farm in Nebraska. Her mother called Josh, said Reagan was acting really weird—depressed, reclusive. Josh said she was always very outgoing and friendly, never depressed.

So they wanted him to come there, but we had so much going on with getting ready for the wedding," she said with a wave of her hand. "He called her, but he said she was not herself at all. So something's going on with her."

"And you want me to do what? Babysit?"

"She's a little old for that. She's your age, if not older." Stephanie shrugged. "I've only seen her twice and both times, she was very nice. Pleasant to be around."

"Maybe her boyfriend broke up with her," she said. And wouldn't that be fun—consoling a straight woman.

"I'm fairly certain that's not the case," Stephanie said pointedly. "You both have the same taste in dates, if you know what I mean."

"Oh, great. She's gay?" Shelby pointed her finger at Stephanie. "I swear, if you're trying to set me up with Josh's sister, I'll kill you."

"Of course not. She's not your type, anyway. She's...well, really out."

Shelby frowned. "And I'm not?"

"You don't go out of your way to advertise it. She's kinda... manly. It's very obvious she's a lesbian, unlike you."

"Manly? You mean butch?"

"Whatever you want to call it," she said with a shake of her head. "But can you try to make friends with her? Maybe find out what's going on with her? They're really worried and I don't want anything to spoil the wedding."

Shelby sighed. "Okay. I'll try to make friends with her. But it doesn't sound like we have anything in common."

Stephanie squeezed her arm. "Thank you. I assume she's coming up tomorrow with her parents. They're staying outside of Denver tonight, waiting until the storm passes."

Shelby sighed again. "Okay. Can't wait," she said with a fake smile.

"You're the best." She glanced at her watch. "I need to go meet the florist. You want to come with me? It shouldn't take long."

Shelby shook her head. "I think I'll stay in the bar. Come find me when you're done. We'll have dinner in town somewhere." she offered.

Stephanie stood. "Trying to sneak away from Mother? You know she's already got every meal planned. Why else would she bring in her own chefs?"

"I know. And I hate that."

"Josh hates it too." She bent down and hugged her quickly. "I'll be back."

She nodded when Zach pointed at her empty glass. Two weeks of being pampered by the hotel staff would spoil her by the time she got back to Denver. She and Stephanie had been working for her father ever since they'd finished college. He owned three hotel resorts in Colorado and the corporate office was still in Denver. Lately, her mother had been hinting at moving the operation to Aspen since her father spent so much time there. So far, her father had resisted. For that, Shelby was thankful. Not that she didn't like Aspen—she did. Only she couldn't see herself living there full-time. It was far too pretentious for her taste. If anywhere, here at Estes Park would be her choice. She loved it here. But she knew her mother would never go for that. Estes Park was too tame, too...*normal.*

The massive mirror behind the bar reflected the activity behind her and she watched as a woman approached the bar. She was attractive, her dark hair cut short in a boyish style. As if feeling her watching, the woman glanced at her, their gazes meeting in the mirror. Their eyes held for a long moment, and Shelby was shocked by the profound sadness she saw in the woman's dark eyes. As if trying to chase the sadness away, Shelby offered a slow smile. The woman's handsome face lightened some as she returned the smile. Shelby finally pulled her eyes away, wondering at the haunted look on the stranger's face. To her surprise, the woman walked over.

"Is this chair taken?"

Shelby glanced at it, as well as at the other three empty chairs along the bar. She shook her head. "No."

"Thanks," the woman said as she sat down. She motioned for the bartender. "Scotch on the rocks," she said. She turned to Shelby. "Your eyes are…incredibly blue." She paused only a few seconds. "Your room or mine?"

Shelby stared at her, shocked. "Wow. You just dive right in, don't you? No foreplay?"

The woman's eyes held hers. "Once we're naked, I'll give you so much foreplay you'll be begging me for release." Her voice lowered to a whisper. "Again and again. I promise."

As Shelby stared into her haunted, dark brown eyes, she felt a tremor travel over her body, landing squarely between her thighs. *Oh…wow.*

She cleared her throat before speaking, hoping her voice didn't fail her. "I think you have set the record for the quickest come-on I've ever had," she said.

The woman laughed quickly, showing off even, white teeth, although the smile never reached her eyes. "I doubt that." Her smile faded altogether. "So? How about it?"

Shelby shook her head quickly. "No. I don't pick up strangers in a bar."

The woman nodded as she sipped from her drink. "I don't blame you, I guess. I wouldn't be great company anyway."

Shelby felt oddly disappointed that the woman had given up so quickly. Not that she had any intention of taking her up on her offer, of course. Because she *never* slept with strangers. That thought amused her. She tried to remember the last time she *had* slept with someone. Was it Katherine? God, that had to have been over a year ago.

She looked past the woman, seeing Stephanie returning.

"As usual, Mother had the flower arrangements already set up. I was allowed to pick a few colors." Stephanie turned to the woman, her eyes widening. "Oh, you've already met. Great."

Shelby frowned. "What? Who?"

"Hello, Stephanie."

Stephanie looked between them. "Oh, God. Were you *hitting* on my sister?"

Shelby narrowed her eyes at the woman. "Who are you?"

"This is Josh's sister," Stephanie explained.

The woman arched an eyebrow as she held her hand out. "Reagan Bryant," she said.

Shelby blew out her breath. "Josh's sister," she murmured. She took the offered hand and squeezed it quickly. "Shelby Sutton. Stephanie's sister."

The woman's eyes shadowed even more. "Well, don't I feel like an ass."

Stephanie sat down beside her. "You really were hitting on her?" She laughed. "That's too funny."

Shelby turned and glared at her, causing Stephanie's smile to fade.

"So when did you get in?" Stephanie asked. "I thought you were coming with your parents."

Reagan shrugged. "I've been in Denver the last few days. I came up early to beat the storm," she said. "Got here about six this morning."

"Does Josh know you're here already? He didn't say anything to me."

"No. I crashed when I got here. I haven't seen him yet." She sipped from her drink. "Have my parents gotten in?"

Stephanie shook her head. "They're coming up tomorrow."

"I hear your father offered to fly down to the farm and pick them up," Reagan said.

Stephanie laughed. "Yes. I think he thought he could land the plane in a cornfield or something."

Shelby knew that Josh's parents still had a working farm in Nebraska, but she could not picture this woman—Reagan—in that setting. She could see her on a horse, maybe working on a cattle ranch in the mountains somewhere. But not on a farm. She was attractive in a nearly handsome way. Taller than most women but not overly so—she appeared to be lean and rugged, strong and agile. But no way would she have used Stephanie's description of "manly." She was too attractive, too pretty for that.

Stephanie elbowed her. "You're staring," she whispered.

Shelby pulled her eyes away but not before she caught the sad smile on Reagan's face. "I should apologize for earlier," Reagan said. "I had no idea you were Stephanie's sister."

Shelby nodded. "No problem." She shoved her empty glass away and looked at Stephanie. "I'm going to go shower. Dinner still on or did Mother demand our presence?"

"She didn't mention it," Stephanie said. "Let me find Josh and we'll sneak away. We can walk and take in the sights."

Shelby nodded again. "That's fine." She turned to Reagan, debating on whether to invite her or not. It would be rude not to include her, but something told her not to issue an invite. "Drinks are on the house," she said instead. She turned to Zach, motioning to Reagan, and he gave a quick nod.

"Well, thanks." Reagan held her glass up. "I'll try not to abuse it." She smiled slightly. "Enjoy your dinner, Shelby."

"You should come with us," Stephanie offered. "You and Josh haven't seen each other in months. I'm sure he'll want to visit."

Leave it to Stephanie *not* to be rude. And of course, Reagan accepted the invitation.

"I'd love to join you. Thank you for asking."

Reagan sounded sincere, making Shelby regret her earlier snub. She was supposed to make friends with her after all.

CHAPTER TWO

The snow on the sidewalks of the quaint downtown area of Estes Park positively glowed from the assorted lights that were overflowing from every available pole, railing and storefront. Reagan soaked it all in, thinking it looked like the perfect scene for a Christmas card. It was with sadness that she realized she had no itch to grab a camera and record the sight. She pushed that thought away, instead absorbing the ambience around her. While cold, it wasn't bitterly so. She found it refreshing after spending so many months in the desert.

When Josh had said the wedding would be a two-week affair, she'd thought he—and Stephanie—were crazy. Who did that? Well, apparently people who owned resort hotels and had more money than they knew what to do with. But it had come at a good time. After what had happened in Afghanistan…well, she needed a break. Her other option would have been to remain at the family farm for a while longer, but she knew she wouldn't be able to escape her mother's questions indefinitely. Her mother had always had a knack for knowing when something was bothering her, no matter how hard she tried to hide it. And this was something she was not ready to talk about. She wasn't even sure she could explain why she was feeling the way she was, explain the pain that she felt.

Josh and Stephanie walked ahead of them and she glanced over at the woman walking quietly beside her. Shelby's boots, like Reagan's, made the icy snow crunch with every step. She was dressed similarly in jeans and hiking boots and a thick, warm sweater. She had a wool cap on her head, covering most of her blond hair. As if feeling her staring, Shelby gave her a curious—and guarded—look. Reagan turned away, instead taking in the sights and sounds of Christmas that flooded the streets around them.

Had she known the beautiful blonde sitting at the bar was Stephanie's sister, she would never have been quite so brazen. In fact, she couldn't remember the last time she'd walked up to a stranger and propositioned her. Maybe it was simply being back in the States after so long. Or maybe it was that she was lonely and still trying to come to grips with the tragedy that had chased her from Afghanistan. When she'd seen Shelby at the bar, her first thought had been waking up in her arms after a night of lovemaking. But was it sex she was after or comfort?

"Have you been here before?"

Shelby's voice broke the stillness, and Reagan looked at her quickly, wondering if perhaps the silence was uncomfortable for her.

"No. First time. I assume you come often?"

Shelby nodded. "It's my favorite of the three that we own," she said. "I come mostly spring and fall. I like to hike in Rocky Mountain National Park. The summers are too busy. It's like a parking lot out there then."

"I wouldn't have taken you for a hiker," she said honestly.

Shelby shrugged. "Looks can be deceiving."

Reagan simply nodded. At the bar, Shelby had looked exactly like what she was—the daughter of a very wealthy businessman. While not overly dressed, it was obvious the clothes were expensive and stylish. Enough makeup to know she wore it but not so much that it took away from her natural beauty. Even the jewelry was understated, yet diamonds twinkled in the lights. Now, though, as they walked along the snowy street, she was dressed for the elements and not for fashion. Unlike Stephanie, who wore high-heeled boots and tights and a thigh-length sweater over a silk blouse. She clung to Josh's arm to keep from slipping on the ice. Reagan had learned from Josh that Stephanie had only followed her sister into the family business out of obligation. What she really wanted to do was be an interior designer. Reagan shook her head as Stephanie's heel got stuck in an ice patch once again.

"I know," Shelby said quietly beside her. "She wouldn't be caught dead in hiking boots."

"I heard that," Stephanie said. She stopped and turned around. "How about here? I know it's Shelby's favorite place. They have, like, thirty varieties of burgers."

Reagan looked at Shelby. "Breaking all the stereotypes tonight, aren't you?"

"Meaning what?" Shelby asked.

"Oh, I thought we'd end up at a fancy restaurant where I wouldn't know which fork to use," she said.

"Quit acting like you grew up on a farm," Josh said with a laugh as he held the door open.

"The fancy restaurant in town is at the hotel. Mother brought in three extra chefs from Denver just for the wedding party. And I will avoid it as often as I can," Shelby said.

"I love eating gourmet meals with five or six courses," Stephanie said. "Shelby would rather eat at places like this."

While they waited to be seated, Reagan leaned closer to Shelby. "So how did these two hook up anyway?"

"What do you mean?"

"He's a farm boy. Stephanie's probably never even seen a farm."

Shelby looked at the man who was about to become her brother-in-law. "He is *so* not a farm boy," Shelby said with a smile. "Are you still a farm girl?"

"Hardly." Then she shrugged. "Well, I could probably still milk a cow if I had to."

* * *

"So let me get this straight," Reagan said. "Your grandparents had a shitload of money, and your father needed something to do."

Shelby glanced at Josh with raised eyebrows. A blush lit his handsome face.

"I'm sure I didn't say shitload of money," he said.

Reagan waved her hand at him. "Whatever. So, he takes the money and builds a resort in Aspen. And of course, it's a success."

"Why do you say it like that?" Shelby asked. "You act as if there's no work involved in making something a success."

Reagan finished off her beer and slid the empty glass toward Josh, who refilled it from the pitcher they'd ordered. "So then he built another one."

"Yes. This one," Shelby said. "And then one in Steamboat Springs."

"And they're all successful?"

"Yes. And seasonal, to some extent," she said. "Estes Park is booked solid summer and fall. Less so during the winter. Steamboat Springs is booked solid winter and spring, for skiing. Aspen is pretty much booked solid all year."

"It's a resort, so the prices are—"

"Outrageous," Shelby said, saving Reagan the trouble. "Especially in Aspen."

"And the rich get richer," Reagan murmured.

Shelby leaned her elbows on the table. "Why do I get the feeling that you have an issue with money?"

"I don't have an issue with money. I like it as much as the next person," Reagan said. "But I've been in countries where poverty is commonplace. Putting a meal on the table is a big deal." She shrugged. "I come back here and see all of the excess, the waste, and it's such a contrast. People don't know how lucky we have it here."

"Let's don't get into a political discussion, please," Josh said. "We're celebrating. Nothing more." Then he smiled. "So did you really hit on Shelby in the bar?"

Shelby was surprised by the slight blush on Reagan's face. "I did. I was an arrogant ass. And I apologized."

"And I accepted," Shelby said.

Reagan smiled, breaking some of the tension that had crept into the conversation. "You don't really look alike. How was I to know you were sisters?"

"We do look alike," Stephanie said. "Only I like makeup more than she does."

"And high heels," Shelby added.

"How did you even know she was gay?" Stephanie asked. "She always gets hit on by men. They normally don't have a clue."

Reagan looked at her and Shelby held her gaze. The dark, haunted look in her eyes was still there but not nearly as profound as when she'd seen her that first time in the bar. Maybe the dinner, being with her brother, had lightened her some. She was skeptical, though, that they could be friends. Despite that, Reagan's words at the bar echoed in her brain. *I'll give you so much foreplay you'll be begging me for release.* Shelby pulled her eyes away, wondering if that would indeed be the case.

Reagan was saved answering Stephanie's question by the arrival of their burgers. They were as big and delicious-looking as always and Shelby swiped at the cheese melting on the side.

"You weren't kidding," Reagan said. "They're huge."

"And so good you'll finish the whole thing."

"This is kinda what I meant by excess," Reagan said. Then she took a bite and moaned. "God, that's good. You're right. I'll finish the whole damn thing."

CHAPTER THREE

Shelby sipped her coffee as she browsed through the local newspaper. She wasn't surprised that there was an article about the upcoming nuptials. Her mother's doing, no doubt.

"There you are."

Shelby looked up, finding her mother approaching in all her usual flair. Hair and makeup done to perfection, her dress and heels matching impeccably—Shelby wondered if she'd brought her wardrobe manager along with her.

"Good morning," she said.

"We have a fitting in ten minutes," her mother said, clapping her hands together. "What are you doing?"

"Breakfast."

"There's no time for breakfast." She looked around. "And where is Josh's sister?"

Shelby shrugged. "Haven't seen her this morning." She frowned. "Wait. What fitting?"

"For the dresses."

"Dresses? Oh, God. You *did* bring Bernie?"

"Of course I brought Bernie. Who else do you think I would trust with the dresses?"

Shelby signed. "There are only two of us. I thought Stephanie didn't want traditional bridesmaid dresses," she said.

Her mother gave a quick smile. "She didn't. I did."

"Does she know?"

"Does it matter?"

Shelby shook her head. "Mother, you can't keep planning everything. It's *her* wedding."

"Of which she has no concept of how to do things the proper way."

"No wonder she wanted to elope."

Her mother gasped. "*Elope?*"

Shelby saw a familiar figure walk in. Reagan was dressed in jeans and a Colorado sweatshirt that looked brand new. Most likely she'd picked it up at the gift shop in the lobby. She motioned with her head. "That's Josh's sister."

Reagan was headed to the bar when she saw Shelby. She raised her eyebrows questioningly and Shelby waved her over.

"Reagan Bryant, meet my mother, Christine Sutton."

Reagan stuck her hand out. "Nice to meet you, Mrs. Sutton."

"Nice to finally meet you, Reagan. You and Josh favor each other." She dropped her hand. "And please, call me Christine."

"Thank you." Reagan glanced at Shelby. "Have you eaten? After that burger last night, I don't think I even want breakfast."

"I know. I only had coffee and a piece of toast."

"Well, good," her mother said. "Because there's really no time for breakfast. We have a fitting. Come along, girls."

Reagan's eyebrows shot up. "A fitting?"

"For the dresses," Shelby said as she headed after her mother.

Reagan stopped in her tracks. "Oh, no. No. No. No," she said with a shake of her head. "I don't do dresses."

Shelby's mother spun around and stared at her. "What do you mean, you don't *do* dresses?"

"I don't wear dresses. Ever," she said. "Well, not since I was about twelve or so."

Shelby hid her smile as her mother's face transformed from shock to indignation. "Twelve? You are in the wedding party. You will be in a dress like everyone else."

"No, ma'am, I won't."

Oh, well, this should throw a kink in her mother's plans, Shelby thought. She wondered if Josh had relayed the "no dress" rule to Stephanie.

"We can't have the bridesmaids dressed differently," her mother insisted. "How will that look in pictures?"

"Don't care," Reagan said with a shrug. "I'll wear a tux if you want me to."

The look of horror on her mother's face caused Shelby to laugh out loud. Her mother looked at her sharply, and Shelby tried unsuccessfully to hide her amusement. Her mother then fixed her gaze on Reagan.

"You will *not* wear a tux."

Reagan simply shrugged. "Okay. And I also won't wear a dress."

Her mother looked at Shelby with pleading eyes. "Will you *please* do something?"

"What should I do?" Shelby asked. "I can't make her wear a dress."

"*You're* going to wear a dress," she said pointedly.

Shelby put her hands on her hips. "Okay, so you're trying to lump all the lesbians together?"

"I'm simply saying, if you can wear—"

"I'm not wearing a dress," Reagan said again. "I don't care what scenarios you come up with. Not doing it."

Shelby's mother let out a frustrated sigh. "We'll see about that," she said as she stormed off.

Shelby was still grinning. "Oh, that was awesome. It's not often my mother doesn't get her way."

Reagan again headed to the bar. "I'm no longer in the mood for coffee," she said. "How about a Bloody Mary?"

Shelby shook her head. "No. But I will have a mimosa," she said as Reagan sat down beside her. "So, haven't worn a dress since you were twelve?"

"If that," Reagan said. The bartender came over. Ty. He'd worked there for years and he gave Shelby a friendly smile. "Bloody Mary for me and she'll have a mimosa," Reagan said.

Ty nodded. "I have your favorite champagne, Shelby."

"Thank you. You must have known how stressful these two weeks were going to be."

"Stephanie warned me," he said as he walked away.

"You seem to know the staff," Reagan said. "How often do you come here?"

"I actually stay here for most of May, into June and most of September, into October," she said. "Like I said last night, the summer months are way too busy."

"So you work from here or just take the months off?"

"Yes, I have an office here." She smiled at Ty as he brought their drinks over. "Thank you."

"Put it on the house tab?"

She nodded. "Yes. Reagan is with the wedding party." She turned to Reagan. "They *did* tell you what that meant, right?"

"Josh said he wanted me to be a part of the wedding, that's all. He knows damn well I'm not going to be a bridesmaid."

Before Shelby could comment, she saw Stephanie and Josh heading their way. "Here come the troops," she warned.

Stephanie put her hands on her hips. "A *tux*?"

Reagan glanced at Josh. "You didn't tell her?"

"I think you'd look cute in a dress," he teased.

"No. Not happening."

Stephanie looked at Shelby. "Can't you do something?"

"Me? What am I supposed to do?"

"Mother is about to have a breakdown and we still have ten days to go before the ceremony."

"You didn't even want bridesmaid dresses to begin with," she reminded her.

"I don't. But Mother is adamant."

Reagan stood up. "Look, it's not going to hurt my feelings," she said. "Replace me with a cousin or something. I'm not wearing a dress." She paused. "Unless you want me to be your best man," she said to Josh with a hint of a smile.

She walked out with her Bloody Mary in hand and did not look back. Shelby wasn't exactly crazy about being a bridesmaid either, but she would never be as audacious as Reagan and refuse to wear a dress. She turned her gaze from Reagan's retreating back and looked at Stephanie.

"Well?" Stephanie asked.

"Well, what?"

"Do your lesbian bonding thing with her and get her in a dress," Stephanie said.

"Look, you wanted me to try to make friends with her and I will. But that's as far as it will go. I'm not planning to *bond* with her enough to get her in a dress." She looked at Josh. "Surely you knew this ahead of time."

He shrugged. "Stephanie said there wasn't going to be a big deal with the bridesmaids. I just wanted Reagan to be a part of the wedding too."

"Please do something. Please?" Stephanie pleaded. "For me?"

Shelby rolled her eyes, but nodded. "Okay. I don't think it'll do any good, but I'll talk to her."

Stephanie clapped her hands together. "Great! Now, come with me. I want you to meet Josh's cousin, Doug. He's the best man. Your partner."

"I thought Mother wanted us to do a fitting."

"She's too distraught. She went back to her suite."

Shelby shook her head. "She normally thrives off drama. What's the deal?"

"She seems really stressed. Maybe the two-week celebration was a bit much," Stephanie mused as she linked arms with her.

"You think?"

Stephanie nodded. "Again, it was not my idea. I wanted a Christmas wedding, that's all. I didn't want all this," she said with a wave of her hand toward the nearly thirty-foot-tall tree that took up most of the lobby.

"I warned you it would be too much," Josh said as he walked beside them.

"You know how Mother is. Everything has to be a production," Stephanie said. "Oh, there he is. He's *so* cute."

Shelby followed her gaze, landing on a very handsome man who was smiling as he headed their way. He had just enough stubble of a beard to be fashionable, and he surprised her by pulling her into a hug.

He laughed as she pulled away. "You *are* Shelby, right?"

"I am."

"And you are as beautiful as Josh said you were. I've got to be the luckiest man here," he said, still smiling. "Doug Bryant. Pleased to meet you."

Shelby returned his smile, albeit with not quite as much enthusiasm as he exhibited. "Nice to meet you too," she said politely.

"Doug is a professor," Stephanie explained. "University of Nebraska."

"Really?"

"My alma mater so it's extra special to be able to teach there," Doug said.

Shelby looked at Josh. "You grew up together?"

"Yes. More like brothers than cousins. Same age, same grade in school," he said.

"My family's farm is right down the road from theirs," Doug said.

"So you're close with Reagan too?" she asked.

"Reagan? I didn't expect her here," he said to Josh. "I'm surprised she took time out from her career to make your wedding."

"No, she wouldn't miss it," Josh said. "She's a bridesmaid."

Doug laughed out loud. "No way. Ray Ray? A bridesmaid? This I gotta see."

Ray Ray? Childhood nickname, no doubt, Shelby thought. But from his tone, she assumed there was no love lost between Doug and Reagan. She wondered what the story was with them.

"Speaking of that," Stephanie said. "Don't you need to go find her?"

Oh, yeah. She was supposed to talk her into wearing a dress, wasn't she? Well, at least it would give her an excuse to escape the over eager best man.

"Yes, I do need to find her." She held her hand out to Doug.
"It was nice to meet you."

He took her hand, but instead of shaking it, he brought it
to his mouth and kissed the back. She didn't know why, but the
stubble of is beard irritated her and she barely resisted wiping
her hand where his lips had touched.

"I understand there's a sleigh ride tonight out in the park,"
he said. "As best man and maid of honor, it will be a privilege for
me to share it with you." He smiled into her eyes. "I'm looking
forward to getting to know you better, Shelby."

Oh, God. Surely they'd told him she was gay. She forced a
smile. "I'm looking forward to the sleigh ride too. Perhaps I'll
see you there."

"Of course you'll see me. I'll save you a seat."

She took Stephanie's arm and pulled her to the side. "Excuse
us one moment," she said quickly to the guys. As soon as they
were far enough away, she glared at her. "Really?"

"What?" Stephanie shrugged. "He likes you."

"You didn't tell him?"

"You always say there's no need to forewarn people when I
introduce you."

"Yes. *People*. Not men who think they're going to spend the
next two weeks trying to get into my bed," she said as quietly as
possible.

"Oh, he'll figure it out," Stephanie said with a wave of her
hand. "But he's so nice. Please don't be rude to him."

"I won't be rude to him," she said.

"Good. Now go find Reagan. Sweet-talk her if you have to."

"I will *not* sweet-talk her," she murmured as she walked off.

CHAPTER FOUR

Reagan shivered and shoved her hands more firmly into the pockets of her jeans. The bright sunshine belied the temperature, even if it was melting the snow. Or maybe she'd spent too many months in the desert. Before that, she'd been in the jungles of Colombia. No wonder she was cold. Of course, leaving the hotel without a jacket hadn't been very smart.

Bridesmaid.

"Hell, no," she murmured.

She turned her attention to her surroundings, feeling disoriented for a moment. She had no clue where she was. The sidewalk she'd been on had taken her here. A golf course. A frozen golf course, but still a golf course. She looked more closely at the patches of snow that hid the brown grass and frowned. It was littered with droppings of some kind. Deer? Elk?

She squatted down, studying it. Too large for deer. Must be elk. And a hell of a lot of them.

"They winter in town."

She turned her head, surprised to find Shelby watching her. She stood back up. "You following me?"

"You weren't hard to find. Stevie pointed me in the general direction of where you'd headed."

"Stevie?"

"The doorman," Shelby said.

"Stephanie sent you?"

"Yes. I'm supposed to convince you to wear a matching dress with heels and be a part of the wedding party," Shelby said. "Will it work?"

"Save your breath," she said as she started walking again.

Shelby fell into step beside her. "If I could, I would opt out too. Thirty is too old to be a bridesmaid."

"Try thirty-two," she said.

"Oh, and I met your cousin, Doug."

Reagan glanced at her. "Dougie is here? Let me guess, he turned on the charm for you?"

"At our introduction, he hugged me," Shelby said. "Then he kissed my hand."

Reagan laughed. "Oh, that's Dougie. He thinks he's a ladies' man." She turned to look at her. "Did they not warn him ahead of time?"

"No, they did not."

"Oh, this is going to be fun. He doesn't take rejection well."

"I got the feeling that there's some animosity between you two."

Reagan nodded. "Goes back to high school," she said. "He caught me kissing Becky McFarlane—his girlfriend."

"Oh, bad. Was she gay?"

Reagan shook her head. "No. Just fooling around. She put a stop to it when I got inside her panties," Reagan said with a laugh. She hadn't thought of that in a long time.

"I hate it when straight girls play games."

"You have a story?"

Shelby nodded. "College. I thought I was in love. Turns out she was doing it on a dare."

"Were you sleeping together?"

"Yes. I should have known she had never been with a woman before but I was…young and stupid," she said bluntly.

They walked on in silence for a moment, going up a hill. Reagan grabbed Shelby's arm, stopping her. "Look at that."

Shelby smiled. "Yes. They're all over town."

The elk herd numbered maybe thirty or so. Most were lying down in the sun. Others were nibbling at the shrubs that lined the course. Out of habit, she reached to her side where her camera would be. Of course, there was no camera. She was afraid there would never be a camera again. Maybe that was a good sign, that she'd at least reached for it. It was the first time in the last month she'd even had an inkling to hold one in her hand again.

"What is it?"

Reagan shook her head. "Nothing."

Shelby continued to stare at her. "I'm a good listener," she offered.

"Do you think I need to talk?"

Shelby continued to stare at her. "Do you?" She finally looked away. "Look, I don't pretend to know you or know what you're thinking, but when I first saw you in the bar yesterday, I thought you looked so…so terribly sad."

Reagan knew she wasn't good at hiding it, knew her mother was worried about her. Hell, she was worried too. But she'd thought she was putting on a good enough façade to cover it up. To think that this stranger could see that in her frightened her. Maybe it *was* time to talk about it.

But not now. She was cold. They were in the middle of a frozen golf course surrounded by elk. And was Shelby Sutton really the best choice to bare her soul to? She was surprised when Shelby reached out a hand and squeezed her arm.

"Are you okay, Reagan?"

Reagan slowly shook her head. "No. I feel kinda…well, depressed seems way too dramatic. I'm just feeling kinda…blue, I guess." She squared her shoulders. "But I have a handle on it," she said, knowing she was lying.

"Well, if you ever want to talk…" Shelby offered again, then turned and left without another word.

Reagan blew out her breath, then shoved her hands inside her pockets. Instead of following Shelby back toward the hotel, she kept on walking up the hill. Images of that fateful day tried to worm their way into her mind, but she shut them out, like she'd been doing for the last month.

She'd always taken pride on being able to separate herself from the images her camera captured. She'd seen death many times over. She had been in Iraq and Afghanistan. She'd been to Syria and Bangui in Central Africa. She'd seen the drug wars in Colombia and Mexico. She'd captured pain on people's faces. She'd captured the cruelty of torture and the anguish and distress of the tormented. She'd captured disease and famine. She'd captured it all, yet she'd remained detached. It's what made her successful where others might have failed, and her images had appeared in countless magazines and newspapers.

Yet here she was, unable to pick up a camera. Unable to shoot even the most benign of images, such as beautiful Estes Park at Christmastime.

Because she'd captured one too many images. And it was that last shot that she could not get out of her mind, that last shot that kept coming to her over and over again.

Oh, she could say she'd shut it out. She could say she pushed the image away. But in her dreams, at night when she had no defense, the image came…over and over again.

She looked to the sky, then took off in a run, up the hill and behind the golf course. She didn't stop until she came to a street where she nearly got run over by a car, the loud honking of its horn stopping her in her tracks. She put her hands on her knees and tried to catch her breath. After a few minutes, she straightened up again, still taking deep breaths. She thought she was in pretty good shape. Apparently she wasn't adjusted to the altitude yet.

"Yeah, let's use that excuse," she murmured as she started walking again. She followed the street and ended up in the downtown area. In the light of day, it was still as pretty as it had been last night. Every shop was decorated on both sides of the road as far as she could see. She walked aimlessly, looking through windows at the various items offered for sale, most targeted to the mass of tourists that invaded the town.

Scattered between the shops were a few cafés and restaurants and she came upon the burger place they'd been to last night. She walked past it, then crossed the street to the other side and headed back toward the hotel. The walk had helped warm her and clear her head. She felt almost normal by the time Stevie held the door open for her. She nodded at him and headed for the bar.

The bartender from yesterday was there—Zach. He obviously remembered her.

"Scotch?"

She shook her head. "A little early for that. How about a beer?"

"Got Coors on draft," he offered.

"That'll do." She pulled a bowl of peanuts closer to her. She'd skipped breakfast. The olives in her Bloody Mary didn't count. Her stomach told her she'd also missed lunch.

"Here you go."

"Thanks."

"No problem. I put it on the house tab."

She raised an eyebrow. "So for the whole time I'm here for the wedding, my bar tab is being picked up by the Suttons?"

"Yes, ma'am. That's what Shelby said."

She smiled at him. "Now that's almost worth being in the wedding party for."

Almost.

CHAPTER FIVE

"Mother, please," Shelby said as she grabbed the bridge of her nose. "You can't force her."

"Well, can you imagine what everyone will say?"

Shelby looked over at Stephanie, who was lying on the sofa in their parents' suite, one arm thrown across her face dramatically. "So ask Holly to be in the wedding instead."

Stephanie rolled her head toward her. "Who?"

"Our cousin. Holly. We saw her yesterday," she reminded her.

"Holly Durkin? Are you serious?" her mother asked. "How would that look?"

Shelby threw up her hands. "I don't care. I'm through discussing it. Reagan in a tux or get someone else. That seems to be your choice." She stood up and headed for the door.

"Where are you going?" Stephanie asked. "I need you here."

"I can't take all this drama," she said. "This was supposed to be a two-week celebration, not two weeks of hell."

"Shelby Lynn Sutton," her mother said loudly. "This is your sister's *wedding*."

"I know, Mother. It's all we've talked about for the last year. And it's your thing and it's her thing. It's not *my* thing. So, I'm going to the bar. See you at dinner."

She slammed the door on her mother's protest and hurried to the elevator. Couldn't have a Saturday wedding like normal people, no. Had to have two damn weeks of it. Who *did* that?

She wasn't surprised to find Reagan in the bar. She wondered if she had a drinking problem. She smiled to herself as she sat down beside her. Of course, what did that say about her? It was two in the afternoon and she was craving a gin and tonic.

"You look stressed," Reagan said.

"If you only knew," she murmured. Zach came over immediately, eyebrows raised. She shook her head. Too early for gin. "I'll have a beer too."

"I hope it's not still because of me and the bridesmaid thing," Reagan said.

"Afraid so. The world is apparently going to come to an end." She turned to her. "I suggested they replace you with our cousin, Holly. That didn't go over too well."

"Why not?"

"We're not exactly close. My mother came from a normal, middle-class family. And she married into a very wealthy family. And, sadly, she enjoys reminding her sisters of that any chance she gets. For example, having a two-week wedding celebration and inviting them all to stay here for free during that time."

"I see. And they all took her up on the offer?"

"Most are only coming next week, but I did see Holly yesterday." She took a drink of her beer. "Maybe I could set her up with Doug."

Reagan laughed. "No. I think it'll be much more fun watching him try to get into your bed."

"It is definitely turning into hell week," she said.

"The two-week thing…that was your mother's idea?"

"Yes. Stephanie simply wanted a Christmas wedding. It morphed into all this." She took another drink of the cold beer. "I wanted a July wedding," she added.

Reagan nodded. "And all the events that are planned? My invitation had something listed almost every day, I think."

"My mother is…crazy," she said with a smile. "And organized. Well, with the help of her staff."

"And your father?"

"He was smart enough to fly back to Denver. He's not coming back until the weekend," she said. His excuse was a problem at the Aspen hotel needed his attention. She knew very well that the manager there could handle any "problem" that came up. And if he couldn't, he would have called her and not her father.

"So you work for your father?"

"Yes."

"What do you do?"

"My degree is in marketing," she said. "I'm not certain what my father's vision was as far as Stephanie and me going to work for him. I don't think he thought we would actually *do* anything."

"Look pretty and collect a nice paycheck?"

She laughed, not offended in the least. That was probably exactly what her father intended. "It took almost a year for me to earn his trust," she said. "And it wasn't until I threatened to quit and go get a *real* job that he started letting me get involved more."

"And now?"

"Now, after eight years, I head up the marketing department, but I'm involved in a lot more than just marketing." She smiled. "The department has all of four employees, counting me."

"Is Stephanie one of them?"

Her smile faded a little. She loved her sister to death, but Stephanie was content to "look pretty and collect a nice paycheck" as Reagan had said.

"Yes, she is."

Reagan laughed. "I take it she doesn't have your drive?"

Shelby looked at her sharply.

"You're very easy to read," Reagan said. "And Josh mentioned once that Stephanie wanted to be an interior designer, so I imagine the marketing department isn't her thing."

She nodded. "Yes, you're right. I keep telling Dad that we need to upgrade some of the suites in Aspen and let Stephanie design them. So far, he's put it off." She finished her beer and pushed it away. "She hasn't quite earned his trust yet." Perhaps not something she should share with Reagan, Josh's sister, but it was the truth. And no, Stephanie did not have her drive. That comment she kept to herself.

Without being intrusive, Zach motioned to her empty glass. She shook her head. One beer was enough for her. Reagan, too, declined his offer.

"Earlier, when you asked if I wanted to talk," Reagan said, surprising her with the change of subject. "Was that simply out of concern, or something more?"

Shelby met her eyes, searching them. They were still shadowed, still harbored sadness, but it wasn't as profound as yesterday when she'd first seen her. Or maybe it was and she was getting used to it. She decided to be honest with her.

"Josh and your parents are worried about you. Stephanie asked me to…well, make friends, as she put it."

"I see."

"I'm sorry. Whatever is going on with you is certainly none of my business. I don't know you, I don't know how you normally are," she said. "I was told that you seem depressed and not yourself." She reached over and touched Reagan's arm lightly. "They're worried about you."

Reagan nodded. "Yeah, I know. My mom, she's tried to talk to me, but I wasn't ready. Not sure I can even explain."

Shelby sensed that Reagan wanted to talk but she wasn't certain a public bar was the proper place. She was curious, though, about her work.

"Stephanie said you are a photojournalist."

Reagan glanced at her, then gave a subtle nod. "Yes."

"And you travel a lot, she said."

"It's not as exciting as it seems," Reagan said. She motioned to her empty mug and Zach immediately pulled out a clean one from the freezer and began filling it.

"I would hate it," she said. "I hate flying, for one thing. And I'm a bit of a homebody. I don't think I could take the travel."

"I know what you mean. Sometimes I'll only stay at a place a week or two. Sometimes only a day." She paused. "And then others, months and months."

"Hard to make friends that way, I suppose." She hesitated before continuing. "And to develop relationships of any kind... lovers."

Reagan smiled. "Oh, you're right about that. Not to mention, there are a lot of different cultures in the world." She shrugged. "I'm not always welcome."

"I imagine you have to be very careful."

Reagan looked at her, a smile hovering on her lips. "Are you fishing for information?"

Shelby felt a blush light her face. "Is it that obvious?" She nodded when Zach brought Reagan's beer. One more wouldn't hurt, she thought. "Did you have a breakup?"

Reagan laughed. "God, no. In *Afghanistan*?"

"Well, there are soldiers there, other Westerners, aren't there?"

The smile left Reagan's face. "Yeah, there are. I was actually traveling with a British group," she said. "Officially, the war has ended and most of the troops have been pulled out."

"May I ask what you were doing there?"

"What? You think it's classified?"

Shelby smiled at Zach when he placed a beer in front of her. "No, I mean, what were you doing there?" She looked at her. "What I really mean is, what the *hell* were you doing there?"

Reagan laughed. "I know. Not exactly a glamorous assignment." Again, the smile faded. "I was working with a friend, a journalist, who was doing a story on one of the villages there. I owed him a favor from years earlier so that's why I was there." She shrugged. "The last time I left, I swore I wouldn't go back. Yet there I was again."

Shelby nodded. "So? Did he get his story?"

When Reagan looked at her, Shelby wished she hadn't not asked the question. Reagan's sad eyes were shimmering with unshed tears.

"No. He didn't."

With that, Reagan stood, leaving her unfinished beer on the bar, and walked away.

CHAPTER SIX

"I saw you in the bar with Reagan earlier," Stephanie said. "Did you find out anything?"

"No."

"So what did you talk about?"

Shelby sighed. "I am not going to tell you every little thing we discussed. You asked me to try to make friends with her and I am."

Stephanie's eyes widened. "Do you *like* her? She's so not your type."

"I didn't say that. I said I'm trying to be friends, that's all. And you have no idea who my type is anyway."

"I've seen some of your dates."

"What? One? Two?" Shelby slipped on her sweater. "And I can't believe you called her manly."

"Well, she is. I mean, she said herself she hasn't worn a dress since she was twelve."

Shelby stared at her. "When's the last time you saw me in a dress?"

Stephanie blinked stupidly at her. "Umm, well, there was the…the office party last year."

Shelby shook her head. "I wore a suit. Try again."

Stephanie waved her hand in the air. "I've obviously seen you in a dress, I just can't think of a time right this minute." She got off the sofa where she'd been lounging. "And even if you don't wear a dress, you don't look gay. She does." Stephanie reached out and brushed her hair. "Please don't ever cut your hair short."

Shelby laughed. "When I cut it last summer like this you almost freaked out."

"I know. I'm used to it now. But no shorter."

"Whatever," she said. "Now come on. We'll be late. You don't want to send Mother into another tailspin, do you?"

"She's going to have me so stressed out by the time the wedding is here," Stephanie said as she followed her out of the suite. "I wish I could ignore her like you do."

"Well, I've had three more years' experience than you," she said with a laugh as she pushed the elevator button.

Josh and their mother were waiting at the entrance to the restaurant. The look on Josh's face told her that he'd been subjected to one of their mother's rants.

"Sorry we're late," Stephanie said as she moved closer to kiss him. "Shelby took *forever* to get dressed."

Shelby rolled her eyes as Josh laughed. "Are you sure it was Shelby?"

Stephanie grinned. "I guess you do know me by now, huh?" She looked around. "Where's Reagan?"

"I don't know. She's not answering her cell. I left her a message to join us though."

Stephanie turned to her expectantly and Shelby shrugged. Granted, their earlier discussion in the bar hadn't ended well, but no alarms had gone off. Well, other than Reagan abruptly getting up and leaving.

"What about your parents?" Stephanie asked Josh.

"They should be here soon, but they said we should go ahead to dinner."

"Ah." Shelby turned to her mother. "So that's what has got you upset?"

"I've never even met them," she said. "I think it's rude for us not to wait on them. They've been traveling for two days."

"Why stress them out with dinner? It'll probably be easier to meet them at the sleigh ride later." She motioned to the entrance. "Shall we?"

Josh glanced at his watch. "Still waiting on Doug," he said.

Great. Dinner with Doug.

"Is that what you're wearing?" her mother asked.

Shelby looked down at her sweater and jeans, then back at her mother. "Oh, gosh no, Mother. I only put this on to walk down here," she said sarcastically. "I've got my formal attire on underneath."

Stephanie laughed beside her, but her mother's glare never lessened. She finally shook her head. "I tried so hard," she said. "I don't know why Stephanie is the only one who got my sense of fashion." She leaned closer. "It's not like you don't have a date for dinner."

Shelby frowned. "Who?"

"Well, the best man, of course. He's so delightful." She smiled. "And handsome," she added.

Shelby turned to Stephanie, her voice a whisper. "I guess she forgot I'm a lesbian."

"There he is," Josh said and they all turned. Doug was hurrying toward them, a smile on his face.

"Sorry, guys. I did a little exploring in town and the time got away from me." He turned to their mother. "You look fabulous, Mrs. Sutton. That color is perfect for you."

Shelby playfully elbowed Stephanie as their mother blushed.

"Thank you. And I told you to call me Christine."

"That you did." He then turned to her, and Shelby clutched her hands behind her back, fearing he would want to kiss them again. "You look lovely, Shelby." Then he winked at her. "I'm looking forward to that sleigh ride tonight."

Shelby held her hand up. "Okay, look. They didn't tell you this, but I'm not—"

"Oh, there's Reagan," Josh said, interrupting her.

Shelby turned, thankful to see her there. Josh went to her and hugged her quickly. Their conversation was too quiet for her to hear. When they came closer, some of the swagger had left Doug's face.

"Well, Ray Ray, been a long time."

Reagan glanced at him, finally giving him a slight smile. "Dougie. How's it going?" she asked, holding out her hand to him.

"Great. Couldn't be better. You?"

Their handshake was brief, and even her mother seemed to sense the tension between them.

"Okay, I guess." Reagan slid her eyes to Shelby and Shelby met them. Whatever Reagan had done, she seemed to be better. Her eyes weren't quite as haunted as before. "Do you and the best man have a dinner date or is this a group thing?"

For having known her only two days, Shelby recognized the teasing in her voice, even though Reagan's face remained serious. Shelby smiled quickly.

"Definitely group," she said. "Glad you could join us."

* * *

God, if she had to listen to one more boring story about grad students, Reagan was going to scream. It was almost as bad as the continuous loop of Christmas songs playing in the background. How many versions of "Silver Bells" would they be subjected to?

Christine Sutton's laughter rang out; she seemed to be completely captivated by Dougie's charm. Reagan tuned it out as her gaze moved to Shelby. As if sensing her watching, Shelby turned and offered a quick smile.

Damn, but Shelby was cute. If she had all her wits about her, she should be trying to get to know her better. But she didn't have her wits. And hell, she'd made a pass at her already. Shelby probably thought she picked up women in bars all the time. Far from it.

"So Ray Ray, where have you been? Last I heard, you were in the jungle," Doug said.

Ray Ray. Did he know how she hated that nickname? Yes, of course he did. *Dougie*. But she would play nice. She hadn't seen the guy in years. No sense in letting him get under her skin now.

"Yeah. I switched the jungle for the desert," she said. "Back home now."

"Out at the farm?" He laughed. "You always hated the farm."

"I use to hate a lot of things," she said, staring at him.

There were a few seconds of uncomfortable silence, then Stephanie cleared her throat.

"So...that prime rib was great, wasn't it?"

The others picked up the conversation, but Reagan tuned that out as well. She felt uncomfortable being here, claustrophobic, nearly. She shifted in her chair, wondering how rude it would be if she got up and left.

She flinched when a hand touched her shoulder. It was Shelby, standing behind her. Reagan turned, meeting her gaze.

"How about a drink before the sleigh ride?" Shelby asked quietly. "I could use a break."

Reagan nodded and stood up, pausing to glance back at the table. "Thanks for dinner," she said, directing her comment to Mrs. Sutton. Then, with relief, she followed Shelby out of the restaurant and into the bar.

"It's not so much a drink I need as a break from Doug," Shelby said as they settled onto the barstools.

"Yeah, he's a little over the top. But thank you. I was about to—"

"Bolt," Shelby finished for her. "You okay?"

Reagan swallowed, then looked at Shelby. "No. Not really."

But Shelby didn't ask more questions and Reagan was thankful. She wasn't in the right frame of mind to talk now. She'd end up bawling like a baby if she did.

"I'll just have a water, Zach. Reagan?"

Reagan nodded at Zach, then let out a sigh. "So, this sleigh ride thing..."

"Not really a sleigh ride," Shelby said. "There's not enough snow in the valley. So it's more like a hay ride. It's a trailer loaded with hay and it'll be pulled by a tractor." Shelby shook her head. "And don't ask me why. Another of Mother's brilliant ideas."

"It's not that cold out. It should be fun."

Shelby raised her eyebrows. "Fun? Doug thinks we have a date."

Reagan laughed. "Oh, Dougie, he doesn't have a clue."

"And why not? He knows you're gay. Why doesn't he have a clue?"

Reagan smiled at her. "Because he can't see past the package. You're very attractive, Shelby. That's all he sees. He doesn't care what's inside." She shrugged. "I haven't known you long, of course, but I think what's inside might be better than what's outside." She smiled again. "And that's saying something, because the outside is gorgeous."

Shelby stared at her for a moment, then looked away. "Thank you."

Reagan leaned closer and playfully bumped her shoulder. "And I'm being sincere. I'm not hitting on you or throwing you a line."

Shelby laughed quietly. "I know. And thank you."

Reagan nodded her thanks at Zach and took a sip of her water. Sitting at a bar with a beautiful woman and drinking water. Something was wrong with that picture.

"Oh, honey, there you are."

Reagan turned at the sound of the familiar voice, smiling as her parents came into the bar. She stood quickly, accepting the tight hug from her mother.

"Don't let Brother Thomas know you're in a bar," she teased, referring to their Baptist minister.

"Brother Thomas doesn't need to know everything," her mother said. "How are you, honey?"

"I'm fine, Mom. Quit worrying." She turned to her father and hugged him quickly. "How were the roads?"

"Nasty coming out of Denver," he said. "Be glad you came early."

Her mother glanced at Shelby, who had been sitting quietly, watching. Reagan turned to her with an apologetic smile.

"Sorry. Mom, Dad...this is Shelby Sutton."

Shelby stood and held her hand out. "Pleasure to meet you," she said with an easy smile.

"You're Stephanie's sister," her mother said, taking her hand. "Although you don't really look alike."

"See," Reagan murmured.

"I'm Margie. This is Frank," she said, introducing her husband. Shelby shook his hand as well.

"Nice to meet you."

"Well, I had no clue as to what to wear on a sleigh ride," her mother said. "I'm glad to see both of you in jeans."

"You're dressed perfectly," Shelby said. "And please don't use my mother to gauge what you should wear," she said with a laugh.

"It's an old-fashioned hay ride, anyway," Reagan said.

"Really? Well, that will be fun."

"Oh, yeah. A blast. Cousin Dougie is already here."

"He and Josh were always close," she said. "Has he even spoken to you?"

"Mom, the Becky McFarlane thing was fifteen years ago."

"And he hasn't gotten over it yet. I'm certain that's the reason he's never married."

"Oh, please. He's obnoxious. *That's* the reason he's never gotten married," she said.

Her mother laughed. "Well, there *is* that," she said.

CHAPTER SEVEN

Shelby cringed when Doug took her elbow to guide her to the flatbed trailer loaded with hay. Apparently he thought she wasn't capable of climbing up on her own. She glanced over her shoulder, seeing Reagan's amused expression as she helped her mother up.

"What a great idea Christine had," Doug said. "This is going to be such fun." He looked skyward. "Clear skies. A million stars twinkling." He leaned closer. "Such a romantic setting, isn't it?"

Seriously?

"Do you mind if we sit by you?"

"Please do," Shelby said quickly to Reagan.

"Hello, Doug."

"Hello, Aunt Margie, Uncle Frank," he said with a quick nod at them.

Shelby smiled her thanks at Reagan as she sat down beside her. She glanced at Doug, noting how perturbed he looked.

Good.

"So...nice night," Reagan said quietly, a smile in her voice.

Shelby turned to her, their eyes holding for a moment. "I plan to push him off into a snowbank once we get going," she whispered.

Reagan laughed out loud, causing Doug to jerk around. "What?"

"Nothing," Reagan said, wiping the smile from her face.

Shelby blew out her breath and leaned back against a hay bale, tuning out the quiet conversations around her. Actually, it was a nice night. Clear skies, no moon overhead yet. There *were* a million stars twinkling in the sky and it was kinda romantic. On one side of her sat Doug, a clueless man who thought he had a chance with her. On the other side, Reagan, an attractive—and troubled—woman who had blatantly hit on her the first time they met. Since she'd found out she was Stephanie's sister, she'd shown no other signs of interest.

But now, sitting close like this, their shoulders nearly touching, Shelby felt herself drawn to her. She couldn't help but wonder what troubled her so. Sometimes when she looked at Reagan, she could see it all over her face, in her eyes. Other times, she seemed lighter, less burdened by whatever demons haunted her.

The jerking of the trailer brought her out of her musings. There were perhaps fifteen people on the hay ride, only a few she didn't recognize. She assumed they were relatives of Josh and Reagan. Josh and Stephanie sat by her mother and Shelby was shocked to see her mother in jeans. Expensive designer jeans, but jeans nonetheless. They were tucked into black, knee-high boots and she had a bulky sweater on. She looked almost normal. She smiled slightly as she saw Stephanie was dressed nearly identically.

Yes, it was a shame she didn't get their sense of fashion, she thought dryly, as she crossed her legs, her loose jeans comfortable and her hiking boots practical.

"So Shelby, I understand you like to ski," Doug said. "I've skied a few times myself. Are there slopes nearby? Perhaps we could take a day trip," he suggested.

I'm going to kill Stephanie.

She forced a quick smile to her face as she shook her head. "No, there aren't any slopes right around here. This area is mostly for cross-country skiing. Which is fun, if you have the stamina," she said. "The closest ski area is in Nederland."

"Well, maybe we could take a trip," he suggested.

"I don't think so. I'm really only here for the wedding. And as you know, my mother has quite a bit already planned."

"I saw the agenda. Quite impressive."

Reagan bumped her shoulder and she turned, smiling as Reagan winked at her. "He's trying so hard to win you over," she whispered. "Go skiing with him."

Shelby met her gaze, her voice low. "I will not." She leaned closer. "I told Stephanie I wouldn't be rude to him but it's so hard."

Reagan leaned closer too, her mouth nearly touching Shelby's ear. "Oh, I'm sure *it* is *very* hard right about now."

Shelby couldn't contain her laughter, causing several people to glance at her, including her mother.

"What's so funny?" Doug asked. He leaned closer too. "I didn't realize you and Reagan knew each other so well."

"We don't. I only met her yesterday," she said.

"She's gay, you know."

"Really? What a coincidence," she said. "So am I."

His eyes widened. "What?" Then he smiled skeptically. "Oh, come on. No way."

She nodded. "Yes. Very gay. Very, very, very gay."

He smirked. "If you need an excuse, at least be realistic. If you don't want to get to know me better, just say so. No need to fabricate something as crazy as that."

She sighed. Why didn't men ever believe her? Why did it always have to be this way? But she'd promised Stephanie she wouldn't be rude to him. He was Josh's best man, after all.

"Okay, Doug. Let's do it this way then. You're not my type, so there's no point in spending the next two weeks getting to know one another better."

He smiled broadly. "Now, was that so hard to say?" Then he leaned closer. "But I'll warn you. Be careful if you're ever standing under mistletoe. You're fair game then."

Seriously?

She felt movement beside her and leaned closer to Reagan. Reagan's mouth moved to her ear and Shelby felt her breath as she spoke.

"There's a snowbank coming up," Reagan whispered. "Want me to help you push him?"

Shelby turned slowly, finding Reagan's mouth only inches from her own. It was too dark to read her eyes but still, she found her closeness unsettling. And not in a bad way. As Reagan slowly pulled away, Shelby saw a smile on her face and she returned it.

"I'll warn you too about standing under mistletoe," Reagan murmured. "You never know who might sneak in for a kiss."

"Consider me warned."

CHAPTER EIGHT

Reagan walked past the restaurant without glancing inside. A group breakfast at the buffet followed by a "shuttle ride to Estes Park's shopping district" was on the wedding agenda.

No, thank you.

She might be persuaded to join the group for dinner though. It was Josh's lone contribution to the activities, she'd learned. It was at a local steakhouse that boasted the state's biggest T-bones. She couldn't remember the last time she'd had a good steak.

"Where are you sneaking off to?"

She turned, finding Shelby coming toward her. She returned her smile, then motioned to the restaurant.

"Hiding from the group. You?"

Shelby nodded. "Me too. I was going to head into town for a quick breakfast, then find a hiking trail. I just want to get out of the hotel for a while."

"Hiking? Are there trails without snow?"

"Sure. Down at Big Thompson Canyon. It's on the dry side of the mountain. There may be some pockets of snow in shaded areas, that's about it," she said. "You want to go?"

"Sounds like fun," she said. "Beats your mother's agenda for today."

"I know." Shelby's cell rang and she sighed. "Speaking of Mother," she said.

Reagan noticed the smile left Shelby's face, and she wondered if their relationship was strained or if it was just the stress of the wedding.

"I'm not joining you for breakfast, no," Shelby said. A slight pause, then another sigh. "Because I'm going hiking." She glanced at Reagan. "I'm showing Reagan the sights," she said. Then she nodded. "Yes, we'll be back in time for dinner."

Shelby slipped her phone back into her pocket, then looked Reagan over. "You might want to grab a jacket."

Reagan had a long-sleeved T-shirt on under one of the new sweatshirts she'd bought. She glanced outside, seeing blue skies and bright sunshine. It looked warm, but it was still probably in the low 30s. So she nodded.

"Be right back."

When she returned to the lobby, another woman was approaching Shelby so Reagan paused, not wanting to interrupt their greeting.

"You're Shelby, aren't you?"

Shelby smiled. "Hi, Holly. Are you enjoying yourself?"

"Oh, gosh, yes. Two weeks free vacation. It's great."

Shelby gave a forced smile, one Reagan had seen her give to Dougie before.

"Well, good. What about the rest of your family? I haven't seen them."

"Oh, they couldn't get off work, but they'll be here for the weekend. But I'd been saving my vacation for a cruise. When this offer came up, I jumped on it," she said. "Two weeks free at a resort hotel? Free food and drinks? Woo hoo," she said with a laugh. "It was a no-brainer!"

"Of course."

"Well, see you later," she said with a wave as she walked away.

Reagan moved closer, shaking her head. "Wow."

"Yeah," Shelby said dryly. "Cousin Holly. I told you we're not really close."

"You don't say."

They went to the entrance and Stevie held the glass door open for them as they stepped out into the sunshine. Shelby headed toward a 4-wheel-drive Jeep Cherokee that was running, the exhaust steaming in the cold air.

"I had them bring my car around," she explained as she got inside.

Reagan got in the passenger side, enjoying the heated seat. "New?"

Shelby nodded. "A few months. I got it in September."

"Not what I pictured you driving," she said.

"Why not? Did you expect a sports car or something?"

"A Mercedes or something," she said. "Not anything quite this practical."

Shelby laughed. "I am very practical. You should know that by now. I had a very reliable Subaru before this," she said as she pulled away from the hotel. "Do you have a preference for breakfast?"

"Whatever. As long as there's coffee involved, I'm fine."

"Good." Shelby's phone came up on the console screen and she scrolled through her contacts, finding the one she wanted. The call was answered on two rings.

"Dave's."

"Good morning. This is Shelby Sutton. I'd like to order a couple of breakfast sandwiches to go, please."

"Sure, Shelby. Sausage, bacon or ham?"

Shelby glanced at her with raised eyebrows. "Bacon," Reagan said.

"Two with bacon."

"Swiss, mozzarella or cheddar?"

"Mozzarella for me. Reagan?"

"Swiss."

"And two large coffees," Shelby said.

"Give me ten minutes," he said.

"Thank you." She disconnected the call as she turned toward town. "You'll love these."

"Eggs?"

"Fried eggs, loaded with bacon, crispy hash browns and cheese. On thick buttered Texas toast. They're sinful."

"God, how do you stay so thin? That burger the other night, now this?"

"I only allow myself one of these breakfast sandwiches when I'm here. I'm scared to even ask how many calories and fat grams they have," she said with a laugh. "We'll work it off on our hike."

Dave's looked like it used to be an old house and Shelby said as much.

"Yes. A lot of the shops are renovated old homes," Shelby said. "Except in the original business district, of course." She pulled to a stop in the small parking lot. "Be right back."

Reagan watched as Shelby hurried inside, then she leaned back in the seat, realizing how relaxed she felt. When she'd first gotten up and looked at the "agenda," knowing she would not be participating in it, the day ahead loomed desolate and bleak... and depressing. She'd thought about calling Josh but knew that he would be hanging with Stephanie. And Dougie, no doubt. She'd thought briefly of finding her mother and seeing if she wanted to do something, but she knew her mother would enjoy the shopping excursion into town with the group. And yes, she'd also considered looking for Shelby to see what she had planned for the day. She hadn't known her long, but she suspected a group shopping trip was not something Shelby would enjoy.

But in the end, she'd escaped her room alone with no plans other than avoiding the wedding party for the day. Apparently Shelby had had the same idea. And thankfully, she'd included Reagan in her plans. Because her loneliness—depression— seemed to disappear in Shelby's presence. The day no longer seemed desolate and bleak. It was filled with sunshine and a new friend to share it with.

She smiled quickly as Shelby walked out of the café, carrying two bags and holding a cardboard tray with two coffees. She reached across the console to open Shelby's door for her.

"Thanks," Shelby said as she handed over the coffees.

Reagan took them from the tray and sat each of them in the cup holders in the console. She then took the large bag from Shelby and peeked inside, the aroma of bacon making her mouth water.

As if reading her mind, Shelby laughed. "I know."

"Will you be able to eat and drive?" Reagan asked.

Shelby nodded. "Yes. This is my normal routine when I head out hiking. Grab breakfast to eat on the way." She handed her the smaller bag. "Sugar and cream. I didn't know how you took your coffee."

"Thanks. A little of each. You?"

"Black with one sugar, please."

Reagan readied their coffee as Shelby pulled away. Then she could wait no longer as she pulled the two sandwiches from the bag.

"They're huge," she said, finding the one with "Swiss" scribbled across the wrapping. She handed the other to Shelby, wondering how she could possibly eat it and drive at the same time.

But, true to her word, she seemed to be an expert at it, tearing only a corner of the wrapping away from the sandwich. She took a large bite, moaning as she chewed.

"So damn good," she murmured with her mouth full.

Reagan, too, took a bite, her taste buds exploding with the first bite. "Oh, my God," she said. "That's—"

"Sinful," Shelby finished for her with a laugh.

"Very."

They ate in silence as Shelby drove them south of town toward Big Thompson Canyon. The river flowed on their right and Reagan enjoyed watching the shimmering rapids as the sunlight reflected off the water. Bare trees—aspen and cottonwood—were intermingled with the evergreen spruce, fir and pine that lined the river. The warmth of the car belied the winter scene. There was hardly any snow along the banks of the river, only pockets here and there where the trees kept it shaded.

"We cross the river up ahead and take a forest road to the trailhead," Shelby explained.

"I'm not in the best of shape," Reagan warned her.

Shelby stared at her for a moment. "I wouldn't have guessed. You seem to be very fit."

"I do a lot of walking, that's about it."

"In your job, you mean?"

Reagan nodded. Yeah…her *job*. Was that still her job? She felt darkness try to settle over her again and pushed it away, staring instead at the tranquil scene outside the window, the ever-flowing river taking some of her dark mood with it.

She finished her sandwich and wadded up the wrapping before putting it back inside the bag. She was stuffed and couldn't imagine taking a strenuous hike after eating that.

Before long, Shelby turned to the right, taking a small bridge across the river, the paved road turning to gravel on the other side. She handed Reagan the rest of her uneaten sandwich.

"I can't eat another bite," she said.

"You did a pretty good job," Reagan said, noting that only a small corner remained. As full as she was, she couldn't resist pulling off the last piece of bacon and popping it in her mouth.

The trailhead parking lot was carved into the forest and she was surprised to see that there were already six other cars there.

"Good. We beat the crowd."

"There'll be more?"

"It's a beautiful morning. It's the holiday season. I'm sure by noon the lot will be full. This is a popular hike in the winter," Shelby said. "There's only a short climb at the start, then it's pretty level until it dips down to the river," she said. "The last part of the trail follows the river back here. It'll take about two hours."

"Okay. I guess I can handle that," she said, wondering what Shelby meant by a "short climb."

They crossed a large patch of slushy snow that covered the trail, then it turned to dirt and rock as they moved into the sunshine again. She looked up into the clear sky, wondering if she'd ever seen it this blue before. She turned to stare at Shelby, finding the same color in her eyes.

"What?"

"Your eyes," she said. "Mirror image of the sky. Beautiful blue."

Shelby stared at her for a moment, then looked up into the sky as if assessing her comment. Her eyes were striking.

No doubt she'd had countless compliments before. Reagan wondered if it made her uncomfortable.

Shelby finally looked back at her. "Thank you," she said quietly.

Reagan gave voice to her earlier thought. "You hear that all the time, I guess."

"Not often with as much sincerity," Shelby said as she continued up the trail.

Reagan didn't offer a comment to that. She suspected Shelby would be wary of any compliment directed her way, whether it be about her looks or anything else. Having access to the family fortune had its benefits, surely, but she wondered if—when it came to dating—Shelby ever trusted anyone.

A large dark blue bird swooped down onto a low spruce branch in front of them, watching as they approached. He didn't appear to be concerned with their closeness.

"Stellar's jay," Shelby said. "Don't know if you've seen one before."

"No, I don't think so."

The bird fluttered up a few branches as they walked past. "I love the different shades of blue and the way it blends with the black on their head," Shelby said. "Do you take pictures of wildlife?"

Reagan shook her head. "My subjects are mostly people." She hoped Shelby wouldn't ask more questions.

Shelby paused. "You don't like to talk about your work, do you?"

They were starting the climb, and Reagan had a hard time catching her breath. Shelby didn't seem affected by the altitude at all.

"I'm kinda...taking a break from my work," she said. "I haven't told Josh or my parents." she admitted.

Shelby stared at her for a long moment, holding her gaze. Reagan wondered what she was seeing there. Could she see the pain? The heartbreak? The guilt? She must have seen something because her eyes softened and she finally nodded.

"Let's go hike."

CHAPTER NINE

Shelby was painfully aware of the quiet woman who hiked beside her. She'd offered bits of information about the area, hoping to draw Reagan into a conversation, but her attempts had failed. Most of Reagan's comments were one syllable, if anything at all.

She should let it go. Whatever was bothering Reagan, she obviously didn't want to talk about it. But, God, the pain in her eyes was almost too much to take. She couldn't imagine what had put that sorrow there. Had she lost someone she cared about? A lover? She had indicated that there had been no breakup, but could it have been something else? Something more tragic than a breakup?

"Wow. That's breathtaking."

Shelby glanced at her, surprised that Reagan had spoken. She then followed Reagan's gaze, seeing the snowcapped peaks to their north. The pristine white of the mountaintops was in sharp contrast to the deep blue sky.

"That's the southern edge of Rocky Mountain National Park," she said.

"Why is there so much snow there and not here?"

"We're quite a bit lower in elevation here, for one thing," she said. "And we're on the eastern slope, so it's dryer."

Reagan had stopped walking, her gaze still fixed on the distant peaks. Shelby studied her, again wondering at her sadness. Reagan turned then, capturing her eyes. They were as haunted as the first time she'd looked into them. Reagan looked so sad, so vulnerable at that moment that Shelby had to stop herself from going to her and embracing her.

"I'm sorry I'm not very good company," Reagan said, her voice not much more than a whisper.

"Tell me what makes you so sad," Shelby replied, her voice as soft as Reagan's. Their eyes held and Shelby could see the uncertainty in Reagan's, could see her warring emotions. Then Reagan pulled her eyes away, looking again to the mountains.

"I can't...can't pick up a camera. I can't even bear to look at one."

Shelby frowned, not understanding. Reagan looked back at her again, and Shelby knew she was ready to talk.

"Let's get off the trail," Shelby suggested. "We'll sit in the sunshine and talk." She hesitated. "Okay?"

Reagan finally nodded. "Yeah. We'll talk."

Shelby led her between two trees, up above the trail. There were several boulders to choose from and she picked a flat one, facing the sun. But Reagan didn't sit. She stood, her back to Shelby. Shelby waited patiently, letting Reagan decide the pace of their conversation.

Reagan finally turned, facing her. Shelby didn't comment on the tears she saw in Reagan's eyes.

"I owed Richard a favor. He wanted me to shoot for him in Afghanistan. He was doing a story on a village, on the civilians there." She shrugged. "I followed him around, getting whatever I could. Some of the villagers, well, they weren't exactly excited to have us there."

Reagan moved closer and sat down beside her. It was a long moment before she spoke again.

"It was a British group, like I said. I was the only American. Richard was the only one I knew but after being there six months, we all became friends."

Shelby sat silently, watching Reagan. She had a faraway look in her eyes, and Shelby knew, in her mind, Reagan was going back there.

"There was this kid. He was so cute. Couldn't have been more than five, six at the most," she said. "He'd come by all the time. We'd give him candy or whatever." A smile lit her face. "He never spoke, we didn't know his name. Cutest kid I've ever seen," she said. "We called him George. Little George," she said with another smile. "Don't know where he lived or who his parents were. He always came alone." She turned to her, her eyes swimming in tears. "Little George. I must have taken a thousand shots of him." She looked away again. "One day, he came like usual, and I had my camera, like always." She took a deep breath, then stood and moved away, pacing. "I'm just focusing on what my camera sees, nothing else. I'm capturing the scene, faces, people, Little George." She turned, looking at her again. "A young man came up, grabbed George. He had a bomb strapped to him. I'm sure I knew what was happening. Surely to God I knew," Reagan said, her voice cracking with emotion. "But I'm still holding my camera, shooting away. I sense Richard run to Little George, to try to help him. I could hear George screaming." She balled her hands into fists, tears streaming down her cheeks freely now.

"And I'm still working the goddamn scene, still shooting away like nothing's happening," she said. "The bomb goes off and I still have my camera, I'm capturing it all. The blast knocked me off my feet, threw me twenty feet back." She looked to the sky. "Only then did I put my camera down, only then did it register what had happened. Screams, crying, chaos. Little George, Richard...nothing much left of them. Twelve people killed, three from our group." She hung her head. "I never even tried to help him, to help George. I couldn't put my goddamn camera down. And now I can't…pick it up again."

Shelby got up then, moving closer. She touched Reagan's arm, but Reagan flinched away from her.

"No. I don't deserve to be comforted," she said through her tears. "What kind of human being am I? Richard was my *friend*. George…George was an innocent little kid. And I did *nothing* to help him. I never once lowered my camera, never missed a shot." She wiped her nose on the sleeve of her sweatshirt, but her tears never lessened.

Shelby tried again, lightly touching Reagan's arm. This time, she did not pull away. "Reagan, all of that probably happened in a matter of seconds," she said. "I can tell the guilt is eating you up, but if you'd tried to help, you'd be dead too." she said quietly.

Reagan looked at her. "I know. But it was just human nature for Richard. He tried to help, not considering the consequences. And I did *nothing*," she said again.

"You did what was instinctual for you," Shelby said. "I know nothing of your work, only what Stephanie has told me, but I gather you're very good at it. I don't know anything about cameras or taking pictures, but I would imagine you did what comes natural to you."

"Yeah. But what the hell does that say about me? It's as if I cared more about getting the shot than I did about their wellbeing."

"Is that true? Or were you simply focused on what you were doing? Maybe it didn't really register with you what was happening," she said. "Like I said, it probably only took a few seconds."

Reagan nodded slowly. "Yes. I've reduced it to slow-motion, frame by frame," she said quietly. "I try not to think about it, but I can't help it sometimes." She looked at her quickly. "I have dreams. Nightmares," she said. "Sometimes in my dreams, I throw the camera down and run to George. I always get there right when the bomb goes off. Other times, I see myself standing at a distance, not watching through the camera at all, just watching it unfold in front of me, doing nothing."

Shelby squeezed her arm. "Were you injured?"

Reagan shook her head. "Not really. A few scratches." She blew out her breath. "I packed up my things, my cameras, and came back here. And now I can't even think about holding a camera again."

"Don't you think you should talk to someone…a professional?"

"Yes. And they'll tell me like you've told me—I shouldn't feel guilty." Reagan shrugged. "But I do." She turned to her. "I've seen a lot of…of death. I've seen a lot of *shit* over the years," she said. "This was the first time it was personal. I didn't know Little George, yet I did. Richard, of course, we'd been friends for years." She snapped her fingers together. "And they were gone just like that." Tears came again. "And I captured it all. Frame by frame, right up to the explosion."

"Why do you think the bomber grabbed Little George?"

Reagan met her eyes. "He didn't want to die alone."

"He was planning on killing others with the bomb though. He wouldn't have really been alone," she reasoned. "Maybe he knew him. Brother? Father?"

"I don't think so. George was terrified."

Shelby moved closer to her. "When did this happen, Reagan? How long have you lived with this?"

Reagan rubbed her eyes with both hands, drying her tears. She cleared her throat before speaking.

"It happened the last week in November," she said. "I never told the authorities that I had any usable images. I couldn't bear the thought of someone looking at them." She shrugged. "We split up. They went back to London, I went home to the farm."

"Did you know Richard's family?"

"No. I mean, I knew of them, but I'd never met them. He had a wife, two kids," she said.

"I'm so sorry, Reagan. I wish I knew what to say to ease your pain." She let her hand slide down Reagan's arm, to her hand, squeezing it gently. "Am I the first one you've told about this?"

Reagan nodded. "Yes. I don't want to tell my family. I don't want them to judge me for not taking action. It would disappoint them."

"Oh, Reagan, you can't possibly think that. You were so close to being a victim yourself."

Reagan dropped her hand and took a step back. "Yeah. But I wasn't. And I have a camera full of images to prove it."

CHAPTER TEN

Reagan stood under the warm spray of water. Her shower long over, but it felt too good for her to want it to end. When they'd returned to Estes Park after their hike, she'd left Shelby in the lobby with a hasty "thank you" and fled to her room. She felt drained, both physically and emotionally. So she'd stripped off her clothes and climbed into bed, pulling the covers up tight, and fell into a surprisingly peaceful sleep.

Maybe talking to Shelby had been good for her after all. Hell, she hadn't cried like that in more years than she could remember, if ever. Yes, she felt guilty. Yes, she felt sorrow. Had she truly even grieved yet or had she merely been wallowing in the guilt?

She finally turned off the water and stepped out, reaching for the thick towel to dry herself. If she was honest with herself, no, she hadn't grieved. She'd pushed the images away, out of her mind, much like she'd done her camera...hidden away, out of sight.

She paused in her task, meeting her reflection in the mirror. If she had to do it over again, would she do it differently? Even if she hadn't had a camera, would she really have chased after a man with a bomb? A man running with a little boy she didn't really know?

She stared into her own eyes, seeing the truth there.

No.

And her tears came again, this time for her. Not for Richard. Not for Little George. She felt weak...cowardly. If she hadn't had a camera, if she'd had time to take stock of the situation, she would have most likely run in the opposite direction of the bomb.

A coward.

She tossed her towel on the floor and headed back to the bed. She wanted to hide. Hide under the covers, hide from people...hide from herself.

She pulled the covers over her head, shutting out the light. The depression settled around her like a thick cloak, weighing heavy on her body...her mind, her soul.

She closed her eyes, but the images remained, playing over and over again in her mind. She curled into a tight ball, her tears turning to sobs in the quiet, lonely hotel room.

CHAPTER ELEVEN

Shelby glanced toward the entrance of the bar once again. She'd come down early, hoping Reagan would be there, but there'd been no sign of her. The group dinner was in an hour, and her mother had two vans waiting to take them to the steakhouse where she'd reserved the back room for the wedding party. Reagan had said that she planned to go, but after their hike—after their talk—Reagan had seemed even more distant than before. That haunted look in her eyes was more pronounced, overshadowing any semblance of light.

Maybe she shouldn't have pushed Reagan to talk. It seemed to only have reinforced her guilt. It was as if Reagan took full responsibility for her friend's death, which was absurd, given the details that Reagan had shared with her.

She sighed. It really wasn't any of her business. She'd offered an ear to Reagan and that was it. There wasn't anything more she could do.

"Figured I would find you here."

Shelby turned, smiling as Stephanie sat down beside her. "Hi."

"Where have you been all day? We had so much fun shopping," Stephanie said.

"I went hiking down at Big Thompson Canyon," she said. "I took Reagan along."

Stephanie leaned closer. "You two sure seem to be getting along. Something I should know about?" she teased.

"Simply being friendly," she said. "Nothing more."

"Oh, and Doug said you told him you were gay." She laughed. "He doesn't believe you, of course, and he said he would spend the next week trying to, and I quote, 'get some sugar' from you. Beware of mistletoe."

Shelby rolled her eyes. "Some *sugar*? God," she groaned. "Who *says* that?"

"He's quite taken by you, apparently. He said he loves it when women play hard to get." She laughed again. "Josh and I didn't have the heart to tell him it was true."

"Thanks a lot," she said dryly. "You'll be lucky if I even stick around for the wedding."

"Now *that* would push Mother over the edge." Stephanie leaned closer again. "I bet Dad is thankful there was a problem in Aspen and he doesn't have to be here. She would drive me crazy if I had to live with her every single day."

Shelby knew all too well that the alleged problem in Aspen was only an excuse…but yes, her mother would drive her crazy as well. Actually, she found it amazing that they'd stayed married all these years. Neither she nor Stephanie would be surprised if he divorced her. She also wouldn't be shocked if he was having an affair. She suspected that he was, based on his numerous absences, but her mother had never said one word to her that suggested she was aware of an affair.

"There *was* a problem, right?" Stephanie prompted.

Shelby looked at her. "What do you mean?"

"I know we've talked about this before, but do you think—"

"It's none of our business, Steph," she said.

"I can't believe Mother doesn't suspect," she said, her voice low. "He's never around anymore."

"I know. But Mother lives in a different world, you know that."

"Yes, she does." Stephanie sighed. "Well, I'm not going to worry about it. Like you said, it's none of our business." She pointed at her empty glass. "Gin and tonic? I may join you for one."

"Sure." She got Zach's attention and pointed at her glass and held up two fingers. "So where's Josh?"

"Oh, he and Doug and two of their cousins were playing cards. He said it's like a family reunion. He hadn't seen Duke in nearly five years." She laughed. "Don't you just love that name? Duke?"

"For a Great Dane, sure."

Stephanie laughed again. "Oh, I know. I thought it was a nickname, but Josh said it's his given name. Duke," she said again. "It kinda grows on you."

"Speaking of cousins, have you spent any time with Holly?" She took the glass Zach placed in front of her. "Thanks."

"Thank you, Zach," Stephanie said. "She went shopping with us today. I think she thought Mother was going to pick up the tab for everyone's shopping excursion. And frankly, I'm shocked that Mother didn't," she added with a laugh. "But it was fun. Holly's sister Hannah is coming tomorrow. Her and her two kids. Her husband has to work this week but is coming on Sunday and staying through Christmas for the wedding."

"Don't you find it strange that they're here?" she asked. "We haven't seen them in years."

Stephanie shrugged. "It's a free vacation for them. Why wouldn't they come?"

"That doesn't bother you that they're coming for the free room and meals and not for your wedding?"

"Like you said, we haven't seen them in years. Whether they're here or not, it makes no difference to me. Mother only invited them—like you said—to show off the hotel and her money." She took a sip of her drink. "And if I ever get married again, please remind me of this chaos."

"Saturday wedding in July. Just sayin'," she said yet again. "And you and Josh are perfect for each other. If he can put up with you, that is," she teased.

Stephanie sighed dreamily. "I really do love him. He is perfect, isn't he?"

Shelby nodded. "As perfect as they come. For a man," she added with a quick laugh.

Stephanie looked at her, her expression turning serious. "I really wish you could find someone. I wish you could find your Josh," she said.

"I know. And someday I will. It's not something I want to force, though. If it happens, it happens." And honestly, that's how she felt. She wasn't lonely. She wasn't concerned that she was over thirty and still single. She had a full life and she enjoyed spending time with her family and friends. Even those friends who continued to set her up on disastrous blind dates.

"Hey."

The voice was quiet beside her and she turned, finding Reagan standing there. She searched her eyes, noting the puffiness. Had she been crying again? That thought made her heart break and she motioned to the chair beside her.

"Join us."

"I'm not interrupting?"

"Oh, no," Stephanie said. "Just chatting. You're joining the group for dinner, right?"

"Yes. My parents want to go and I haven't really spent much time with them." She looked at Zach who was standing by patiently. "Scotch," she said.

Shelby leaned closer to her, away from Stephanie. "You okay?" she whispered.

Their eyes held for a moment and Reagan nodded. "I guess. Thanks."

Shelby reached over and squeezed Reagan's thigh before she even realized what she was doing. She removed it just as quickly, embarrassed for touching her with a familiarity that they didn't have. But it brought a smile to Reagan's face so that was good, she thought.

"I understand Shelby made you go hiking with her," Stephanie said.

"I did not make her," Shelby protested.

"It was fun," Reagan said. "Really, having those breakfast sandwiches made it worth it."

"You took her to Dave's? God, how can you eat that stuff? It's *so* not good for you," Stephanie said.

"Yeah, but it was *so* good," Reagan countered.

Stephanie shook her head. "Oh, your mother joined us today," she said. "She's very sweet." She lowered her voice. "Normal. Unlike you-know-who."

Reagan laughed. "Yeah. I'll give her that. So how did she and your mother get along? This wedding celebration is the first time they've met, right?"

Stephanie nodded. "Yes. And I suppose they got along fine. Mother was being her usual bossy self. I made Josh go with us, so that helped."

"Speaking of you-know-who…" Shelby said, motioning to the entrance.

"There you girls are." Their mother looked disapprovingly at them. "Isn't it a little early to be drinking?"

"Never," Shelby said with a smile. "We're celebrating the wedding. Every hour, every day."

"Well, you'll have to make do with wine for dinner. I had several bottles brought in from your father's collection." She looked at Reagan. "He's a collector of fine and rare vintage wines." She paused. "Are you familiar with wine?"

"Mother," Shelby warned.

"What? I'm merely asking."

"I'm not a big wine drinker, no," Reagan said. "But a sweet sangria goes down pretty good on a hot summer day."

Her mother stared at Reagan blankly as if she'd uttered a blasphemy, and Shelby couldn't contain her laughter. Reagan, too, sported a teasing smile. It was nice to see that the smile actually reached her eyes.

"Does Dad know you've snatched some of his wine?" Stephanie asked.

"He picked it out personally." Their mother squared her shoulders. "We leave in five minutes. The vans are out front. I trust that Josh will make it on time?"

"I'll call him," Stephanie offered.

"Please do. I don't want to keep the other guests waiting. How would that look?"

Reagan tossed back the last of her drink and Shelby did the same to hers. She loved her mother, she really did. But this extra-long wedding celebration was proving to be an exercise in patience. She no longer lived near her parents, but they had a standing dinner date twice a month. That was about the extent of her interaction with her mother. Her father, on the other hand, she saw daily at the office, unless it was during the months that she worked here at the hotel. She and her father were very much alike and got along wonderfully. She and her mother... not so much.

"Is she always like this?" Reagan whispered.

"Unfortunately, yes," Shelby said.

Her mother turned around, addressing Shelby.

"Oh, and I have the seating already arranged. You and Doug will be dining at the head table with Stephanie and Josh. And me, of course." She turned to Reagan. "I took the liberty of seating you with your parents and I believe a cousin of yours... Duke."

"Thank you so much," Reagan murmured dryly as her mother turned away again.

"Who is Duke?" Shelby asked. "Stephanie said he was playing cards with Josh and Doug earlier."

"Duke is a cousin on my mom's side. He's the same age as Josh and Doug."

"He grew up with them too?"

"Yeah. They lived in town though. Not on a farm."

"And do you get along with him?"

Reagan shrugged. "He and Dougie are close. Besides, you know, once I started working—traveling—I don't get back to the farm that often. Whenever I'm in between assignments, I usually go to Denver to see Josh, then head to the farm for a day or two to see my parents," she said. "It's not often that I see anyone else."

Shelby groaned. "And there's Dougie now," she said, using Reagan's nickname.

He smiled broadly as they walked up to the van. "My maid of honor," he said dramatically as he bowed at the waist. "What a privilege to be dining with you this evening. I can hardly wait."

Reagan laughed. "Are you this dorky all the time?"

Doug's smile faded. "Shame you don't get to sit at the head table, Ray Ray. I'll miss visiting with you. I think you're somewhere in the back of the room."

As she saw the shadow settle on Reagan's face, Shelby suddenly got angry with her mother. Why wouldn't Reagan—Josh's sister—get to sit with them? In fact, why not her parents too?

"Actually, there's been a change in plans on the seating arrangements," Shelby said. "Only *immediate* family will be at the head table. I believe you'll be seated with your cousin, Duke."

Before he could protest, she took Reagan's hand and led her into the van. Her mother was already seated and Shelby could tell by the look on her face that she'd heard her announcement to Doug. She smiled sweetly at her mother.

"The family should all sit together," she said pointedly.

"But my instructions to the staff were—"

"I'm sure it won't be a big deal to change." She looked around. "Where's Steph?"

"She and Josh are in the other van with his parents."

Shelby nodded and leaned back with a sigh. Her mother really was too much sometimes.

"I think your mother has a crush on Dougie," Reagan whispered into her ear.

Shelby turned, their eyes meeting. Sometimes, making a little teasing comment like this chased some of the sadness from Reagan's eyes. She smiled at her, hoping to keep the lightness of Reagan's mood intact for a little longer. So she leaned closer, her mouth inches from Reagan's ear.

"My mother is pretending I'm not gay. She's actually trying to play matchmaker," she said quietly. "She does this every once in a while, thinking I'll snap out of my gayness." She paused. "If I wasn't gay, Doug would make me seriously consider it."

Reagan contained her laughter, but her eyes were swimming in merriment. Shelby returned her grin, knowing that—at least for a few moments—Reagan's mood had lightened and quite possibly, for the first time in a long while, her personal tragedy wasn't first and foremost on her mind.

They sat quietly as the van pulled away. Shelby listened absently to the conversations going on around them. She was content simply sitting next to Reagan. Their shoulders were touching and she didn't find it odd in the least that they were sitting as close together as they were. She found it comforting.

"Do you have anything planned tomorrow?" Reagan asked, breaking their silence.

Shelby turned to her. "No. You?"

"It's supposed to be another nice day," Reagan said. "I thought maybe you'd take me into the national park and show me around."

Shelby smiled and nodded. "I'd love to. We can only go as far as Bear Lake though. The road is not maintained past that during the winter. But there's an easy hiking trail around the lake." She sat up, already mentally making plans. They could make a day of it. Maybe have lunch in the park. "We really need to drive out there in the evenings too, right at dusk. The elk herd—thousands of them—come down into the valley to graze and you can usually find bighorn sheep too." She recognized the excitement in her voice, and she tried to temper it. "I mean, if you want to. That may not be anything you'd be interested in."

"I wish we were doing that right now instead of heading out to dinner with the group," Reagan said quietly.

Shelby leaned back again, their shoulders touching once more. "Me too."

CHAPTER TWELVE

"Sangria wine?"

"Yes. Surely you have a bottle," Shelby said.

"Your mother inventoried the wine selection. I'm pretty sure sangria wasn't allowed in here this week," he said.

"Oh, come on, Ty. When she threw out all the cheap wine, where did you put it?"

"Okay. I'll go see if I can find a bottle. Will you watch the bar?"

Shelby grinned. "I always wanted to be a bartender."

He pointed at her. "Please don't mess anything up. Your mother will have me fired."

"Ty, my mother may *think* she runs things, but she doesn't." She motioned him away. "Hopefully, we'll have no bar customers this early in the morning. At least for nothing more than coffee."

She sat down on a barstool and spun it around to face the entrance. There were two people in the bar, sitting in a quiet corner, both drinking coffee. She'd told her father that they needed to add a small coffee bar with breakfast options like pastries or muffins. Not everyone enjoyed a big breakfast like the restaurant offered. Some, like her, simply wanted a cup of coffee and something light to eat while enjoying the morning paper. You couldn't do that in a noisy restaurant. Maybe she would talk to him again about it.

Of course, having a full-service restaurant did have its advantages. Especially when the kitchen staff didn't mind doing favors. Like fixing a picnic lunch for her on the spur of the moment. She knew Reagan wasn't expecting anything other than a trip into the park, a short hike around Bear Lake and some sightseeing. But it was a sunny, cloudless day and the temperature was going to be near fifty. It was too pretty a day to waste. They would find a picnic table in the sun and have lunch…and a bottle of sangria wine, if Ty could find one.

"Here you go," he said, holding up two bottles. "There's a whole case."

"I only need one. Put the other in the cooler for me."

"Your mother—"

"Will not come in here and inspect the bar," she told him. She took a twenty-dollar bill and shoved it in his tip jar. "Thank you."

He grinned. "Any time."

She turned and left with her treasure, heading to the lobby and the front desk. She shook her head at Bruce, the manager, as he looked at her questioningly.

"I don't need anything," she said. "I'm sneaking through the back to get to the kitchen," she explained.

"Well, do you have a minute?"

She stopped. "Sure. What's up?"

"Your mother."

She groaned. "Now what?"

"The Christmas tree in the lobby," he started.

"Yes? It's beautiful, as always," she said. "She doesn't like it?"

"Quite the opposite," he said. "She wants me to have it moved into the ballroom."

"Oh, God…for the *wedding*?"

"Yes, for the dance and then the wedding. I've already told her that we plan to decorate the ballroom with several smaller trees as it is. But she—"

"No. No, no, no," she said with a shake of her head. "The tree in the lobby stays. How did she think you were going to move it? Bring in a forklift?"

"I have no idea."

"Look, just decorate the ballroom as you planned. I'm assuming she's already given you instructions on that as well," she said.

"Oh, yes. And you wouldn't *believe* what all she wants," he said.

"Oh, I'd believe it all right." She smiled. "Don't worry about the tree. I'll talk to her," she promised.

"Thanks, Shelby. I appreciate it."

"No problem."

"What's up in the kitchen, anyway?"

"I commandeered the staff into making me a picnic lunch," she said. She held up the bottle of wine. "To go with this cheap sangria."

He laughed. "After your mother got through, I didn't think we had any cheap wine left."

"Ty found it for me." She smiled. "I know you'll all be glad when my mother is out of your hair and things can get back to normal."

"Let's hope this is the only wedding of hers we'll be hosting."

"Given up hope on me, have you?" she teased as she walked away.

"Your wedding would be out in the park somewhere, I'd guess," he called after her.

"For sure," she agreed.

* * *

"I can't believe how warm it is," Reagan said as they stepped onto the trail at Bear Lake. "Feels like spring."

"I know. Isn't it beautiful?" Shelby asked, staring up into the blue, blue sky. "I love days like this," she said. "No wind, no clouds…simply beautiful sunshine."

"There's more snow here than where we hiked the other day though," Reagan noted.

"This is one of the lone trails still open for hiking," she said. "Most of the others are for cross-country skiing, which I hate."

"Do you? I thought you told Dougie that you skied."

Shelby smiled. "Yeah, downhill. Now that's fun. I find nothing enjoyable about slugging along on thin skis, especially uphill. Too damn much work."

They fell into step along the trail which circled the lake. By late January, the lake would be mostly frozen over, but today it was shimmering in the warm sunlight. She recognized the call of a Clark's nutcracker in the trees, and she looked up, hoping to spot it.

"So when you stay up here at the hotel, what do you do? Hike every day?" Reagan asked.

"I buy a season pass to the park so I come here a lot, yes. But there are other hiking trails in the area that aren't in the park," she said. "And I'm not really a rabid hiker," she explained. "A couple of miles is about my limit." She motioned to the trail they were on. "I love this trail. It's long enough to get you out in the forest, but not too long. Unfortunately, it's the most popular hike in the park for that very reason. If you want solitude, this is not the trail."

"Not crowded today though," Reagan said.

"I know. I'm surprised, since it's such a nice day."

"So if I wanted to stay at the hotel, what would a room cost me?"

"Two hundred a night for a single."

"Wow. How do normal people afford that?"

She shrugged. "It's a luxury hotel. You get what you pay for," she said easily. "It's not for everyone. And sometimes, people just want to experience it once, so they save during the year so they can splurge on it for a long weekend."

"Do you have a particular room or something different each time you come?"

"I have a suite," she said. "Nothing huge—a bedroom, a small living room and a mini-kitchen."

"A suite, huh?"

"Top floor, corner," she supplied.

"Let me guess. Facing the mountains?"

She smiled. "Yes, facing the mountains."

"And do your parents have a suite too?"

"Yes. Larger than mine and it rarely gets used."

"And it faces town," Reagan guessed.

"Wow. Didn't take you long to figure out my mother," Shelby said with a laugh. "I think she likes to pretend she's a queen looking down on her subjects."

The trail snaked away from the water and into the trees. The snow was deeper here, but others had come before them and they followed in their tracks. The sunshine and warmer temps had turned it slushy.

"Are you dating someone?" Reagan asked after a while.

Shelby shook her head. "It seems the older I get, the less patience I have for dating," she said. "Actually, I find myself completely bored on most of my dates." She glanced at Reagan. "Blind dates," she added.

"Why blind dates?"

"Well-meaning friends," she said with a wave of her hand. "They insist they have the *perfect* date for me. And that's never the case." She paused. "Besides, I always have this fear that the only reason they want to go out with me is because of the family business."

"You mean the family *money?*"

"Yes. Which is crazy. I mean, someday, sure, I'll inherit some of it. But right now, I work just like they do. It's not like I get an allowance or anything."

Reagan looked at her skeptically.

"I don't," she said. Then, "Well, my salary might be a little higher because I'm his daughter," she admitted. "And bonuses."

Reagan laughed.

"But I *do* work for it."

Reagan raised her eyebrows. "You think I'm judging you?"

Shelby blew out her breath. "I sometimes judge myself."

Reagan shook her head. "You shouldn't have to apologize for being born into a wealthy family, Shelby."

"I know. And I try so hard to keep things *normal*." She nudged Reagan's shoulder. "And I shouldn't even be telling you this, but Stephanie is too much like our mother. I hope Josh can keep her grounded."

"Well, the short time I've known you, I can say without a doubt that you are *nothing* like your mother. I haven't met your father, but I assume you're more like him."

She nodded. "Yes. My mother came from a middle-class family," she said. "She and my father met at a college party. By all accounts, they shouldn't have hit it off. They were from two different worlds." She smiled. "But my dad said he fell in love that very night." She glanced over at Reagan. "Probably because she was so different from the girls he was used to dating. And according to him, my mother used to be fun, used to be carefree. He blames himself for her change. He brought her into the family…she suddenly had servants, cooks, an assistant to handle even the most mundane of personal chores for her. By the time I was born, he said she was a completely different person." Shelby shrugged. "Of course, how she is now is all I know. She's always been this way."

"What about her family?" Reagan asked. "I know you and Holly aren't close."

Shelby shrugged. "Average family…normal. But after she married, she kinda shunned them. She doesn't have a whole lot to do with her sisters now at all, so we really never got to know that side of the family," she said. "I didn't know my grandparents at all. I could count on one hand the number of times we saw them."

"Are they still alive?"

"She is. She's in a nursing home, which my mother pays for but that doesn't mean she goes to visit her. And she doesn't ever let her sisters forget that she pays for it." She glanced at Reagan. "I hate that about her."

"What about your dad's side of the family?"

Shelby smiled at her. "Inquisitive today, aren't you?"

Reagan shrugged. "Just curious."

Shelby nodded. Surprisingly, she didn't mind sharing her family history with Reagan. Normally, she avoided talking about her family, thinking it really wasn't anyone's business. But she found Reagan easy to talk to. And maybe later, she could learn more about Reagan, if she felt like sharing, that is.

"Well, as my mother used to say, 'as luck would have it, your father is an only child.'"

Reagan laughed. "Ah...so all the money goes to him."

"Already has," she said. "They're both gone. And it was a very sad time. They were very down-to-earth. You would have never guessed that they were so wealthy. They were very ordinary people, and Stephanie and I were so close to them."

"They lived in Denver?"

"Yes. We lived close enough to walk to their house," she said. "My grandmother had a stroke at a young age...she was only seventy-two. Then died a year later." She shook her head. "They were so in love...right up until the end. He died only four months after." She smiled sadly. "It was like he died of a broken heart." She paused, remembering the looks her grandparents would share, their love there for all to see. "Growing up, we were around them a lot. They were my role models for the perfect couple. They were always happy, always affectionate with each other, always in love."

Reagan arched an eyebrow. "Your parents?"

Shelby sighed. "Oh, I don't know. My mother is hard to live with." She gave a quick laugh. "As you can probably imagine by being around her the little you have."

"She would try my patience, yes."

"I know. Maybe that's why my dad is not here. And maybe that's why their marriage has survived this long...he's not around her that much anymore. But I don't know...she's more concerned with outside perception than anything else. It's like this wedding. It's consumed her for the last year. I mean, *consumed* her. It's like this is her sole purpose in life."

"So...happily married...not so much?"

"No. Oh, they pretend they are," she said. "My father is absent a lot."

"Like now, even at the wedding?"

"Yes. When you own three hotels, there's always an excuse to be made as to why you must visit one or the other. The current excuse is a problem in Aspen."

"Does he have a mistress?"

Shelby hesitated. Was she really having this discussion with Reagan? Should she be having this discussion with *anyone* outside the family? Reagan apparently sensed her hesitation.

"What? Too personal?"

She shrugged. "Stephanie and I were just talking about that. Even though we suspect that maybe he does, it's not any of our business."

"It's not any of your business or you really don't want to know?"

Shelby sighed. "Both, I suppose."

CHAPTER THIRTEEN

Reagan laughed as Shelby handed her the bottle of sangria wine. "You found a bottle of my favorite, huh?"

Shelby smiled. "It's not a hot summer day but it'll have to do."

Reagan fingered the corkscrew, watching as Shelby unpacked the picnic basket. When she'd asked for a tour of the park, she hadn't anticipated all this. She was pleasantly surprised that Shelby wanted to spend this much time with her. She knew she hadn't been the best of company on some of their outings. She turned the corkscrew over and inserted in, turning it quickly and pulling out the cork.

"You know your way around a wine bottle," Shelby said.

"Because I can open a bottle of wine doesn't mean I like the stuff."

"I know. I'm not really a wine drinker either, which is surprising. As my mother said, they have quite a collection of wine and I grew up drinking it."

"Gin and tonic more your style?"

Shelby nodded. "When I'm stressed...gin and tonic. When I'm relaxed and mellow...a nice brandy will do."

Reagan met her gaze. "I don't recall you having a brandy even once."

"You're right." Then she smiled. "But I am relaxed now so the sangria will have to suffice."

Reagan nodded. "So, what do we have here?"

"Not quite sure," Shelby said. She opened one of the containers, finding a nice, thick sandwich, cut in half. "Appears to be roast beef." She opened another and found turkey. "Do you have a preference?"

"How about half of each," Reagan suggested.

"Deal." Shelby pulled out two small bags of chips. "It's like a real picnic," she said, sliding one bag across the picnic table toward her.

"It was nice of you to do all of this," Reagan said.

"Too pretty a day to be indoors," Shelby said as she pulled out two wineglasses.

Reagan filled both of them, sliding one in front of Shelby. Then she picked up the thick roast beef sandwich and inspected it. The beef was covered with onions and some sort of white sauce. Horseradish? The bread was smeared with brown mustard. She closed it back up and took a bite, moaning at the taste.

"Really good. Spicy."

"The turkey is good too," Shelby said. "It's got a cucumber-cilantro mayo on it. They make it fresh in the restaurant."

"This has a nice horseradish sauce," she said as she took another bite.

They ate in silence for a moment, and she could feel Shelby watching her. She finally met her gaze with an arched eyebrow.

Shelby smiled slightly, then wiped her mouth before speaking. "We've talked about me. What about you?"

"What about me? You want to know about growing up on a farm?" she asked.

"I imagine it would be fun," Shelby said.

"Not so much. Lots of work. And as a kid, you don't think of the animals as a food source, they're pets. So when one of them disappears and ends up on the dinner table, it would be quite traumatic."

"Oh. I didn't think of that," Shelby said. "What kind of farm?"

"Corn and wheat. We kept a few cows and chickens. Those were for us to eat, not sell." She shook her head. "I learned pretty quickly to stop naming them. In fact, I stopped eating meat at home, knowing it was one of my friends." She looked at Shelby. "I didn't have a lot of real friends," she explained. "I preferred the company of farm animals to the kids at school."

Shelby took a sip of wine. "When did you know you were gay?"

Reagan smiled. "You think that's why I avoided friends? Because I was gay?"

"Some do."

"Did you?" Reagan asked.

"For a time, yes. I was afraid they would find out and shun me so it was easier to shun them first," she said. "I didn't tell a soul until I was in college."

"I'm guessing your mother didn't take it well," Reagan said.

"That's an understatement," Shelby said. "But we were talking about you, not me."

Reagan nibbled on a chip, remembering the conversation with her mother like it was yesterday.

"I was young. Tenth grade," she said. "I had a huge crush on Tammy Melton. She played basketball. So I tried out for the team too." She laughed. "And I sucked. So Tammy offered to coach me."

"Ah…Tammy had a crush too," Shelby guessed.

"Yep."

"She was your first?"

Reagan sighed. "She was my first kiss. And my first make-out session." Then she shook her head. "But she freaked out when it got a little heated. She called me a freak and a pervert," she said.

"Oh, you're kidding me. The little bitch."

Reagan laughed. "That she was. I think she assumed I would tell everyone what we'd been doing, so she got it out first. She said I'd forced her and...well, it wasn't a real fun time for me."

Shelby reached across the table and squeezed her hand. "I'm so sorry. Kids can be cruel."

"Don't I know," she said. "I went home and locked myself in my room and cried like a baby," she admitted. "Of course, my mother knew why. One of the other mothers called her to let her know what had happened." She smiled. "And she was so great. She brought dinner into my room, just for the two of us. And we talked. And I told her what had really happened."

"She already suspected you were gay?"

Reagan nodded. "Yes. So she wasn't shocked by it. I wouldn't go so far as to say she was happy about it, but she wasn't shocked. And she didn't go crazy over it or anything. And she told me she loved me and that mean people like Tammy didn't deserve my tears."

"Oh, that's so sweet."

"Yeah. But school wasn't a whole lot of fun for a while after that," she said. "Not a lot of them wanted to hang out with me, if you know what I mean."

"Did you and Tammy ever talk about it?"

"Oh, she avoided me for the next year, at least. Then one day out of the blue, she came up to me and wanted to apologize." Reagan shook her head. "I wanted to tell her to go to hell." She shrugged. "But I no longer had a crush on her and it didn't matter to me one way or the other. I knew what I was, who I was. And I knew she was struggling with it."

"Was her apology before or after Becky McFarlane?" Shelby asked.

Reagan smiled. "After. But then I left for college and didn't go back. Well, other than to the farm now and then. I haven't seen anyone I went to high school with since the day we graduated."

Shelby finished her turkey and picked up the roast beef half. "So how was college?"

"Fun. Made a few friends."

"And your choice of a career?" Shelby asked.

Reagan realized she had spent almost the entire day without the heavy weight of Richard's death hanging over her. And all it took was an innocent question from Shelby to bring it back. Shelby seemed to sense this as, again, her hand reached across the table and found hers.

"You can't carry that guilt forever, Reagan. You have to let it go," Shelby said gently.

"Am I that easy to read?"

"To me you are. Your eyes have been clear today, not shadowed. Not until I asked that one simple question," Shelby said. "So answer it."

Reagan closed her eyes for a moment, chasing away images she wanted to forget. She opened them again, then nodded.

"I needed a one-hour course to meet my financial aid requirements," she said. "A friend talked me into taking a photography class. I fell in love with it."

Shelby took a sip of her wine, but her eyes never left Reagan's.

"Do you want to talk some more about...about what happened?"

Reagan shrugged. "Not much more to say. But I think it did help to talk about it," she said. "I feel better today." She tapped her head. "Up here."

"I know it's none of my business, Reagan, but I really think you should talk to a professional."

Reagan shook her head. "I'm afraid they'll want me to take a look at the images on my camera. Some sort of closure or something. And I don't think I can do that. Not yet."

Shelby rested her chin in her palm, her eyes thoughtful as she watched her. "I didn't know Richard, of course, or know anything about him...but he assembled this team, right?"

Reagan nodded. "Yes. Mostly colleagues he'd worked with before on other projects," she said.

"Do you think he felt responsible for their safety?"

"Of course. It was his project."

Shelby nodded. "So then maybe Richard wasn't trying to save George, but rather he was trying to protect his team."

It wasn't something she had considered before. "I don't know. It all happened so fast. I'm shooting…the guy with the bomb, he looks like anyone else. He's dressed in traditional garments." She closed her eyes for a moment, seeing it again in her mind. "When he grabbed George, his top—I think they call it a *perahan*—came up on the side, I could see the bomb strapped to his waist," she said. "But I was shooting George." She opened her eyes, meeting Shelby's. "I keep shooting but I'm thinking, Jesus Christ, that's a bomb…but I keep shooting. The next thing I know, Richard is in my frame and it registers that it's Richard…but I keep shooting." She paused. "And the bomb goes off. And I see what happens. I get blown back by the blast and instinctively I shield my camera, I guess, because it wasn't damaged at all."

"And then what?" Shelby asked gently.

"And then chaos…crying…screaming…people running."

"What did you do?"

"I don't…I don't remember, really," she said. "I remember looking around and it was like everything was happening in slow motion. And I remember thinking, you've got your camera, you should be using it to capture the scene. That was my job." Reagan shook her head. "But I couldn't." She ran a hand through her hair. "Bentley was injured, bleeding badly. I went to him first. He was in shock. Hell, I guess we all were."

"So why do you blame yourself, Reagan?"

"I should have done something," she said.

Shelby was watching her intently, so much so that Reagan had to pull her eyes away, afraid of what she might find there.

"You say you don't want to pick up a camera," Shelby said. "But is it because of the images that are on it…or is it because you blame the camera somehow?"

A simple observation, but it hit home nonetheless. She nodded. "If I hadn't been holding the camera, if I hadn't been shooting George, then maybe I could have done something. Or at the very least, stopped Richard." She closed up the container on the turkey sandwich, unable to finish it. "I have no idea what I'm going to do now," she said. "I only know I can't go back to what I was doing. There was always too much pain and suffering...too much tragedy. Darkness, never light," she murmured.

"So maybe you need to change your subject matter," Shelby suggested. "Instead of chasing wars and tragedies...maybe you should chase smiles and happiness."

Reagan looked at her doubtfully. "What? Like a wedding photographer or something?"

Shelby smiled. "That would be a good start. Or kids' birthday parties. Or parades. Or—"

Reagan laughed. "Okay, I get it. Smiles and happiness." She paused and looked around. "Or maybe I should be chasing mountains and sunshine. It certainly makes me feel good to be out here." She met Shelby's gaze. "Or maybe it's you that makes me feel good."

Shelby smiled sweetly at her. "Maybe both."

CHAPTER FOURTEEN

Shelby shook her head. "There's nothing going on," she insisted.

"Then why have you been sneaking off with her?"

"Steph, I have *not* been sneaking off. She asked me to show her the park, so I did."

"And a picnic lunch?"

Shelby raised her eyebrows.

"Bruce told me."

"It was a beautiful day." She sat down on the sofa and kicked off her boots. "Besides, you wanted us to be friends, didn't you?"

"I wanted you to be friends so you could find out what was going on with her, that's all." Stephanie sat down beside her. "So? What have you found out?"

Shelby debated whether to tell Stephanie or not. If she told Stephanie, then she'd tell Josh, who would then tell his parents. She didn't think Reagan would appreciate that. "I think...that she's going to be fine," she said instead.

"What does that mean?"

"It means that if she wants anyone to know, she'll tell them. It's not my place."

"But she told you?"

Shelby nodded. "Yes. We've talked about it a couple of times now and I think she's going to be okay. She needs some time."

Stephanie eyed her suspiciously. "So why did she tell you and not her family?"

Shelby smiled. "We bonded. Like you suggested."

"Oh, my God. You *do* like her," Stephanie teased. "I knew it. I told Josh there was something going on with you two. You can tell by the way you look at each other."

"There is *nothing* going on," she said again. "Now, what has Mother got planned for dinner?" she asked, changing the subject. "And is it something I can get out of?"

"I must have been out of my mind when I agreed to all this," Stephanie said with a wave of her hand. "She's got the seafood extravaganza on the menu tonight."

Shelby bit her lip. Seafood was her favorite, especially when it involved shrimp. It was going to be hard to pass it up. "Only Mother would do seafood at Christmas in Colorado. Where? Here?"

"Yes. They're sectioning off part of the restaurant."

"Well, I guess I'll have to suffer through it. You know me and seafood."

Stephanie laughed. "Yes, I knew I could count on you. Tomorrow is spa day. I'm really looking forward to that. Josh and I are going to do a mud bath and a couples massage," she said.

"Spa day? Okay. I guess I'm going to have to go to that too," she said.

"Thought you would." She paused. "Have you heard from Dad?"

Shelby shook her head. "No. Why?"

"I asked Mother if she knew when he was coming up again. She said she didn't have any idea, and Shelby, she didn't even try to make up an excuse or anything. You know how she normally says that he's got this or that going on and how he's so busy. Well, she said nothing like that."

Shelby shook her head. "No. I know that look, and no, I am not going to talk to her."

"You're the oldest. She might need someone to talk to."

"So? You're closer to her than I am. You talk to her."

"No way. How about you talk to Dad?"

"Stephanie, do we really want to know what's going on? I mean really?" she asked, echoing Reagan's earlier remark.

"Yes, I do. I don't want to bury my head in the sand and act like everything is rosy. Because it's not." She grabbed Shelby's arm. "It's my wedding and he's not even here."

"Your wedding is not until next Friday," Shelby reminded her. "I'm fairly certain he'll be here by the weekend."

"The ballroom dance is Monday. He better be here by then. He's supposed to do the first dance with me."

Shelby rubbed her forehead. "I had forgotten the big dance Mother had planned. I hope enough guests are here by then."

"I think the weekend is when most everyone is coming," Stephanie said. "Did you hear Mother wants to move the Christmas tree from the lobby to the ballroom? How is that even possible?"

"It's not. And I forgot I promised Bruce I would speak to her about it." Now she rubbed her temple, hoping to ward off her fast-approaching headache. The relaxed feeling she'd had after spending time with Reagan in the park was fading fast.

"And one other thing…she's back on the bridesmaid dresses."

"Great. You're really full of good news, aren't you?"

"Well, I told her that I was perfectly fine with Reagan wearing a tux and so is Josh," Stephanie said. "Mother wouldn't hear of it. She said if Reagan won't wear a dress, she would not be a part of the wedding party."

"Jesus Christ, Steph, is it her wedding or yours?"

Stephanie laughed. "Well, it's hers, obviously."

"It's not funny," she said. "She's obsessed with this. It's like it's life or death to her. She's surely not enjoying herself."

"I know. But you can't do anything but laugh."

"How many times have you thought about eloping?"

Stephanie's expression turned serious. "Counting twice today? About fifty."

"Oh, Steph…why did you let her talk you into all of this?"

"Come on, you know Mother. This is her big splash."

"And when are all of her friends coming?"

"Monday for the dance, I think," Stephanie said. "Of course, some of them won't stay for the wedding on Friday. They've got their own Christmas obligations." She sighed. "That's one reason I wanted a Christmas wedding," she said. "I thought it would only be us. Just the family. Mine and Josh's. A small, intimate Christmas wedding. That's what I wanted."

"And instead, it's this big production lasting nearly two weeks."

"Well, two weeks for some. I get to get out of here bright and early Saturday morning and go to Hawaii," Stephanie said. "And it can't come soon enough."

"Yes. I'm thinking I'm heading back to Denver on Saturday too," she said.

Stephanie shook her head. "Wouldn't it be sad if the only people still here are her family taking advantage of the free rooms?"

"It would serve her right," Shelby said. "And I know that's mean to say, but she rubs it in their faces any chance she gets."

"Do you think we'll even recognize our aunts? I haven't seen any of them since I was a kid, I think."

Shelby tried to picture them. "Aunt Laura is the oldest. Holly's mother is Kathleen, isn't she?"

"I think so. Holly is what? Between us?"

"I think she's a year older than you," Shelby said. "And then Aunt Kay, the youngest. I think I would know them," she said. "We went with Mother when they put their mother in the nursing home, remember?"

"Talk about depressing," Stephanie murmured.

Shelby stood up. "Okay, enough of this. I need a drink." She went to her mini-kitchen and opened a cabinet, finding her bottle of brandy along with a cognac. She chose the cognac. "You want one?"

"It's three o'clock, Shelby."

She sighed. "God, I know." She put the cognac back. "What is it about our mother that makes me want to drink so?"

"Stress."

She grabbed a water bottle from the fridge instead. "I'm sorry, Steph, but I can't wait for your wedding to be over with."

"You and me both," she said. "And Josh has been hanging out with his cousins, leaving me with Mother. And she is non-stop about the wedding."

Shelby sighed. "Well, I guess I need to find her and have a talk about the tree in the lobby."

"It's an hour before dinner. Why don't you wait until then?" Stephanie suggested. "She'll be less likely to cause a scene."

"I guess I could go down a little early."

Stephanie stood. "Well, I'll let you shower. I should go get ready too." She paused. "And you should consider something other than jeans tonight, Shelby. Mother wants it to be fancy and jeans won't do it."

"For a seafood buffet? I think jeans will be fine."

Stephanie shook her head. "I'm wearing that new silk blouse Mother got me with a skirt."

"And I'll be wearing a sweater over a turtleneck," she said. "And if my mood hasn't completely soured by then, I'll wear khakis instead of jeans."

Stephanie laughed. "You do that just to piss her off, don't you?"

"Yes. Because she makes such a big deal out of it. I dress up every day at the office. When I'm here, I'm wearing what makes me comfortable. You'll be lucky to get khakis."

Stephanie walked over and gave her a quick hug. "Just so you know, what you wear to the office every day...I wouldn't exactly call it dressing up."

Shelby frowned. "You don't consider my expensive power suits 'dress up'? Not even the one with pinstripes?"

Shelby shook her head. "Maybe if you paired them with skirts. You have sexy legs, Shelby. Why don't you show them off?"

"And who do I want to show them off to at the office?"

"You never know who you might meet. What if—when I met Josh at that Christmas party—I hadn't been wearing what I was? He may not have even noticed me."

Shelby waved her away. She was long weary of this conversation. "Okay. Whatever. See you down at dinner."

"Reached your limit, huh?"

"Yep."

"Okay. See you at dinner."

She sighed heavily when the door closed. Stephanie would never admit it, but she sure was an awful lot like their mother.

"Poor Josh," she murmured.

CHAPTER FIFTEEN

Shelby walked into the restaurant about fifteen minutes early. The back portion had been walled off by a partition and she heard her mother's voice giving instructions. She nodded politely at Sonya—who was seating an elderly couple—as she made her way to the partition. She had to admit, it looked nice. The tables were covered in alternating green and red tablecloths. Freshly cut spruce boughs were arranged on each table and red and green candles were already lit. She spied her mother talking to one of the chefs and she went over.

"I specifically asked for three types of cocktail shrimp, not two. And what about the crab legs?"

"Yes, ma'am, we'll have crab legs. But if you want three kinds of cocktail shrimp, then I'll have to go short somewhere else. We were going to fry some and sauté some with a mushroom sauce for the pasta you wanted."

"Fry? I don't like fried. That seems so—"

"Delicious," Shelby said, interrupting her. She turned to the chef. "Two types of cocktail shrimp are sufficient," she said. "Please don't cut short my fried shrimp."

He nodded with relief. "Thank you. Yes. I'll get right to it."

Her mother stared at her. "Since when have you taken an interest in the menu?"

"Since you were about to cancel the fried shrimp," she said. "Mother, there aren't that many guests yet. There's no need to have three varieties of cocktail shrimp."

"Well, I think having only two lacks focus and planning. I wouldn't want anyone to think that I'm skimping on this meal."

"No one will think that." She clasped her arm at the elbow and led her away from the tables. "I need to talk to you. It's about the Christmas tree in the lobby."

"Yes. I meant to talk to you too. I tried to call you this morning," she said.

"I was at the park," Shelby said, completely forgetting about the missed call from her mother. "Reagan wanted a quick tour."

"What park?"

"The national park."

"Oh. I should have guessed that's where you were. Well, about the tree. I want it moved into the ballroom in time for the dance Monday. And of course it'll be there for the wedding on Friday. Bruce has yet to do it. I need you to talk to him."

"Yes. About that. The tree is not going to get moved, Mother. It stays in the lobby."

Her mother's eyes widened. "It's one thing for you to override me in regard to the menu. But how dare you override my directive to Bruce?"

"I dare because it's a whim on your part," she said bluntly. "They already have several trees planned for the ballroom. This particular tree is in the lobby every year at Christmas. Would you have us not have a tree this year?"

"I simply want the tree for the wedding. He can put one of the smaller trees in the lobby."

She shook her head. "No. You have no idea what it takes to put up the tree in the first place. It's in four parts. It takes several hours to put it together and get it anchored safely. Then it is painstakingly decorated. It's nearly thirty feet tall. You can imagine the difficulty they have."

"That is not my concern," she said. "I want—"

"It's *my* concern, Mother. All three hotels have the same tree in the lobby. The tree stays."

"If your father were here—"

"He'd agree with me and you know it." She paused. "When is he coming back?"

"I have no idea. He's still in Aspen, he said." She lowered her voice. "Perhaps you could call him?"

She sighed, remembering Stephanie's earlier concern. "Yes, I'll call him." She raised her eyebrows. "So? We're okay with the tree?"

"Not really but I suppose I have no choice. It's only...well, I want everything to be perfect for the wedding. You know my sisters will be here. I don't want them to think that this is some ordinary wedding," she said.

"No one would ever call any of this ordinary, Mother."

"Well, I'm trying to make it special for Stephanie. I've given up on you ever getting married."

"I hope you mean to a man," she said. "Because you know, me getting married now is a possibility."

"Yes, well, so they say." Her mother stood up straighter. "Have you met Doug's parents? They're delightful people. Perhaps you would like to join us at our table for dinner?"

"We'll see."

"He's such a nice man, Shelby."

"Yes, I'm sure he is. It's a shame I don't *like* nice men," she said pointedly.

"Oh, here they are now. Right on time."

Shelby turned, silently groaning as Doug's eyes swept over her. Instead of a turtleneck, she'd decided on a lavender button-down shirt. The dark lavender sweater matched perfectly. And instead of khakis, she'd decided on black jeans. Tight black jeans. Doug apparently approved. Before she could protest, he'd captured her hand and brought it to his lips for a kiss.

"You look absolutely stunning, Shelby. Please, won't you give me the pleasure of dining with me and my parents?"

"Of course she will," her mother answered for her. "I have our table reserved."

Shelby smiled politely and nodded, all the while looking around for Reagan or even Stephanie to come to her rescue. No luck as neither was there yet.

"My parents, Henry and Lenora," Doug introduced.

"Nice to meet you," she said as she shook both of their hands.

"Oh, you too, dear. We've heard so much about you."

"Josh's father and Henry are brothers," her mother supplied. "They are also in the farming business."

"Yes, so I've heard," she said.

"Well, let's take a seat, shall we?" her mother directed. "I'll have them bring out some wine for us while we wait for dinner."

Shelby cringed as Doug placed his hand on the small of her back, guiding her to the table. She glanced once more at the door, pleased to see Stephanie and Josh walk in. She gave Stephanie a pleading look, but Stephanie only waved. She was either ignoring her plea or she didn't recognize it. The smile on Stephanie's face told her it was the former.

I'll kill her.

But her mother saw them too and beckoned them over. "Come join us."

"Yes, come join us," she said through gritted teeth.

* * *

"Should we sit at the table with Josh?"

Reagan shook her head. "It looks a little crowded," she said. "Let's take this one."

"I wonder when Lenora and Henry got here," her mother mused as she sat down. "She had said at one time that she didn't think they were coming until the weekend."

"Hard to pass up free rooms and meals," she said.

"Oh, I know. I can't imagine what this is costing the Suttons." Her mother touched her arm. "Doug seems quite smitten with Shelby."

"Yes. He doesn't believe she's gay."

Her mother's eyes widened in shock. "She's gay?" she whispered. "I would have never guessed. Did you know?"

Reagan smiled. "I made a pass at her in the bar."

"Well, at least you have good taste," her mother said with a laugh. "I take it she turned you down?"

"I didn't know she was Stephanie's sister at the time," she said. "But yes, she turned me down."

"Well, maybe she's seeing someone," her mother offered. "Oh, she's coming over," she whispered.

Reagan met Shelby's gaze, an involuntary smile lighting her face. She glanced down quickly, taking in Shelby's tight jeans. Damn, but she was cute. Too cute.

"Hi. When did you sneak in?"

"Just got here," she said.

Shelby's gaze slid to her parents. "Hello, Mr. and Mrs. Bryant," she greeted.

"It's Margie and Frank, please," her mother corrected.

Shelby smiled. "Of course. Habit." She glanced back at the table from where she'd come. "Why don't you join us?"

"I'm not sure we'll fit," Reagan said. "Besides, Dougie—"

"We'll make room." She placed her hand on Reagan's shoulder and leaned closer. "Please, come rescue me," she whispered. "He's driving me crazy."

Reagan grinned. "Okay, but you'll owe me."

"Whatever you want, it's yours."

Reagan's glance slid from her eyes to her lips, then back up. "Really? You may regret that."

Shelby's lips were fighting a smile. "Maybe."

Reagan turned to her parents. "So? You want to join them?"

"We would love to," her mother said.

"Great," Shelby said. "Let me rearrange some chairs."

As soon as she walked away, her mother leaned closer. "I think she was flirting with you," she whispered.

"You think? See what lengths people will go to to get away from Dougie?"

Her mother laughed. "He's not that bad. He just tries too hard."

"No, he *is* that bad," she countered.

She stood and held out the chair for her mother. As her father walked past her, he leaned closer.

"She's cute. You might want to make another pass at her."

Reagan laughed. God, she loved her parents.

And as luck would have it—or maybe Shelby's creative seating arrangement—she was between Shelby and Stephanie. Doug was on the other side of Shelby, along with his parents. She leaned forward, looking past Shelby and Doug and giving her aunt and uncle a quick smile in greeting. She hadn't seen them in years.

"You'll need to come visit later, Reagan, and tell us what you've been up to," Aunt Lenora said.

"Sure," she said, knowing she would do no such thing.

"Not close to them either?" Shelby asked quietly.

"Not really, no." She leaned closer. "Doug is pouting."

"I know. And I don't care," Shelby said. "All I want is some fried shrimp. Maybe some crab legs. And I think there's going to be smoked salmon." She rubbed her hands together. "Can't wait. I love seafood."

Reagan motioned to the bottles of wine that were being placed on the tables. "What kind?"

"I think chardonnay and sauvignon blanc," Shelby said. "I believe the chef picked out tonight's wine, not my mother."

"I'm thinking a cold beer sounds pretty good right about now," she said.

"Then you should get one." Shelby raised her hand, getting a server's attention. He came over immediately. "Coors on draft, please. Two," she said.

"Certainly, Miss Shelby. Be right back."

"Can't beat the service," Reagan said.

Shelby smiled at her. "Well, you said I owed you."

Reagan smiled too. "That wasn't exactly what I had in mind."

"No?" Shelby rested her chin in her palm. "You look good."

"Thank you. So do you. I love the jeans."

Shelby laughed. "That wasn't what I meant." She leaned closer. "Your eyes…they're clear, bright. You look relaxed."

Reagan nodded. "I feel good." She met her eyes, holding them. "And I should thank you for that," she said quietly. "It's been good to talk about it. You've put some things into perspective for me."

Shelby reached over and touched her arm, squeezing gently. "I'm glad. Because I hated seeing you look so sad…so unhappy."

"I suppose a month is enough time to wallow in my guilt," she said.

"And again, your guilt is misplaced, I think," Shelby said.

"So you say."

"Yes. Because—"

"I understand there's a spa day tomorrow," Doug said, interrupting them. "Josh says it's for guys and girls."

Shelby looked at her with exaggerated wide eyes before slowly turning toward him. "Yes, that's what I hear."

"You're going? Because I'd like the two of us to have a spa date. We could—"

Shelby held up her hand. "Doug, I told you, you're not my type. At all. It's not going to happen."

"But your mother—"

"She's already got a date for the spa, Dougie," Reagan said. "Me."

Shelby turned around, eyebrows raised.

"You said anything I wanted," Reagan reminded her quietly. "That's what I want."

"Come on, Ray Ray, don't try to—"

"I'm sorry, Doug," Shelby said. "I have a spa date with Reagan. But have you met my cousin Holly?"

CHAPTER SIXTEEN

Shelby stared across the room, picking Reagan out of the group of similarly dressed women, all sporting thick white robes. Reagan wasn't looking, and she allowed herself a quick perusal…starting at her bare feet and ending at…damn, she *was* looking.

Reagan smiled and walked her way.

"I hear we start with a facial and while the cucumbers are sprouting or something, we'll get a pedicure and a manicure," Reagan said.

"I'm pretty sure cucumbers don't sprout," she said with a smile.

"And I'm pretty sure if I end up with red toenails or fingernails, someone will have hell to pay," she said.

Shelby laughed. "Then tell them you want it natural."

"And you?"

"Well, it's Christmas. I'll at least do my toes red." She held up her hands to Reagan. "Not big on nail polish though."

"You have nice hands," Reagan said slowly, her voice low.

Shelby swallowed, feeling a bit out of sorts. What game were they playing today? Or was it still a game?

"Hey you two," Stephanie said as she linked arms with them both. "I heard a rumor that you have a spa date. I also heard from a good source that Doug and Holly are spending the day together."

Shelby laughed. "Good. I thought they might hit it off."

"Poor Holly," Reagan said dryly.

Stephanie laughed. "Oh, Holly will be fine. So, what all have you signed up for?"

Reagan shrugged. "I let Shelby do it. Facials are first, then pedicure. After that, I don't know."

"Wait until the naked mud bath. That is so cool," Stephanie said. "You two have fun. Josh and I start with the Jacuzzi and then a massage followed by the sauna. I hope it's a room for two," she said with an exaggerated wink. "We might not ever come out."

"Have fun," she said, smiling as her sister sauntered away. She looked happy and relaxed, something Shelby hadn't seen in several days.

"So? Shall we?"

"Facials," Shelby said. "It also includes hands and feet. To prep us for the manicure and pedicure."

"Whatever. I'm just looking forward to the naked mud bath."

* * *

"No," Reagan said. "No color."

"How about this one?"

"No," Reagan said with a shake of her head. "Natural."

"How about this? It's an understated red. It'll be great for—"

"No. Nothing. Now I'm going to lay back and put these cucumbers over my eyes. There better not be any color on my toes when I take them off," she said.

"Yes, ma'am."

Reagan took a moment to glance over at Shelby, who was two chairs down from her. She looked content and sported a smile on her face. No doubt she had heard the exchange. Reagan let her eyes linger, down past the knee-length robe to her exposed legs. Nice legs. Really nice legs.

"All ready?"

"Yes."

She leaned back and covered her eyes with the cucumbers, trying to relax. The facial had been nice, but the room held six stations and all had been full. She and Shelby were not next to each other. And again in here, eight stations were lined up against the wall and all were full. So far, this "spa date" wasn't affording them much alone time. Well, it wasn't really a date. It was only something to save Shelby from Dougie's obnoxious ass.

The music was soft in the background, but several conversations were going on around her and she couldn't concentrate on any of them so she tried to tune them all out. And for once, her mind wasn't filled with the constant reminder of bombs and war, death and destruction. No, instead, memories of their walk around Bear Lake, the clear water, the green trees, patches of snow, bits of conversation...and Shelby's smile, her reassuring voice, her gentle comforting touch.

She'd made a new friend. An unexpected occurrence, for sure. She'd left the farm early because she couldn't stand her mother's worried look for another day. The guilt had eaten at her and eaten at her until it had all but consumed her. Yet it wasn't something she wanted to talk to her mother about. She'd told Shelby that her family would be disappointed in her. That was just the guilt talking too. No, her mother would have been terrified for her safety if she'd known how close she'd been to the bomb...how close she'd come to being another casualty of the never-ending war there.

So she'd fled the farm and headed to Denver, but she hadn't gone to Josh's place. She'd stayed at a hotel for two days, never venturing out and living only on room service. The expected storm had pushed her to Estes Park a day early. After hiding in her room all day, letting her guilt eat at her some more, she'd finally ventured down to the bar, intending to drown her sorrows in booze.

And she ended up making a pass at the most beautiful woman in the bar. She smiled, remembering Shelby's words.

"Wow. You just dive right in, don't you? No foreplay?"

For those few seconds of their exchange, Reagan had actually forgotten about Afghanistan. For a few seconds.

And now? Now the trauma that she'd been through was slowly subsiding, fading to the background...all thanks to Shelby Sutton.

Who would have thought?

"Ma'am?"

Reagan pulled the cucumbers off and blinked several times. Had she fallen asleep?

"All done."

"Already?" She looked down at her feet. No color. "Thank you."

"Come on, sleepyhead," Shelby said. "Sauna."

Reagan got up. "What about the crap on our faces?"

"Come with me. They'll peel the mask off and give us a hot towel. Then we'll hit the sauna for twenty minutes."

"And then?"

Shelby wiggled her eyebrows. "Then you get your naked mud bath."

"Do they have tubs for two?"

Shelby laughed. "Sorry."

Ten minutes later, they were entering the sauna door precisely as Doug and Holly exited. Holly smiled broadly at them, as did Doug. They both looked like they were enjoying themselves. In fact, Doug hardly gave Shelby more than a passing glance.

"I think you're off the hook now," she said. "Doug has shifted his focus, it seems."

"Yes. Good," Shelby said. "I think Holly would be perfect for him."

There were only four others in the sauna and Shelby led them to a back corner. The steam was swirling and Reagan tightened the towel around her breasts. What she really wanted to do was take the damn thing off. There was nothing better than sitting in a sauna completely naked. Now *that* would open your pores.

"I know what you're thinking."

She grinned. "Do you now?"

"And in case you didn't notice, that's your mother over there on the side. So leave your towel on."

Reagan laughed, causing some of the others—including her mother—to look at her. She waved to her mother, then leaned back next to Shelby.

"How often do you get pampered like this?" she asked.

"Not often enough," Shelby said. "I normally don't have several hours to kill. And if I do, I'd rather be out hiking. But I do try to come here at least once when I'm at the hotel. If not for the whole thing, I'll do a mud bath and then a massage. The hot mud really loosens up your muscles. And then a massage afterward?" She smiled. "I'm like Jell-O when I leave here."

"You would think the sauna would come after the mud bath," she said.

"I think normally it does," Shelby said. "But we had such a large group, they staggered everything. After the mud bath, we'll get rinsed off, then go into the Jacuzzi. It's got some kind of herbal salt or mineral water or something. Then we'll get wrapped in cool sheets after the warm water. Then the massage." She smiled. "Then Jell-O. It's all I can do to take my shower and dress."

A buzzer went off and the four others got up. Her mother turned around and pointed a finger at her.

"Behave."

Reagan laughed and nodded.

When the door closed, she turned to Shelby. "So...looks like we're alone."

Shelby wiped at the moisture on her face, then reached over and brushed Reagan's cheek. "Yes. We're alone." She met her eyes. "How do you feel?"

Reagan knew Shelby's question was for her mental state and not physical. "Good. Really good."

"Then the spa day is helping."

"You're helping," Reagan said honestly. "The more I think about it, you may be right."

Shelby raised her eyebrows.

"About Richard. He did feel responsible for everyone's safety. It was something he stressed constantly before the project started. So I think you're right. He wasn't trying to save George. He was trying to save his team, me included."

Shelby nodded.

"He was brave and selfless," she said. "And I don't know if I'd have had the courage to do what he did," she admitted. "And that truth still bothers me. I think I would have run."

Shelby leaned closer, letting their shoulders touch. "Let's hope you don't ever have to make that choice, Reagan. Because I'm really glad you're here." Then she smiled. "And that's being selfish on my part. Because honestly, I was dreading this whole wedding celebration. You've made it fun."

"Thanks. I was actually dreading it too. And after the first day and the whole thing with your mother and bridesmaid dresses, well, I was ready to leave."

"Speaking of that, I believe she's ready to pursue that subject again."

Reagan stretched her legs out. "She can pursue it all she wants. She ain't getting me in a damn dress."

Shelby laughed. "I vote for the tux. I bet you would look very handsome."

Before she could answer, the sauna opened and Josh and Stephanie came in, both wrapped in towels. She guessed Stephanie didn't get her wish for a private sauna. She felt Shelby sit up straighter and move away from her a little.

"Hey, you two," Stephanie greeted. "Having fun?"

"Yes. How about you?" Shelby asked.

"The Jacuzzi was great and private," she said with a laugh and Reagan noticed Josh blushing. "But everything is all out of order. Our mud bath will be last. We go to facials next."

"We're doing mud baths next," Shelby said. The buzzer went off. "In fact, right now."

She got up and Reagan followed. Shelby turned around, smiling. "Remember, this isn't a private sauna," she teased.

"I think after the Jacuzzi, we're good," Stephanie said, causing Josh to blush yet again. "Enjoy your naked mud bath, Reagan."

"I plan to."

Of course, she had no idea what to expect from a mud bath. In fact, she was totally speechless when Shelby dropped her towel and climbed into the tub. So shocked, in fact, that she hardly had time to register that Shelby was standing in front of her naked.

"Ma'am?"

Reagan turned, seeing the young girl pointing at the tub next to Shelby. She glanced over at Shelby who was smiling at her.

"Well? Get in. You wanted a naked mud bath, didn't you?"

What the hell, she thought. She dropped her towel where she stood and got in the tub. She'd never been modest. Why start now?

She relaxed back against the pillow as warm mud was poured into the tub and the girl packed it down around her. The mud had a bit of a doughy feel to it, warm and thick and heavy. As soon as their tubs were full, they were left alone.

"How's it feel?" Shelby asked.

"Nice. Not what I expected."

"I know. It's hard to describe without actually experiencing it." Then she smiled. "You have a nice body."

Reagan arched an eyebrow. "Are you flirting with me?"

"I was making an observation," Shelby said.

"Yeah, well, you disappeared in the tub so fast I hardly had a chance to take note," she said.

"Well, there's always the Jacuzzi. Maybe you'll have another shot."

Reagan stared at her. Yes, Shelby was definitely flirting with her. Before she could reply though, the girls came back, signaling an end to their mud bath.

"That was quick."

"Ten minutes," one said. "Time for your rinse."

The mud was very heavy and Reagan needed help getting out. She laughed as both she and Shelby were covered in the thick goo. They stood in a tiled stall and she held her arms up as she was literally sprayed down, head to toe, with warm water. Before long, the water ran clean and she was handed a towel. She watched Shelby, who simply wrapped the towel around her instead of drying off. Reagan did the same.

They were led down a tiled hallway to another small room. It contained nothing more than a bubbling Jacuzzi. On the side were two tall glasses of a light green-colored drink.

"Cucumber juice," Shelby said. "So you don't get dehydrated."

It was surprisingly refreshing, and she drank the whole glass. She and Shelby stood facing each other, then Shelby smiled and let her towel drop. Reagan stared at her, her eyes landing on her breasts...full and firm. She felt her breath catch as Shelby's nipples hardened under her stare.

Jesus.

Then Shelby swung her legs over the side and sunk beneath the water, letting out an audible sigh.

"Fabulous. Come join me."

Oh my. Oh my oh my oh my. She blew out her breath, then dropped her towel. No big deal. She was getting into a Jacuzzi with a naked woman. No big deal. A naked woman who was flirting with her. Well, kinda a big deal, maybe.

So she averted her eyes and landed on the opposite side as Shelby. Jets of warm spray hit her body from every direction, it seemed. But she felt Shelby's eyes on her and she looked up.

"I can't believe you're shy," Shelby said. "Not after your great pickup line in the bar."

"Yeah, well...I wasn't really myself that night."

Shelby moved through the water, coming to sit beside her. "So? Are you shy or scared?"

Reagan smiled nervously. "Okay, look, you're kinda freaking me out here."

Shelby laughed. "What? I thought you wanted a spa date."

"Yeah, but I didn't really know what a spa date was," she said. "I've never been to a spa before."

Shelby leaned back and closed her eyes. "Relax, Reagan," she said. "Enjoy the water, the jets. Relax," she said again.

Sure. Relax. I'm sitting next to a beautiful naked woman. Relax, she says.

But she needn't have worried. Before too long the door opened, signaling an end to the Jacuzzi session. Of course, when Shelby rose out of the water like a goddess, Reagan nearly drowned as she slipped on the step and fell backward. When she righted herself, Shelby was smiling, blatantly watching as Reagan stepped out and quickly reached for her towel to cover herself. Really...was she shy or scared?

"Massage is next," Shelby said. "So I'll meet you in the shower."

Reagan nodded. She meant dressing room, right? Not...*in* the shower.

Right?

CHAPTER SEVENTEEN

Shelby was in such a state of bliss after her massage, she could hardly walk. Only the prospect of sharing a shower with Reagan moved her along.

Oh, Reagan. For all her bravado in the bar that first day, she certainly looked like she was in over her head now. Shelby wondered, had she taken Reagan up on her offer that day, if Reagan would have been able to go through with it. Knowing her as she did now, she'd have to say no.

And knowing her as she did now, the offer in the bar was more about human contact—the result of her trauma—than sex. She paused, remembering the haunted look in Reagan's eyes that day. The thought that Reagan had been reaching out for some kind of comfort—from a complete stranger—made her heart break…that Reagan had reached out to *her* and she'd rebuffed her. Knowing what she knew now, would she have accepted her offer and taken her to bed? Taken her to bed and eased some of her pain for a few hours?

Yes.

But Reagan seemed to be healing. She hadn't seen that shadowed look in a couple of days. Certainly not today.

No. Today they'd been playing. Flirting. She smiled. Well, *she'd* been flirting. Which was a little out of character for her. She was usually so guarded—protective—of her personal life, she wouldn't dare flirt like that on one of her dates. Which is probably why she usually came across as being cool…aloof.

It was different with Reagan. She'd talked freely to her about her family, her job. She wasn't really harboring any secrets that she was afraid for Reagan to find out. There was nothing more to be guarded about.

"Are you daydreaming?"

She looked up, realizing that she had stopped walking and was standing in the hallway outside of the dressing room. And yes, daydreaming.

She smiled at Reagan. "So, how was the hot oil massage?"

Reagan nodded. "You were right. I feel like Jell-O. It was fantastic."

"I know. I feel like I've been drugged."

Reagan raised her eyebrows. "So…what about that shower you mentioned?"

Shelby laughed quickly. "Oh, so *now* you're getting brave. Naked in the Jacuzzi, not so much," she teased.

But alas, the dressing room—and showers—were crowded as most of their party had worked their way through the spa cycle. In fact, Stephanie and their mother had just come from the showers, both covered in thick, terrycloth robes.

"What an absolutely fabulous day," Stephanie said. "I hope you two enjoyed it as much I did."

Regan laughed. "Well, probably not *quite* as much. I'm assuming my brother enjoyed it too."

Stephanie winked. "I should hope so."

Shelby looked at her mother. "Did you enjoy it?"

"Yes. It was very relaxing. Although I'm not crazy about the mud bath." She turned to Reagan. "Your mother just went back to the showers. She said it was her first spa."

Reagan nodded. "Mine too. Thank you."

"Well, I think you two are the last of our group. I'll have the vans waiting."

"So much for a leisurely shower," she murmured. She turned to Reagan. "You missed your chance in the Jacuzzi, it seems."

"My, my, but you are a tease, aren't you."

Shelby grinned as they headed to their lockers to retrieve toiletries. "Actually, I'm not. You must bring it out in me."

"If you're not careful, I'll embarrass you at the dance Monday night. I'll be on the lookout for mistletoe."

"Honey, I would guess you'd be more embarrassed than me," she said as she patted Reagan's stomach as she walked past her to the showers. "By the way, I'm a very good dancer," she called over her shoulder.

Reagan was simply staring after her, and Shelby wondered if she was playing with fire. Oh well. It didn't matter. She was having fun. And really, she couldn't remember the last time she'd thought that. Fun? No. Her interaction with other women—dates—hadn't been fun in a very long time.

CHAPTER EIGHTEEN

Reagan was actually nervous as she waited in the bar. Things were beginning to happen that she wasn't really prepared for. Things with Shelby. Oh, Josh had called and said he and Stephanie were joining them for dinner. It wasn't like they would be alone. But still...

Was she scared of Shelby? Really?

Well, Shelby was a little out of her league. A *lot* out of her league, she clarified. For all her world travels, she was still a farm girl from Nebraska. Sure, there'd been a handful of brief affairs over the years, in many different countries, yet none were really memorable. But Shelby was different and not only because her sister was marrying Josh. She was different because she'd been able to touch her, been able to reach her when she was in her darkest hours. She had been so certain she'd never tell a soul about what had happened in Afghanistan. She'd lived nearly a month with it. Not living, really. Existing. Painfully... lonely. Shelby had gotten it out of her on only two tries.

And now things were relaxed between them—fun and teasing. And flirting? It wasn't something she was really used to.

The places she'd been, where she'd worked…there wasn't much fun going on. Had she become so accustomed to that lifestyle that she forgot how to play? Forgot how to *live*?

She felt eyes on her and looked up into the mirror, finding Shelby standing behind her, a soft smile on her face. Reagan returned it.

"I was hoping you'd be early," Shelby said as she sat down beside her. Zach came over immediately.

"Your usual?"

Shelby shook her head. "I think I'll have what Reagan is having."

"Scotch. Coming right up."

"So only gin and tonic when you're stressed, huh? Does that mean you're relaxed?"

"Yes. The spa day still has me feeling mellow," Shelby said. "How about you?"

Reagan nodded. "I'm still trying to wrap my head around the fact that I saw you naked."

Shelby leaned closer, her eyes teasing. "I saw *you* naked too," she said quietly. Then she smiled. "Do I make you nervous?"

Reagan swallowed. "Yes."

"Why? *You* are the one who wanted a spa date and a naked mud bath," she reminded her.

Reagan waited until Zach placed Shelby's drink in front of her and walked away. She turned sideways in her chair, facing Shelby.

"You make me nervous because…well, it's been a really long time since I've had any interactions with another woman." She met her gaze. "A *really* long time."

Shelby's expression turned serious. "And your pickup line in the bar the other night?"

Reagan shook her head. "I'm not usually—*ever*—that forward," she admitted. "I just…I saw you and…well, I…I needed—"

"Someone?" Shelby asked in a near whisper. "Someone to make you feel alive?"

Reagan nodded, then her breath caught as Shelby reached out and placed a warm hand on her thigh.

"If I had to do it over again...your offer...I'd probably say yes."

Reagan wasn't sure what to say to that so she said nothing. Shelby smiled, a sweet and gentle smile that eased some of her anxiety. Shelby then patted her thigh and withdrew her hand.

"Relax," she murmured. "It's all good."

Reagan took a deep breath, trying to do just that.

"So...with all the wedding planning, I completely forgot about gifts," Shelby said, changing the subject to something less personal. "Do you think it would be rude to skip gifts this year?"

"I never do gifts," Reagan said. "It's rare that I'm home for Christmas anyway."

Shelby studied her. "Even if you're in another country, surely there are others there that celebrate, aren't there?"

Reagan nodded. "Sure. But most celebrations involve food and booze," she said with a shrug. "Some miss it more than others. Some will give little trinkets simply to be giving something. Which is why I hate the whole Christmas thing anyway," she said. "Giving gifts only to be giving with little thought put into it. Most of us don't *need* anything. We don't need a new sweater, a new shirt...a new tie. It's all so wasteful. If people could really see those in need, they'd appreciate the holiday more, I think."

"I know. But to most people, Christmas is a feel-good holiday. Parties and gifts. And food. All things in excess." Shelby leaned closer. "Like this wedding. And for as much as Stephanie loves Christmas, I don't blame her for this. I blame my mother."

"Josh hasn't said a whole lot about it," she said. "I do know that initially they wanted only the family here for the wedding and they were going to make it a long weekend."

"Yes. Christmas is on Friday, which is when she wanted the ceremony. They were originally going to stay here for the weekend and head to Hawaii on Monday instead of Saturday," Shelby said. "My mother thought it would be fun to also celebrate the week before too." She sipped from her drink. "In fairness to Stephanie, Mother is hard to say no to. Impossible sometimes."

"So how are we getting out of the group dinner tonight? Josh didn't say."

"We had an argument with Mother and she's too distraught to be a hostess for dinner," Shelby said. "Bruce—he's the manager—will be seating everyone in the restaurant."

"But we're going out?"

"Yes."

She leaned closer. "Why an argument?"

Shelby smiled. "Bridesmaid dresses."

Reagan groaned. "So she's still on that, huh?"

"Like a dog with a bone," Shelby said. "I gave her three options, none of which were acceptable to her. You in a tux. Or only have one bridesmaid—me. Or replace you with Holly or someone else."

Reagan smiled. "Those three are all perfectly acceptable to me."

Shelby bumped her shoulder with her own. "Thought they'd be."

Then Shelby pulled away and put some distance between them. Reagan frowned, then heard a familiar voice. Stephanie. She looked up into the mirror and saw her and Josh coming toward them. Apparently Shelby wanted to keep their budding friendship a secret. She wondered why?

"I'm in the mood for Mexican food," Stephanie stated. "Mexican food and margaritas. And I want to relax and there's to be no mention of bridesmaid dresses or Mother. I've reached my limit."

"I'm in," Reagan said.

"Me too," Shelby said.

CHAPTER NINETEEN

Shelby stood at the large window in her suite, her gaze traveling to the snowcapped mountain peaks west of town. They were still holding onto the gentle pink color of the sunrise. It was going to be another sunny day although a storm was on the horizon. Nothing severe, the weather forecast said, but a few inches of new snow and colder temps. She was thankful there was nothing on her mother's agenda today. She wanted to get out and enjoy the last day of warmer weather. She had hoped to entice Reagan into another hike, but her parents had asked her to take them into Boulder to view the campus and do some shopping. She imagined—with this being the last weekend before Christmas—that most of the shops would be packed, even if it was a Sunday. She did not envy Reagan. Christmas shopping was near the bottom of her list of fun things to do.

She turned away from the view and moved into her small kitchen. The Keurig was ready and she chose a Sumatra blend for her morning coffee. She took her cup and her phone and sat down in the recliner, pausing to stare out of the window for a few more seconds before calling him. She should have called yesterday, but it was late when they'd returned from dinner. And truthfully, she'd been afraid she'd interrupt something had she called that late. Like Reagan had suggested, she really didn't want to know if her father was having an affair or not.

"And how is my favorite daughter this morning?"

She couldn't help but smile, even though he greeted her in the same way most mornings. "I believe she's stressing out over her wedding," she answered. "She's afraid her father is not going to make it."

"Is she now? And what about my other daughter? The sensible, practical one?"

"She is trying to keep Mother in line. That should be *your* job," she said.

"Oh, Shelby, I've long given up trying to keep your mother in line." She heard papers rustling and wondered if he was already at work. "So what do I owe the pleasure? Is there a catastrophe of some sort?"

"There will be if you don't make it up here for the dance tomorrow. What's going on?"

"Is that tomorrow?"

"Yes. We'd hoped you'd be here already." She paused. "What's going on, Dad?"

"I told you, there was a problem in Aspen that needed my attention."

"If there was a problem, I would have heard about it."

"I told William to leave you out of the loop. You have enough going on with the wedding and all," he said.

"I'd have rather been in Aspen," she murmured and he laughed. "So, what kind of problem is it that William couldn't handle?"

She could sense his hesitation, and she wondered if he was debating whether she had a need to know or not. While he had let her delve into most aspects of the business, some things he still kept from her.

"William stumbled across some...well, some improprieties. I had an audit done."

"We have our own audit team."

"Yes. So I hired an outside agency."

"Oh, no," she said. That could only mean one thing.

"Yes. It seems Murray has been doctoring the books."

"Mark Murray? He's been with us for years. I can't believe it."

"Yes, he's worked for me for thirteen years," he said. "And over the last five, he's embezzled over a million dollars."

"I would never have suspected he was capable. He seemed so loyal, so protective of his work. I thought it was simply him not trusting anyone else to do the job." She leaned back, staring at the ceiling, picturing Mark's face. "He oversaw all three hotels. Are you going to audit the others?"

"Yes, of course. He lives here in Aspen and so he has more access, but he's had his hand in the accounts of all three."

"Does he know what you've found?" She paused. "And why didn't you tell me?"

"He knows I've had someone here poking around, yes. I told him we were auditing housekeeping, for starters. But judging by his demeanor, I think he must suspect. And Shelby, I didn't tell you because I didn't want you to worry about it. The wedding—"

"Is Stephanie's wedding, not mine. Or it could be Mother's wedding...it's hard to tell at this point."

"I'm sorry I'm not there to help you, honey. I know how difficult she can be."

"But you'll be here for the dance?"

He sighed. "I suppose I must. I'll fly up tomorrow," he said.

"There's a storm coming overnight. You may want to fly in today," she suggested.

"You never did trust my piloting skills," he said with a quick laugh.

"It's really the plane I don't trust. You know how I feel about flying."

"Yes, I know. You're so much like me in most everything. I always wondered why you never got my love of flying."

"Nor your fondness for expensive wine," she added.

"Well, you do like a fine brandy and scotch. There's that at least," he said.

"So? When will I see you?"

"I'll check the weather. I promise. But I'll definitely be there before the dance." He paused. "Oh, and Shelby...please keep this conversation between us. Other than William, no one else knows. I'd like to keep it that way for now. We'll discuss it more when I get there."

"Of course. I understand. I'll see you soon."

After she disconnected, she realized she had taken only one sip of her coffee. It now held only a hint of warmth, and she went into the kitchen and tossed it out. She shook her head, still not believing that Mark Murray would skim money from them. She knew what his salary was, and it was quite lucrative already. It was simply astounding that he would cheat them—and chance getting caught. She'd known him since she was in high school and he was always an upstanding guy. To find out the opposite was true was shocking.

But her father had a handle on things so she wasn't going to worry about it now. She still had another six days to make it through until the wedding.

So, while another cup of coffee brewed, she pondered her day. A solo hike, which is what she was accustomed to, didn't sound appealing. But still, it would get her outside. And away from the hotel. According to Stephanie, their mother was going to take up the issue with the bridesmaid dresses again. Or, more specifically, Reagan's refusal to wear one.

A smile lit her face as she tried to picture Reagan in a dress. And heels. She shook her head. No, she couldn't see it. Now a tux? Yes, Reagan would look quite attractive in a tux.

She added sugar to her coffee and stirred it, her mind wandering to Reagan. There was an attraction between them, she knew that. Even though they'd done nothing more than tease about it, it was there nonetheless. She felt closer to her than the time they'd spent together warranted. Whether it was Reagan's recent trauma—and her confession—that drew them close, she couldn't be sure. Maybe it was just the circumstances here that they naturally gravitated toward each other. Reagan certainly wasn't like most of the women she dated. But that was more of a product of well-meaning friends setting her up with the wrong kind of women. Reagan was obviously independent and was used to being alone. She was too, for that matter. Reagan was attractive, virile...handsome. She didn't hide her sexuality, something Shelby appreciated. She'd been out with her share of closeted women and found it exhausting...and a waste of time. She could have told each and every one of them that they were only hiding from themselves.

But she shrugged. Not everyone was comfortable being out and open with family and friends. Reagan obviously was.

Knocking on her door brought her out of her musings, and she walked over, glancing through the peephole before opening it. She knew it was too early for Stephanie and feared it would be her mother. She was pleasantly surprised to find Reagan standing in the hallway.

She opened the door, smiling at her. "You found my suite."

"I hope you don't mind. Josh told me. I don't have your cell number," Reagan said.

"Come in," she said as she stepped back.

Reagan came inside and gave a cursory glance around, then brought her attention back to Shelby. Shelby stood still as Reagan's eyes traveled over her. While Reagan was already dressed for the day, she was still in her robe and bare feet.

"You're...you're not dressed," Reagan said. "Am I too early? I assumed you were an early riser."

Shelby shook her head. "No. I was having coffee. Would you like a cup?"

"I probably...shouldn't," she said nervously. "Maybe you should go put some clothes on though."

Shelby laughed. "I have bed head, no makeup on and coffee breath. I doubt that's very appealing."

Reagan's eyes met hers. "Then you obviously haven't looked in a mirror," she said quietly. "You look adorable, coffee breath and all."

Shelby sipped from her coffee cup, a smile on her face. "So...what brings you up here?"

"Oh, yeah. I was wondering if you wanted to go to Boulder with us. Keep me company," Reagan said.

"Christmas shopping? You've got to be kidding," she said.

"Not just shopping," Reagan said. "A drive through the mountains, a stroll around campus." She put her hands in her pockets and Shelby wondered if she was really that nervous. "I'll treat you to lunch," she offered.

Shelby arched an eyebrow. "Like a date?"

"Well, my parents will be there. Not sure we should call it a date."

Christmas shopping...it was at the bottom of her list, she reminded herself. But the prospect of spending the day with Reagan was too appealing to let shopping stop her.

"Okay," she agreed. "On one condition."

"And that is?"

"You let me drive."

"Okay. Deal."

"Good. Then let me get a quick shower and I'll meet you downstairs."

Reagan went to the door, then turned back around. "Are you...are you naked under your robe?" she asked quietly.

Shelby met her gaze. "What would be your guess?" Their eyes held for a long moment, and Shelby noted that there wasn't even a trace of the haunted, saddened look in Reagan's. There was, however, a trace of desire. It caused her heart to beat a little quicker.

"Yes would be my guess," Reagan said, her voice little more than a whisper. "And I should...I should really get out of here now," Reagan said.

Shelby smiled at her and nodded. "Yes. That's probably a good idea. Unless your parents want to go by themselves..." she said, her voice falling off in a question.

Reagan smiled too and took another step toward the door. "You enjoy teasing me, don't you?"

"Who said I was teasing?"

CHAPTER TWENTY

Reagan was still smiling as she got off the elevator. Yes, of course Shelby was naked under her robe. Silly question. She'd seen her at the spa. Shelby was quite comfortable being naked. With a body like that, who wouldn't be? Damn...

She found her parents in the bar sipping coffee. Her father was reading a newspaper, his glasses perched on the end of his nose, and he greeted her with a brief nod. There was another couple in a far booth having coffee and sharing quiet conversation. Other than that, the bar was empty. She sat next to her mother and waited until Ty came over.

"Just coffee," she said.

"Did you have any luck with Shelby?" her mother asked.

"Yep. She also offered to drive us."

"Well, that was nice of her." Her mother gave her a playful poke with her elbow. "That'll give you girls a chance to spend some time together."

"Don't play matchmaker," Reagan warned. "Shelby Sutton is out of my league."

"No more so than Josh and Stephanie," she said.

"Josh is an attorney. Big difference."

"And you're an award-winning journalist," her mother reminded her. "Besides, I've seen the way she looks at you. I think you have a chance."

Reagan laughed. "You think it's time I settle down?"

Her mother's expression turned serious. "Whatever happened to you in Afghanistan, I wasn't able to reach you, to help you. You had such a terrible dark cloud over you when you came back."

"Mom—"

"But she reached you, didn't she? That spark is back in your eyes again."

Reagan nodded slowly. "Yes. Something happened over there. Something terrible." She cupped her coffee cup with both hands. "Now's not the right time to talk about it, but...I haven't been able to pick up a camera." She glanced at her. "And yes, I talked to Shelby about it."

"I told your father that this was the first time in years that I could recall you not having a camera strapped on your hip." She met her gaze. "You know you can talk to me about anything."

"I know. But it's very painful to think about, to talk about." Reagan sighed. "There was a bomb. A very good friend was killed. And that's all I want to say about it right now."

Her mother leaned closer, putting an arm around her shoulder and squeezing. "I'm sorry, honey. If you want to talk, I'll be here for you."

"Thank you. I love you, Mom."

Her mother got tears in her eyes as she looked at her. "You hardly ever say those words, Reagan. It's always so special when you do. I love you too."

Reagan blinked her own tears away. God, how had the conversation turned to this all of a sudden? She would much rather have her mother teasing her about Shelby. But the moment passed and they both smiled.

"So...do you want to window-shop or do you really have gifts to buy?" she asked, changing the subject.

"I know we all decided that the wedding was going to be Christmas for us and we weren't exchanging gifts," her mother said, "but I have a few that aren't family that I want to get something for." She patted Reagan's arm. "And don't worry, nothing for you. I know how you feel about Christmas gifts. Besides, just having you here is gift enough."

"Thanks. I don't want to have to stress over gifts. I've got enough of that going on with Mrs. Sutton trying to get me into a damn bridesmaid dress."

Her mother's laughter rang out, causing her father to glance at them curiously. "Oh, you're kidding. A *dress*?" She laughed again. "Frank, can you see Reagan in a dress? How long has it been?"

"Exactly," Reagan said. "I offered to wear a tux, but that didn't go over with her."

"Speaking of clothes, what do you plan to wear to the dance tomorrow night? It's a dressy affair, Josh tells me."

Reagan groaned. "I don't know. I haven't really thought about it."

"Well, I noticed a couple of shops here in town that rent formal wear."

"What are you suggesting?"

Her mother grinned. "You'd look lovely in a tuxedo, Reagan."

"I agree."

Reagan turned, finding Shelby standing behind them. "You agree?"

"Yes, you would look…lovely." She motioned to the door. "I had them bring my car around. Are you all ready?"

Reagan stood up. "We're ready. Thanks for driving."

"My pleasure," Shelby said easily as she linked arms with her mother. "Now, Reagan says you wanted a tour of the campus. I graduated from there. I can show you around."

Reagan and her father followed, and she realized she had an involuntary smile on her face. Shelby seemed to do that to her. Her father elbowed her quickly.

"I like her."

"Yeah. I kinda like her too."

CHAPTER TWENTY-ONE

After shopping and lunch, they walked for nearly an hour around campus, which Shelby found wonderfully enjoyable. Even though Estes Park was fairly close to Boulder, she hadn't been to the campus in several years. The weather was perfect for late December, and she found Reagan's parents to be delightful.

But after they'd returned to the hotel, she wasn't ready for her time with Reagan to come to an end. So she suggested another outing.

"A quick drive to the park to look for bighorn sheep and elk," she said. "How about it?"

They were alone in the lobby, Reagan's parents having already gone up to their room. Reagan nodded immediately.

"I'd love to."

So back in the Jeep they went, and Shelby drove them north of town and headed to the national park. It was still an hour before dusk, plenty of time to make the loop to Bear Lake and back. They were sure to see elk, but she wasn't always successful with bighorn sheep.

"You love it out here, don't you?"

"Yes." She turned to Reagan. "I could live here."

"At the hotel?"

"Well, if I lived at the hotel, I'd need something a little bigger. And a real kitchen. I like to cook."

"Do you? I'm never in one place long enough to do any cooking," Reagan said.

"So you live out of a suitcase?"

"Yes. And it's exhausting."

"I imagine so. Like I said, I'm a bit of a homebody. I would get tired of all the travel," she said.

"It's all I know, really. But...well, after what happened, I'm not sure when I'll go back." She glanced at her. "Or even *if*," she said.

"Well, as I suggested the other day, you're chasing the wrong things," she said. "Even though I know you're successful at what you do." She slowed. "Sheep!" she said excitedly, pointing to their right. "See them?"

Up on the hill, not far from the road, was a small herd. They blended in well with the rocks and winter vegetation, and she'd almost missed them. She pulled to a stop on the side of the road, trying to get a better look. When she got her binoculars out of the console, Reagan laughed.

"Great. I was hoping you'd have a pair."

She smiled as she handed them over to Reagan. She'd seen bighorn sheep many times before. She doubted Reagan ever had.

"There's a nice big ram in the back," Reagan murmured as she continued to stare out the window. "He's gorgeous."

Shelby's eyes were on Reagan, not the sheep. As if sensing her watching, Reagan lowered the binoculars and turned.

"You want to look?"

Shelby shook her head. "No, you go ahead. Enjoy."

Reagan turned back to the sheep and watched them for another few minutes before turning. "I counted at least twenty-five," she said. "There were four rams that I saw. Do they travel like that? You'd think the rams would have a harem or something."

Shelby nodded. "In the winter, after mating season, they travel together in larger herds. You'll only find them here in the foothills during winter too. Once spring comes, they move up into the high country, then split up. The rams travel together in what they call bachelor groups."

"You seem well versed," Reagan said.

"I've always been interested in nature, animals," she said. "And I visit with the rangers some when I'm here."

"Any of them cute lesbians?" Reagan teased.

"Actually, yes. Julie. Or Ranger Dirksen, as she's known on the job."

"Do you see her on a personal basis when you're here?"

Shelby laughed as she pulled back onto the road. "Do you want to know if we've dated?"

"Okay. Have you?"

"No. She's cute and nice and we've had dinner a couple of times, but no, we've not dated. I'm not attracted to her and I assume she's not attracted to me because she's made no advances at all." She put her blinker on as she took the road into the park. "I imagine if I was here more often, we could become good friends. She's easy to talk to and I enjoyed her company."

"Do you know anyone in town or just the hotel staff?"

"I don't really know anyone, no. Some of the restaurants, cafés—Dave, for instance—know me, but only in passing." She glanced at her. "Why so curious?"

Reagan shrugged. "I was wondering how much you get out when you're here. I hate to think of you holed up in the hotel, only sneaking out for an occasional hike."

"I love sunshine," she said. "It's takes a lot of discipline to stay inside and work. And I'll admit, when I'm here, I'm out more than I'm in. I do a lot of work at night, in that case."

She slowed again as they approached the first meadow. She saw a few elk against the trees but not the large herds that normally grazed.

"We'll go farther into the park," she said. "There'll be hundreds of them."

"Are they like the sheep? They go up higher during the summer?"

"For the most part, but you can still find them, just not in the large herds like now." She turned to Reagan. "If I were a photographer, wildlife would be my subject."

"I thought I was supposed to chase smiles and happiness," Reagan said. "You know, weddings, birthday parties," she reminded her.

Shelby smiled. "I said if *I* were a photographer. I hate weddings and parties."

Reagan studied her. "I haven't known you long, but let me take a guess. You don't like people, do you?"

Shelby laughed out loud. "Well, it's not so much people, it's all of the stuff that goes along with them. It seems everything is a production. I like things to be simple, I like people to be honest. I don't like games. It's exhausting."

"Is that why you said before that you try to keep everything in your life normal?"

"Yes. Normal. Practical." She smiled quickly. "The opposite of my mother."

"More like your father?"

She nodded. "Although I wouldn't exactly label him practical," she said. "He was born into money and then was successful with the hotels. He doesn't shy away from his wealth. But he also doesn't go out of his way to flaunt it, like Mother does."

"So you don't feel like an heiress?"

She laughed again. "Stephanie could play the part of an heiress, never me." She pointed through the windshield. "There's the big herd I was looking for."

"Oh, wow. You weren't kidding when you said hundreds," Reagan said as she reached for the binoculars again.

"During the fall rut, the bull elks will bugle. That's how they attract the females. It's like a parking lot here then with so many people and cars. So I asked Julie to take me out last year," she said. "She knew of a little meadow that's not accessible to the public. It was incredible. You should Google it sometime and listen to them."

"There's a bunch with antlers over there on the left," Reagan said. "Huge antlers. Wow."

"Yes, they're magnificent animals."

Reagan handed her the binoculars, and Shelby couldn't resist taking her turn to look at them. Dusk was fast approaching and the shadows were getting thick. Another car pulled up behind them, so she moved up farther to allow them a chance to view the elk too.

"Thank you for taking me out here. This was pretty cool."

"You're welcome." Shelby leaned back, her gaze still on the elk. "In your travels, do you get to see much wildlife in other countries?"

"No. The places I go are...well, war zones mostly. I spent some time in the jungle in Colombia, but I was covering the drug wars down there so no time for eco-tours or anything like that."

"Why?"

"Why what?"

"Why Colombia? Why drug wars? Why Afghanistan?"

Reagan shrugged. "That's where the money is," she said. "Anyone can stay here in the States and shoot police riots or snarled traffic after a snowstorm or presidential elections. Besides, I was fresh out of college and it all sounded so exciting."

"And dangerous," she said.

"Yes. Sometimes. In most countries, journalists are respected as neutral and left alone. Any publicity is considered good publicity, whether it's the government or the drug cartels," she said. "In the Middle East, different story. You live in fear of being kidnapped or killed. I don't mind saying, I hate the place. More so now, of course."

The car that was parked behind them pulled away as it was too dark now to see the elk. It was also too dark to see Reagan's face, to see her expression, but Shelby sensed she wanted to talk so she remained still.

"And now...well, I don't even know what's going on in the world," Reagan said quietly.

"What do you mean?"

"I was a news junkie. In my line of work, you have to be. Chase the news and all that," she said. "Sad, really, when all you're doing is looking for conflicts and unrest in volatile areas."

Reagan turned to her. "I haven't read a single news article since I've been back. I haven't turned the TV on. I have no idea what's going on and I don't want to know. Because I never realized how stressful it was to live that way. I feel…peaceful now." She paused. "Is that really healthy though? I mean, ignoring what's going on around us?

There are conflicts in some part of the world every day, whether we know about it or not," Reagan said. "But more often than not, we read the newspaper, watch the news on TV…we know about it. We reflect on it, sympathize with those affected, get angry at the aggressors. It keeps us involved somehow." She sighed. "But is it healthy—mentally—to pretend that those things aren't happening? Is it healthy to ignore the news? To pretend that the world is a peaceful place when it's really not?" She shook her head. "Because I know it's not. I've been to all those places you see on the news. The world is not a peaceful place. I've seen it firsthand. And I helped bring those images to people like you, so you could have a front row seat in a conflict that was taking place thousands of miles away."

"If it weren't for people like you, who bring the news back, then there would be no cause for others to take action against the atrocities that are out there," Shelby said. "I can't imagine living in such a vacuum where there was no one reporting the news."

Reagan sighed again. "I know. But it's so much easier to hide and ignore things and pretend all these bad things aren't happening…when I know they are." She shifted in her seat, turning to face Shelby. "Anyway, that's where I am. I'm torn between doing my job, finding these places, recording what's happening and sharing it…I'm torn between that and living a peaceful life, not having to see all the carnage that I've seen and all the…the death, the despair. I've seen my share. And I don't know if I want to see it any more. So I'm torn."

"What do you plan to do?" she asked quietly. She heard Reagan sigh once more before she answered.

"I have…no idea."

While her voice was quiet, there was a slight tremor in it, as if Reagan was worried what the future held for her. Shelby couldn't resist as she reached across the console and found Reagan's hand. Their fingers entwined and she squeezed tightly.

"Thank you," Reagan said. "I sometimes feel lost...alone."

"Lonely?" she guessed.

"Yes."

And again, she simply couldn't resist. She leaned closer, resting her elbow on the console. Reagan turned to her and Shelby tugged on her hand, pulling her nearer. There was a slight hesitation as their lips hovered an inch apart, then she closed the distance, finding Reagan's mouth. The quick, unexpected flash of desire startled her, causing Shelby to moan, albeit softly, unable to contain it as their lips moved together. She was about to deepen the kiss when Reagan pulled away, but she could hear Reagan's shallow breathing, matching her own.

"I'm sorry," she whispered. "I shouldn't have—"

"I've wanted to kiss you since the moment I laid eyes on you," Reagan said. She reached out, her fingers gently touching Shelby's face. "But I don't want your actions to be because you have pity for me."

Was that the reason she'd kissed her? Out of pity? Or empathy? Maybe that's what gave her the courage to kiss Reagan, but it wasn't the sole reason. She was attracted to her...physically, yes. But also on a deeper level. As she'd told Stephanie, she and Reagan seemed to have bonded emotionally. And she didn't think it was totally the result of Reagan's sorrow and anguish she'd been suffering from. She genuinely liked her.

And she liked being around her. Like now. So she smiled and leaned back, away from Reagan.

"I'll expect a dance from you tomorrow night," she said as she turned the Jeep around and headed back to the hotel.

"That's it? We're not going to talk about it? We kissed, right?"

"Right. And I liked it very much. In fact, I'd like to do it again sometime." She glanced over at Reagan, seeing her face in the shadows of the Jeep's interior. "But only when you're sure that it's because I want to and not because I'm taking pity on you."

"And…you want to dance together?"

"I love to dance. I told you, I'm a very good dancer. And with luck, we may find some mistletoe." Then she laughed. "And if Doug comes within twenty feet of me, I'll expect you to come to my rescue. I have visions of him walking around with mistletoe in his hand, holding it over unsuspecting women."

Reagan laughed too. "I thought you'd been replaced by Holly?"

"We can hope. But I'm going to be wearing a very sleek, very strapless dress with a slit up the side."

"Oh my," Reagan murmured. "I'm not sure us dancing is very wise then."

"We'll be fine."

"People might be shocked," she warned.

"Everyone in my family knows I'm gay," she said. "Yours?"

"Definitely."

"Then the only thing our dancing together will do is annoy my mother and, of course, remind her that yes, I *am* still gay." She paused. "You do know how to dance, right?"

"Yes. I can even lead."

"Perfect." She drove out of the park, then glanced over at Reagan. "And by the way, I don't do pity kisses."

CHAPTER TWENTY-TWO

"And how's my favorite daughter this morning?"

Shelby looked up from the paper she'd been reading, smiling as her father came over. "You made it, finally."

He sat down beside her and Ty placed a cup of coffee in front of him. "Yes. Got here very early. Beat the storm by twenty minutes."

"Yes, I peeked out. It's snowing pretty hard now." She took a sip from her coffee. "Glad you're here. I'm sure Mother was happy to see you."

He shrugged. "Your mother is…well, your mother," he said. "I understand the latest crisis has something to do with a bridesmaid dress."

"Oh, yeah. Josh's sister, Reagan…well, let's just say she would feel more comfortable in a tuxedo than a formal dress, if you know what I mean."

He raised his eyebrows, and she smiled and nodded at his unasked question.

"That's a coincidence, isn't it? Do you know her?"

"Met her last week when I got here. Tuesday. Anyway, she's refused to be a bridesmaid if it involves a dress and Mother refuses to let her wear a tuxedo, even though Stephanie and Josh are fine with it. So that's the crisis."

"What's your take on it?"

"I think Reagan would look *very* handsome in a tuxedo," she said with a smile. "In fact, I'm certain it would push Mother over the edge. That would be entertaining." She leaned closer, lowering her voice. "Any more news on Aspen?"

"They're going to wrap up the audit this week. I did speak to Murray, briefly. I was vague with what we'd found. I have a meeting scheduled with him and William next Monday."

"I still can't believe it," she said.

"I'm as shocked as you are. After I meet with him next week, we'll decide how to proceed."

"Surely you're going to fire him."

"Without a doubt, yes. I meant whether we're going to press charges or not."

"Worried about publicity?"

"Yes." He finished his coffee and shoved the cup away. "But let's not let it ruin the week." He stood. "I hope you'll save a dance for me."

"Of course."

She sighed as her gaze followed him out the door. He seemed...a little down and she suspected it wasn't all due to Mark Murray. Her father was usually a cheerful, playful man. It was obvious by his demeanor and the look in his eyes that he would rather be anywhere else than here. But she knew that had nothing to do with Stephanie's wedding and everything to do with her mother.

Or else...maybe he was missing someone, wishing he was with her instead. Should she come right out and ask him if he was having an affair? Would he consider it any of her business? *Was* it her business? She grabbed the bridge of her nose and squeezed. Her father was a handsome man, still young-looking at fifty-eight. She had visions of his mistress being a twenty-five-year-old gold digger. A voluptuous blonde with long, red fingernails and costume jewelry.

Unless he already had her dripping in diamonds.

CHAPTER TWENTY-THREE

Reagan stared into the mirror, adjusting the bow tie a bit. She'd been pleasantly surprised that the first shop she'd gone into had tuxedos for women. There were four places in Estes Park that rented formal wear. She had been prepared to have to hit them all to find what she wanted.

"You look so pretty."

Reagan turned to her mother. "I'm a dyke in a tuxedo. You can't say pretty."

Her mother grabbed her lapel and pulled it tighter. "What should I say? Handsome? You're that too. And I don't like you calling yourself a dyke. It's offensive."

Reagan rolled her eyes. "I am what I am, Mom."

Her mother fussed with her tie a bit, stalling. She finally dropped her hands. "When you were young, a toddler, you were so darn cute," she said. "I'd thought about sending your photo in to a modeling agency."

"Seriously?"

"Yes. You've seen your baby pictures, Reagan. You were adorable." She laughed. "Not to insinuate that you're not still."

"Well, thank you for *not* doing it."

"I had visions of you in commercials or maybe modeling."

"Modeling?" She laughed. "I was a farm girl with skinned up knees."

Her mother waved her hand in protest. "Regardless... you were an adorable farm girl. And you've grown into such a beautiful woman."

Reagan took her mother's hands. "I'm sorry I wasn't the girl you wanted, Mom. You had visions of twirling and cheerleading and dance classes. I'm sorry I wasn't all that."

Her mother squeezed her hands. "Don't you dare say you're sorry. I wouldn't trade you for anyone in the world."

As their hands held, Reagan blinked tears away as she saw her mother's eyes well over too. She finally pulled her mother into a tight embrace.

"You're the best, Mom," she whispered in her ear.

When they pulled apart, her mother dabbed at the tears in her own eyes. "Well, I happen to think that you're the best too."

Reagan took a step away, trying to get her emotions under control. "I should warn you, Shelby expects a dance tonight. With me."

Her mother smiled. "She does? That's great. Did you make another pass at her like we suggested?"

Reagan shook her head. "Actually, she made a pass at me." She smiled, embarrassed. "She kissed me."

Her mother's eyes widened. "What does that mean?"

"It means I'm in trouble. Big trouble."

CHAPTER TWENTY-FOUR

Shelby and Stephanie took a casual stroll inside the ballroom, looking at all the Christmas decorations Bruce and his staff had managed to cram inside. It was so overdone, so jam-packed with colorful trees and lights and red and green garland…and it was beautiful in spite of the excess.

"I'm in love with it," Stephanie said again. "It's like Christmas overload."

"I have to admit, it's very pretty," Shelby said. Christmas carols were playing quietly in the background and she found herself humming along.

"You look gorgeous, by the way," Stephanie said. "I'm jealous. That dress is awesome. Where'd you get it?"

Shelby smiled. "You thought I'd wear a suit, didn't you?"

"It crossed my mind."

"Well, I didn't shop for it. I told Bernie what I wanted."

"Wow. Mother let you borrow Bernie? She was probably shocked that you even asked." She touched the dress. "What shade of blue is that? It has a lavender tint to it."

"Bernie called it midnight blue." Shelby led her to the tables where the staff was beginning to put food out. "What did you finally settle on?"

"You mean, what did Mother finally settle on," Stephanie corrected. "All finger foods. Fancy sandwiches—eleven kinds. Seven varieties of cheese. Shrimp and sushi and caviar. Some tartlets. A bunch of dips," she said. "Oh, you've got to try the seafood guacamole. It was *so* good. And there's a crab and artichoke dip that was awesome too."

"I take it you got to sample the menu?"

"Yes. Remember a couple of weeks ago when Mother and I met with the chefs? They had over seventy items to choose from."

"Sorry I missed it," she lied. "Come on, let's get a drink."

"I'll have a glass of champagne," Stephanie said.

"I'll need something stronger than that to get through the evening," she said as they headed to the bar that was in the back corner. Zach was working it. "They pull you out of the main bar?" she asked him.

"It's my day off so I volunteered to work back here." He motioned to his large tip jar. "Open bar usually means big tips," he said with a grin.

"Good plan," she said. "I'll have my usual. Stephanie wants champagne."

"So you talked to Dad this morning, I guess," Stephanie said when Zach stepped away.

"Yes. He seemed…well, not himself," she said. "What did you think?"

"He appeared distracted," Stephanie said. "Of course as soon as he got here, Mother started in on the wedding and how it's going to be a complete disaster."

Shelby rolled her eyes but didn't comment. When Zach brought their drinks, she reached into her handbag and pulled out some money, being the first to fill his tip jar.

"Thank you very much," he said with a grin.

"You're welcome."

Stephanie touched Shelby's glass with her champagne flute. "Cheers," she said.

"To wedded bliss," Shelby added.

"Speaking of that, have you seen Mother? She looks really nice."

Shelby shook her head. "Have they come in?"

"Mother was here earlier—making her last round to make sure everything was set up like she'd ordered," she said with a laugh. "But I just saw Dad come in."

Shelby scanned the room, finding her father speaking with Josh's parents. Her mother wasn't around. "I don't see her."

"Over there," Stephanie said. "She's talking with Mrs. Harper, one of the friends she invited from her bridge club."

"Oh. She's in red. She blends in with the Christmas decorations."

"I know. But she's festive," Stephanie said. She looked at her, taking in her dress again. "Bernie did her dress too, obviously, but I like yours better."

"Thank you. I'm really glad Mother didn't try to go strapless as well."

Stephanie didn't answer as she stared past her. "Oh, my *God*," she whispered. "Oh my *freakin'* God."

"What?" Shelby turned, following Stephanie's gaze. She very nearly dropped her drink.

"Don't you dare tell Josh this, but Reagan looks better in a tuxedo than he does." She leaned closer. "I think even I would go out with her."

Shelby blinked several times, finally finding her voice. "How about you stick with Josh, huh?"

Unfortunately, she didn't have time to gather herself as Reagan had spotted them and was headed their way. And, as Stephanie had said, "oh my freakin' God." She couldn't take her eyes off her as Reagan walked confidently toward her. Reagan stopped several feet away, her own gaze sweeping over her, then once again, more slowly. Shelby finally took a breath, not realizing she had stopped breathing.

Stephanie cleared her throat beside her, and Shelby pulled her eyes from Reagan and turned to Stephanie. "Don't you have somewhere to be?"

Stephanie gave her a knowing smile and a subtle wink. "Sure. I need to find my fiancé." She walked up to Reagan and touched her arm. "You look fabulous in a tux," she said. "Please wear it to the wedding on Friday."

Reagan gave her a quick nod, then turned her attention back to Shelby. Shelby took a deep breath, then moved closer, smiling as she met Reagan's eyes.

"Had you been wearing *that* in the bar that first day I would have definitely said yes."

Reagan smiled too. "Well, I won't make that mistake again." Then her expression turned more serious as her eyes swept over her once again. "You look...beautiful," Reagan said quietly. "In fact, breathtaking."

"Thank you." She looked down at her dress, the slit in the side much higher than she'd wanted, but Bernie had insisted. As she saw Reagan's gaze follow hers and lock on her exposed leg, she was very glad she'd let Bernie have his way. "It's not often that I...well, this isn't exactly what I normally wear," she admitted.

Reagan motioned to her tux. "Nor I."

Shelby couldn't resist as she took a step closer. "You look *incredible* in a tuxedo," she whispered.

Before Reagan could answer, the lights were dimmed and the Christmas music was muted as the DJ took over.

"Welcome, everyone. Glad you could make it. To kick off our wedding dance, the bride will share the first one with her father. Give them a hand."

Clapping ensued and Reagan leaned closer. "*That's* your father?" Reagan asked with just a touch of surprise in her voice.

Her father was a tall, handsome man and came across as intimidating to some. But he was only her father to her.

"Yes."

"You do favor him, although his hair is more brown than blond."

Shelby laughed. "Well, I have a very good hairdresser." She motioned behind her to the bar. "You want a drink?"

"Yes, please."

They went over to the bar and Zach raised his eyebrows. "Scotch?"

Reagan nodded. "You're a good man, Zach."

"The sign of a good bartender is remembering what the regulars drink," he said with an easy smile.

Reagan laughed. "Not sure I want to be classified as a regular...not at a hotel bar, anyway."

Shelby leaned against the bar next to her. "I didn't see you around today."

"No. We braved the weather and I took my mom out to lunch, then we went shopping," Reagan said. "What did you do?"

"Visited with my father a little, then spent the rest of the time avoiding my mother," she said with a quick laugh. "I had a little work to do too, so I spent a couple of hours with that."

She looked out over the dance floor as the song came to an end. She was surprised to see her father seek out her mother for the next dance. Maybe things were okay between them after all.

"Heads up," Reagan said quietly. "Dougie's on his way over."

Shelby turned, watching as Doug sidestepped an older woman she didn't recognize. One of Josh's relatives, maybe. Doug caught her eyes and smiled, and she tentatively returned it. Then, in a panic, she looked above her head, making sure she was not standing under mistletoe.

Reagan laughed. "I would have already claimed a mistletoe kiss if it was there."

Doug stopped in front of them, his gaze shifting to Reagan, and he slowly shook his head.

"My goodness, Ray Ray, look at you. Did you take a wrong turn at the dress fittings?"

Shelby had to bite her lip to stop herself from coming to Reagan's rescue. Of course, Reagan didn't need rescuing. At least, not from Doug.

"No, they actually make tuxedos for women," Reagan said easily. "You should try it, Dougie. I'm sure they'll have one to fit you too."

Shelby stifled her laugh, but Doug was not amused.

"I think one cross-dresser in the family is enough." He turned to Shelby. "You look absolutely beautiful, Shelby. I was hoping to have a dance with you." He stepped closer. "I won't take no for an answer."

She opened her mouth to protest, but he had grabbed her hand and was tugging her out onto the dance floor. She looked back at Reagan, who was simply watching them with an amused expression on her face.

"You really need to be careful of Reagan," Doug said as he pulled her closer. "She's unscrupulous."

"Really? I've actually spent quite a bit of time with her, and I've found her to be very forthright," she said. His hand was on her bare back and she tried her best to ignore it. But when it moved lower, she stiffened. "If you touch my ass, I'll slap you," she warned. The hand immediately stopped its movement.

"I'm...simply dancing," he said. "But that dress...you are the most beautiful woman here, Shelby."

She didn't acknowledge his comment. Instead, she tried to steer the conversation away from her. "I expected to see you here with Holly. She's very nice, don't you think?"

"Oh, yes. She is. We had fun at the spa together. But she's not really my type," he said. He leaned closer, his lips near her ear. "Now, you, on the other hand—"

She laughed. "Trust me, I am *not* your type." She tried to put some distance between them as they danced. "I know you don't believe me, Doug, but I really am a lesbian."

He shook his head and smiled. "No, you're not. I asked your mother. She said you hadn't met the right guy yet. In fact, she thinks I might be the right guy."

She forced a smile to her face. "My mother is still holding out hope," she said. "But if there is one Bryant here that I am attracted to, it's Reagan, not you."

He nearly stumbled as their feet tangled. When he righted himself, he sported an angry blush on his face.

"Ray Ray? You're attracted to *her*? She's dressed like a man, for God's sake."

Shelby stopped dancing and pulled out of his arms. "She looks stunning. And don't ask me to dance again," she said quickly before heading back to the bar and Reagan.

But she was intercepted by her father, who held a hand out to her. "May I?"

She smiled at him. "Of course."

"Who was that handsome fella you were dancing with?"

Shelby groaned. "Josh's cousin and the best man. Doug Bryant."

"I take it you're not fond of him?"

"He thinks he has a shot with me, thanks to Mother. He tried to grab my ass when we were dancing."

Her father laughed. "Now when's the last time a man has gotten that close to you?"

She smiled. "It would have been Preston Wilcox when I was nineteen," she said.

He nodded. "I remember Preston. I never liked him."

"Mother loved him."

"I would think Christine would love *any* man you brought around."

"I know. And I know she still thinks this is a phase I'm going through."

"Well, you never bring any lady friends around," he said. "In fact, we've not met a single woman you've dated, have we?"

She sighed. "No. Truth is, I don't date much, Dad. One and done, usually," she admitted.

"Why is that? You're a beautiful woman, Shelby. Smart, conscientious, mature. Why one and done?"

"Stephanie says I'm either too picky or I'm paranoid."

"Everyone should be picky when it comes to finding the right mate," he said. "But paranoid?"

She nodded. "Because of you, the hotels, the money."

"Ah. Of course. Hard to trust?"

"Yes."

He spun her around with a smile. "My lovely daughter… you'll meet someone one day who will sweep you off your feet. You'll know when it's right and you'll know you can trust her."

"You think so?"

"I do. These things often happen when you least expect it." As the song faded and another one began, he led her off to the side. "I could use a drink," he said.

She linked arms with him. "You're in luck. I happen to know the bartender. Besides, there's someone I want you to meet."

CHAPTER TWENTY-FIVE

Reagan stared nervously as Shelby and her father headed her way. She turned to Zach, who had just made a martini for someone.

"Can I get another?" she asked as she slid her empty toward him.

"Sure. But don't worry. Mr. Sutton is a great guy."

Reagan turned back, meeting Shelby's gaze as she came nearer. Shelby looked composed—calm—and it helped settle her nerves somewhat. She returned Shelby's smile, then turned her attention to her father.

"Dad, this is Reagan Bryant, Josh's sister," Shelby introduced.

Reagan shook his hand. "Pleased to meet you, sir."

Mr. Sutton studied her for a moment. "You're the photojournalist, right?"

"Yes, sir. I'm kinda…taking a break," she said.

"Dad, what would you like? Scotch?"

"Please. On the rocks," he said. He motioned to Reagan's drink. "Is that what you're having."

"Yes. And thanks for the open bar," she said with a smile.

Zach was already on it, and Shelby found a fresh gin and tonic that he had placed in front of her. She took a sip before turning back to Reagan.

"Dad, by the way, Reagan is the one causing Mother fits," Shelby said with a laugh.

Reagan's eyes widened.

"I told him about the dress," Shelby explained. "Or lack of, I should say."

"Well, I, for one, think you look quite dashing in a tux," Mr. Sutton said. "It gets my vote."

Reagan felt a blush on her face, and she nervously took a sip of her whiskey. *Dashing?*

"I hope you won't mind if Reagan and I dance later," Shelby continued.

"Of course not. There are no secrets here, right?"

Shelby smiled. "Right. But to prevent Mother's stroke, you may want to shield her."

Mr. Sutton laughed at that statement and Reagan assumed his sense of humor matched Shelby's and not her mother's. "Quite the contrary. I think the two of you would make a stunning couple out on the dance floor." He took his drink off the bar and raised it to her. "Nice to meet you, Reagan. Enjoy the dance."

"You too. Thank you."

He leaned over and kissed Shelby on the cheek, then whispered something into her ear. Shelby's eyes met hers and she smiled.

"I'll keep that in mind," Shelby said to him. As soon as he walked away, Shelby moved closer to her. "Why do you look so nervous?"

Reagan gave a shaky laugh. "Do I? I thought I was hiding it well."

Shelby tilted her head. "Are you nervous of my dad or of me?"

"Both, I think." She took another sip of her drink. "So how was Dougie?"

Shelby rolled her eyes. "You're right. He's obnoxious. His hand on my back was getting dangerously close to my ass."

"Oh, that's Dougie," she said, surprised by the jealousy she felt.

"I can't totally blame him," Shelby said. "My mother didn't help matters. He apparently asked her if I was really gay, and she told him I hadn't met the right guy yet."

"Your mother has a crush on him."

"I know." Shelby took the drink from her hand and put it on the bar. "And I'm ready to dance with you."

Reagan swallowed nervously. So they really *were* going to dance? She let her fingers entwine with Shelby's as Shelby led them out onto the dance floor. The lights were dim, but even so, Reagan imagined all eyes were on them.

"Relax," Shelby murmured.

Yes, *relax*, she told herself. Easier said than done, though. Shelby moved closer and put a hand on her shoulder.

"You did say you would lead, right?"

Reagan took a deep breath, then slipped her arm around Shelby, her hand touching her bare back. Shelby's skin was warm and smooth, and she spread her hand out, touching more of it as she pulled her closer. The song was a slow one, but not overly so. For the life of her, Reagan couldn't recall the name or artist or even from what decade it was, but it suited them just fine. She relaxed and tried to forget that her hand was touching Shelby's bare back as she moved with her across the floor. Their dance was fluid and graceful—for that she was thankful.

"Do you think people are staring?" she asked, her eyes darting around them.

"I don't really care," Shelby said. She pulled back. "Do you?"

"I don't care for me, no. I was worried about you."

Shelby met her gaze. "The only person who would have an issue with this is my mother," she said. "And since she's apparently forgotten that I'm gay, I don't mind that she sees us."

The song ended all too soon, but it blended into another one, this one slower than the one before. Shelby looked at her questioningly, and Reagan pulled her closer, their bodies meeting fully for the first time. She missed a step, then laughed quietly as Shelby chuckled in her ear.

"Relax," Shelby said again.

"Easy for you to say," she countered.

Shelby pulled back a little. "I can't believe you're so nervous. I still keep going back to your proposition that first day."

"Yes, well, I was completely out of my mind," she said.

She thought back to that day, only a week ago. Yes, she'd been out of her mind with grief, with guilt. She'd only wanted someone to take her away from that for a few hours. What if Shelby had said yes? Would they be having this dance right now? Probably not. If they'd had sex that first day...and then found out later that they were each sisters of the bride and groom... well, she could only imagine how awkward that would have been. No, they wouldn't be having this dance. They wouldn't have become friends. And Shelby wouldn't have tried so hard to reach her, to urge her to talk about the pain she was feeling. And a week later, she would most likely still be eaten up with guilt, with grief.

Instead, she felt good. Content in some ways. She realized her guilt had been misplaced, and she'd embraced her grief instead of wallowing in it. Her mind felt clear for the first time in over a month. Clear, yes, but she still had no desire to pick up a camera.

So she pulled Shelby a little bit closer, feeling Shelby's hand on her shoulder move slightly, touching her neck, her fingers brushing her hair. She relaxed, allowing herself to enjoy the dance, enjoy this closeness with Shelby. She breathed deeply, savoring—memorizing—the scent that she'd come to associate with her. It was a light cologne, very subtle, almost as if she wore nothing at all. And it was so very intoxicating.

"You're a very good dancer," Shelby said, breaking the silence.

"Thank you. You are too."

"Shame we haven't danced under any mistletoe though."

Reagan recognized the teasing in Shelby's voice, and she smiled, spinning them around dramatically, causing Shelby to laugh in her ear. She hadn't danced in years and was quite proud that she hadn't faltered in the spin. She pulled back far enough to meet Shelby's gaze, returning her grin. She had an almost uncontrollable urge to kiss her, right then and there. Shelby's beautiful eyes turned a darker shade of blue, and as she stared into them, she stopped dancing entirely. Shelby's gaze dropped to her lips and Reagan's breath caught. Would they kiss? *Here?* But the song ended, breaking the spell. She pulled away, looking around them, expecting stares. But conversation and laughter— and more dancing—continued with no one seemingly paying them any mind.

"That was fun," Shelby said.

"Yes. And no one seemed fazed by our dance."

Shelby smiled at her. "Then I'll expect several more." She leaned closer. "I love being in your arms," she whispered.

Reagan felt her pulse spring to life, and she raised an eyebrow. "Are you flirting with me again?"

Shelby laughed quietly as she linked arms with her and headed back toward the bar. "Just stating a fact, Reagan, that's all."

CHAPTER TWENTY-SIX

Shelby sipped her water, watching as Reagan made her way across the room to her mother, who had waved her over. The woman next to her mother was an aunt Reagan hadn't seen in years, she'd said. So she leaned back against the bar, forgoing another gin and tonic for water. She was already feeling too relaxed, too placid. Another dance with Reagan and she might forget where they were...in a public setting. Because the look in Reagan's eyes said she wanted to kiss her. Shelby let her gaze travel over Reagan once again. She already knew that she was attracted to her, but the way she looked in that tuxedo, she simply wanted to devour her. And she couldn't remember the last time she'd thought that about another woman.

"Hey...there's my beautiful sister," Stephanie said, her voice singsong and tinged with amusement as she came closer. "And I see who you're staring at."

Shelby smiled, noting the empty champagne glass she was holding. "Enjoying the champagne fountain, are you?"

"The fountain is flowing. However, Zach has the good stuff back here." She set the glass on the bar. "I'll have another, please."

Shelby shook her head. "You're going to have a headache in the morning," she warned.

"I don't care. Right now, I feel too good and I'm having too much fun." Her voice lowered. "I saw you and Reagan dance."

"Did you now."

"You look so cute together," she teased, her voice once again singsong. "So what's going on?"

"Nothing's going on, Steph," she said.

"Liar, liar," Stephanie said with a laugh. "I can tell something is going on with you two."

"It was just a dance," she insisted.

"That was more than a dance, Shelby."

"Oh, come on. I danced with Doug earlier too. It doesn't mean anything."

"Admit it, Shelby...you like her."

Shelby nodded. "Yes. I like her fine. She's very nice. We get along great."

"That's not what I meant. You *like* her," she teased.

Shelby sighed. "What are we, Steph? Back in high school?"

"She's *so* cute. Isn't she?"

"You didn't think so. You said she was manly," she reminded her.

"Well, she's in a tuxedo, Shelby. That *is* manly. But she looks almost feminine in it, doesn't she?"

Shelby laughed. "I think Reagan would be insulted by that statement."

"You know what? I think *you* would look fabulous in a tuxedo too." Stephanie leaned closer. "That would solve the whole bridesmaid issue. Instead of you both wearing dresses, you could both wear a tux. What do you think?"

"Sure. And then afterward, we could both go visit Mother in the hospital," she said.

Stephanie laughed loudly. "Oh, I know. That would do it, wouldn't it? You in a tux." Then Stephanie elbowed her. "Here she comes," she whispered.

"Yes, I see that," Shelby said, her eyes on Reagan as she walked toward them.

"Aunt Martha," Reagan explained. "Haven't seen her in six or seven years." She turned to Stephanie. "Having fun?"

"A blast," Stephanie said. "And you, my new sister-in-law… look absolutely gorgeous." She pointed at the tux. "I want you to wear that to the wedding."

Reagan raised her eyebrows. "But your mother said—"

"No," Stephanie said, holding up her hand. "It's my wedding, not hers. Besides, Shelby will talk to her."

Shelby frowned. "Why me?"

"Because you're the oldest."

"So?"

"So? You can talk to her like that, I can't. Tell her it's a done deal. I want Reagan in the wedding, Josh wants Reagan in the wedding." She smiled. "She looks so beautiful. You two look beautiful together. I think you—"

"Okay, okay," Shelby said, interrupting her. "I'll tell her. And now you should probably go mingle with your guests, maybe find Josh," she suggested.

Stephanie picked up her champagne glass again, which Zach had dutifully filled. "I should mingle. You two should dance again." She leaned over and kissed Reagan's cheek, then did the same to Shelby. "Love you guys. You're so cute together."

When she left, Shelby turned to Reagan. "Too much champagne," she explained.

Reagan nodded, then glanced at the water bottle in her hand. "I think I'll have water too."

"Good. Because the next slow song that plays…you're mine."

Reagan surprised her by leaning closer, her voice low. "Yes. I'll be yours tonight." Their eyes met. "All night, if you want."

Reagan's voice had a huskiness to it that sent shivers down her spine. Was Reagan saying what she thought she was saying?

She held her gaze, trying to read Reagan's eyes. She saw what she needed to see. She nodded.

"Yes. I think I want that," she whispered.

Reagan smiled slowly. "Then let's dance…and see what the night holds."

CHAPTER TWENTY-SEVEN

Reagan literally trembled as Shelby moved into her arms. She closed her eyes, wondering if she'd ever been so affected by someone before.

"Relax," Shelby whispered once again to her.

Reagan tightened her hold on her. "I want to kiss you. I want...I want to touch you."

She heard Shelby's quickly drawn in breath, felt Shelby's hand move into the hair at her neck, gently stroking, but she said nothing. She simply moved closer to her.

"If you don't stop, I'll end up embarrassing us both," she warned.

Shelby pulled back, enough to meet her gaze. Her blue eyes were dark, smoldering. Reagan couldn't help it...she fell right into their blue depths, knowing she was in danger of drowning there. She didn't care.

Then suddenly, Shelby stopped dancing and pulled out of her arms. Reagan looked at her questioningly. Had she done something wrong? Shelby took her hand and led her off the dance floor and back to the bar. But she didn't stop. She went behind it, tossing a glance at Zach.

"Need to borrow the closet for a minute," she said.

Zach grinned and nodded. "Sure."

Confused, Reagan followed her, wondering what was going on. The closet proved to be a small room filled with bar supplies. Shelby closed the door and locked it. Reagan had no time to contemplate what was about to happen. Shelby moved closer.

"You said something about a kiss," Shelby murmured.

There was no pretense from either of them, no easing into the kiss, no hesitation. Reagan pressed her against the wall, her thigh sliding up between her legs as she found her mouth. Shelby moaned into the kiss, her mouth opening and their tongues meeting in a crazy dance.

Shelby's arms circled her neck, one hand cupping the back of her head, pulling her closer. Reagan's hands moved across Shelby's bare back, then slipped lower, cupping her hips and bringing her up higher against her thigh.

Shelby pulled her mouth away, gasping for breath, then came back, kissing her once again, her tongue sliding into Reagan's mouth. They were moving together wildly, hands roaming at will. When Shelby's hands slid inside her jacket and cupped her breasts, Reagan's hips jerked hard against her.

Jesus…God…how far were they going to go in this closet? But when her hand slipped inside Shelby's dress at her back and moved lower, when she heard Shelby's deep moan, she knew they had to stop.

Her mouth left Shelby's, moving to her neck where she left tiny kisses, then to her ear. "Not here, Shelby," she whispered.

Shelby groaned, then separated from her. Her eyes were as dark a blue as Reagan had ever seen. She stared into them, then pulled Shelby closer again, finding her mouth once more. But this time it was Shelby who slowed things down, easing their kiss from frantic to calm, from mouth and tongue to lips before finally stopping altogether.

They were both breathing hard, fast, and she leaned against the wall beside Shelby, their shoulders touching. Shelby turned her head, a smile on her lips.

"Wow, Reagan...you do just dive right in, don't you?"

Reagan smiled too. "I'm thinking this was your doing, not mine."

Shelby shook her head. "Your fault. You were flirting with me on the dance floor."

"You were flirting with me *before* the dance," she reminded her.

Shelby turned to her, straightening her tie and then her jacket. Then she ran a gentle hand through Reagan's hair, pausing to brush her fingers against her cheek. Shelby met her stare, never blinking.

"I'm quite aroused, in case you didn't know," Shelby said quietly. "It's been a really long time since that has happened."

Reagan wasn't sure it mattered, but she wanted to tell Shelby anyway. "It's been...well, a few years since I've been with anyone." She shrugged. "Three, four. Maybe longer."

Shelby's expression softened, her fingers tracing a lazy path along her cheek. "Why?"

Reagan ducked her head. Why? She didn't really know why. How could she explain the emptiness she'd felt the last few times she'd taken women—strangers—to bed? Or worse, not a stranger but a colleague that she didn't even like as a friend, much less a lover. She looked up, meeting her gaze again.

"I got tired of the emptiness," she said truthfully. Shelby seemed to understand and instead of asking more questions, she moved closer, wrapping her arms around her shoulders and pulling her into a tight, intimate hug.

"There'll be no emptiness tonight, Reagan. I promise." Shelby kissed her lips gently, lingering slightly before pulling away. "We'll make love. It won't be a meaningless encounter." Shelby let out a heavy breath. "Because honestly, I've had my share of those too."

CHAPTER TWENTY-EIGHT

It had been an endless night, and Shelby was ready for it to be over with already. She'd suffered through a handful of dances, even one with Duke, Reagan's cousin. But Doug stayed clear and she'd seen him dancing with Holly several times. Reagan, too, stayed away, visiting with her family for most of the evening instead. That's not to say that they didn't find themselves watching each other on several occasions. Shelby couldn't seem to take her eyes off Reagan.

And now she was wondering how she was going to get Reagan up to her suite unnoticed. She didn't want to answer questions from Stephanie or her mother. And she didn't want Reagan to have to answer questions from her family. She didn't want to broadcast what was happening between them. It wasn't anyone else's business, she reasoned. She only wanted to share the night with Reagan, alone…and naked.

God, if the scene in the closet was any indication, they would be completely compatible in bed. She could already imagine what it would feel like to have Reagan's hands…and mouth…

on her. So much so that she contemplated stealing Reagan away early, before the dance even came to an end. Would it be less conspicuous then?

"Feel like a dance?"

She turned, smiling at her father. "You've been dancing the night away already. Having a good time?"

"Surprisingly so, yes," he said. "You?"

"Yes."

He glanced across the room, and she followed it, seeing his gaze land on Reagan. "You haven't danced together lately," he noted.

"No."

"I hope your mother didn't say anything to you."

"No. I haven't spoken to her," she said. "Why? Was she appalled?"

He nodded with a slight smile. "I told her you had the best-looking date here."

"Well, she's holding out hope for Doug still, I think." She leaned closer, touching his shoulder with her own. "Are you and Mother okay?"

He seemed surprised by her question. "We're...the same," he said evasively.

"None of my business?"

He took a deep breath. "When this is all over with, maybe it's time you and I had a talk," he said. "I sometimes forget that you're all grown up."

She nodded, knowing from his statement that things were *not* okay with her parents.

"Anyway, I've got some business changes I'd like to run by you. This thing with Murray...well, it's got me thinking."

"Changes?"

But he shook his head. "We'll talk when we get back to Denver. Nothing to worry about, Shelby." He smiled. "Now... how about that dance?"

* * *

Reagan turned in her chair to get a better view of the dance floor. Shelby was with her father this time. Much better than when she'd had to watch Shelby with Duke, of all people. At least Dougie had kept his distance. Of course, so had she. After what had happened in the supply closet, she didn't dare take a chance with another close encounter.

"You're staring."

She pulled her eyes from Shelby, smiling at her mother. "Caught me," she said.

"I'd say." Her mother leaned closer. "That dress is beautiful on her. She's a striking woman." She paused. "All of your cousins are fawning over her."

"So I've seen. I thought Duke was going to hyperventilate when they danced."

Her mother smiled as she patted her knee affectionately. "Well, I've seen her watching you too," she said quietly.

"Mom…"

"Oh, I'm not trying to get into your business, Reagan. Just making an observation." She laughed lightly. "And in case you need some motherly advice, don't be shy with this one."

"I told you, she's out of my league," Reagan said.

"Nonsense. There is no *league*, Reagan. We're all just people."

It sounded simple, but was it really? Shelby had said once that she didn't really trust her dates, always wondering if they were more interested in the money than her. Did she think the same of Reagan? No. No, she couldn't possibly. For one thing, they had become friends. Reagan didn't care how much money she had. That was never a consideration when she'd bared her soul to Shelby, sharing all her dark secrets. They were just two people, learning to trust, learning to care.

We're all just people.

She turned to her mother. "I like her. It's been a long time since I've been…emotionally close to someone."

"I know. And I like her too."

CHAPTER TWENTY-NINE

There was no sign of Reagan as Shelby made her way through the ballroom, scanning the faces of the remaining guests. The DJ had already packed up, and the kitchen staff was removing the food items that remained. She snatched up a small sandwich before they took the last tray, then grabbed another bottle of water from Zach. Stephanie and Josh were still dancing, even though the only music was the return of Christmas carols. Stephanie spotted her and waved her over.

"What a magical night," Stephanie said as she held onto Josh. "I love this man."

"I should hope so. You're going to marry him very soon," she said with a smile at Josh.

"Where's Reagan?" he asked.

"I don't know. I was actually looking for her," she said.

Stephanie pointed her finger at her. "And you say there's nothing going on."

"There's not," she said. "But I'm tired. I'm going to head up to my suite. Are you about ready to call it a night too?"

"Mother says we have to stay until all the guests leave. But I am ready for bed," she said with a wink at Josh.

"I'm sure you are." She looked around, seeing Josh's mother. "I think I'll say a quick goodnight to your parents, then head up. I'll see you tomorrow."

"Okay. Goodnight," Josh said.

"Night, sis," Stephanie called as she walked away. "We've got a lunch date tomorrow, don't forget."

Damn. Yes, she had forgotten. Her mother wanted them to go out to lunch with her bridge club ladies.

She smiled as she approached Margie Bryant, who was chatting with another woman. "Sorry to interrupt," she said politely. "Did you have a nice evening?"

"Oh, it was fun, yes. Shelby, this is Dora Ellis, my sister. They got here today."

"Pleased to meet you. I hope the storm didn't delay you," she said.

"Nice to meet you too. No, we live up in Casper, so we're used to driving in the snow," she said.

"Good." Shelby turned to Margie. "I'm heading up to my room. Did Reagan sneak out earlier?"

"Not too long ago. She said she was ready to get into some comfortable clothes." She laughed. "I don't blame her. I helped her dress, and the tuxedo was a bit cumbersome."

She nodded. "Yes, I'm ready to get out of this dress and these heels too." She smiled. "Well, goodnight ladies."

"Goodnight, Shelby."

She steered clear of her mother and headed to the door, feeling a little disappointed—and confused—that Reagan had slipped out without a word to her. Maybe Reagan had changed her mind. Maybe spending the night together was no longer appealing to her.

She frowned. Or maybe her mother said something to her. Shelby wouldn't put it past her. Her disappointment morphed into frustration at that thought, and she pushed the button for the elevator several times. When it arrived, it was empty. She got in, riding up to her floor alone, feeling a bit lonely, which was odd for her. She was used to spending her nights alone.

Of course, that was before Reagan and before a rather intense make-out session in the supply closet. She smiled wryly as the elevator came to a quiet halt. It seemed she was frustrated in more ways than one.

She walked down the hallway to her corner suite, pausing when she spotted a familiar figure leaning casually against the wall. Reagan was dressed in jeans and a sweatshirt, looking more like the Reagan she'd first met. While she loved the tux on her and would even echo her father's words—she looked dashing—she thought she preferred her this way. So she walked on, meeting Reagan's tentative smile with one of her own.

"I'm really glad to see you," she said. "You look nice. Comfortable."

Reagan pushed off the wall, meeting her at her door. "My feet hurt in those shoes."

Shelby laughed. "I know what you mean. I can't wait to get out of these heels."

Their eyes met and the smile left Reagan's face. "Am I being...presumptuous? I mean—"

"No." Shelby moved closer, resting her hand on Reagan's hip. "In fact, I was terribly disappointed when I couldn't find you down there," she said. She leaned forward, kissing Reagan lightly on the lips. "I'd really like to continue what we started earlier," she said, her voice not much more than a whisper. She saw Reagan swallow nervously.

"Yes. Me too."

"Good." She unlocked the door and pushed it open. She found Reagan's nervousness to be endearing, and she took her hand, tugging her inside. She closed and locked the door, leaving them standing in the muted light of the lamp she'd left on. "Would you like a brandy? Or cognac?" she offered.

Reagan shook her head slowly, a smile forming on her handsome face. "What I'd like is to get you out of that dress."

Shelby smiled too and moved closer but not close enough to touch. "You simply amaze me," she said.

Reagan arched an eyebrow questioningly. "Why's that?"

"One minute, nervous and tense, as if you're about to run. The next, confident and charming with no sign of panic."

Reagan took a step closer, leaving them only inches apart. "Yes. Nervous and scared," Reagan said quietly.

It was Shelby's turn to raise an eyebrow. "Why?"

"I told you, it's been a while. I'm not sure what to expect. I'm not sure what you—"

Shelby stopped her with a gentle finger to her lips. "I want to make love with you, Reagan. I don't want empty—emotionless—sex. I like you. I'm attracted to you. And I think you feel the same." She moved the few inches necessary for them to touch. "You said earlier that you were tired of the emptiness. I want to make love tonight. I want you to stay with me and wake up with me in the morning." She met her eyes, holding them, seeing the doubt disappear. "Will you stay with me tonight, Reagan? Because I'm tired of the emptiness too."

* * *

Reagan told herself there was nothing to be nervous about. Shelby was a woman like any other. Yet...she wasn't. She felt almost mesmerized by her as she stood still, watching as Shelby's strapless dress slid slowly down her body. She'd seen her naked—at the spa. But not like this. At the spa, Shelby had been playing...teasing. There wasn't this fire in her eyes then... an ice-blue fire that nearly had her trembling. Trembling with want...with desire...with fear. Fear of what, she had no idea. Fear that she'd forgotten how to make love? Fear that Shelby would find her lacking?

Before she could contemplate that, Shelby's hands were pulling her sweatshirt up and over her head, then urgent fingers went to the button of her jeans. But Shelby only unbuttoned them, she didn't push them down. Instead, a lazy hand ran up her belly, between her breasts, then back down again.

Relax, her mind screamed seconds before Shelby uttered that very same word.

"Your skin...so soft, warm," Shelby murmured.

Reagan stood still as Shelby leaned closer, her lips nibbling gently at her neck, causing all sorts of sensations that were completely foreign to her. God, had it really been that long that she'd forgotten what it was like to make love?

"It's okay to touch me."

Reagan laughed quietly. "I feel like a virgin," she admitted.

Shelby's mouth touched the corner of her lips, then moved across her cheek to her ear. "We can go as slow as you need. We've got all night."

But something about Shelby's words, the gentleness of them, the barest of touches against her ear...the sound of a heartbeat stirred her to life. She turned her head, finding Shelby's mouth. The once-gentle kiss turned heated in seconds and her subtle fear faded away. Shelby recognized the change, it seemed, for her fingers went to the zipper of her jeans, lowering it in one motion before slipping both hands inside to push them and her panties down.

Then Shelby drew her to the bed, down beside her. Reagan let her gaze travel over Shelby's body, lingering on her breasts, then lower. She was...she was simply exquisite. Reagan was certain she'd never been with anyone this beautiful before. She reached out to touch Shelby, her hand following the same path her eyes had moments before.

"Beautiful," she whispered, giving voice to her thoughts. She leaned down, kissing Shelby again, slowly at first, then harder as they shifted, Shelby lying back, urging Reagan on top of her. Their breasts touched, then their hips as Reagan settled between her thighs, moaning as Shelby thrust up to meet her.

She pulled her mouth from Shelby's, her breath coming quickly as her hand moved to Shelby's breast, her fingers tracing her nipple, feeling it harden beneath her touch. Shelby's hands were on her back, sliding up and down slowly, urging Reagan ever closer with each pass.

She shifted again, her thigh pressed hard against Shelby, feeling her wetness as it dampened her skin. Shelby's legs parted even further, and she cupped Reagan's hips, pulling her more firmly against her, rocking slightly against her thigh.

She lowered her head, capturing Shelby's nipple with her mouth, sucking gently on it, then more forcefully as Shelby moaned with pleasure. Fingers in her hair held her there, and Reagan nearly devoured her as she moved to her other breast.

* * *

"Oh…sweet Jesus," Shelby murmured as Reagan's hot mouth closed over her breast. She could no longer stifle her moans as Reagan's tongue flicked against her nipple, making it swell even more. She held Reagan's head, pressing her down hard, urging her to take more. Reagan did, then pulled away slightly, her lips closing over her nipple now, suckling it, causing desire to flow through her at an alarming rate. She arched her hips, thinking crazily that she was about to have an orgasm simply from Reagan's mouth on her breasts.

Then Reagan pulled away entirely from her breast, her mouth coming back to hers, her tongue sliding wetly against her own. Shelby opened her mouth, taking Reagan's tongue inside, sucking it, all the while trying to hold on to her sanity. She couldn't remember another time when she'd been so wildly aroused from a kiss.

When Reagan's mouth went back to her breast, blood pounded in her ears and she couldn't breathe. Only when Reagan's hand moved between their bodies, when Reagan's fingers found her wetness, did her breath come back to her. She was trembling in anticipation and she opened her legs even wider, giving Reagan room. Her breath hissed between her teeth at Reagan's first touch.

"Oh…God…*yes*," she murmured, her hips rising up as Reagan's fingers pushed through her wetness, filling her.

"Tell me what you like," Reagan whispered. "Do you want me inside, like this? Or…like this?" she asked as her fingers found her clit, rubbing against it in a circular motion.

Shelby jerked from the contact, panting now as her hips pushed against Reagan's fingers. She couldn't believe how close she was to orgasm and she gripped Reagan's waist with both hands.

"Don't you dare stop," she breathed.

But Reagan took her hand away. "Not yet. You said you wanted foreplay, remember?"

Shelby growled in frustration, opening her eyes, meeting Reagan's. Her breathing was ragged, but she managed a smile.

"If you don't finish this right now, I'll—"

"You'll what?" Reagan asked as she kissed her, her tongue shoving into her mouth.

Shelby moaned around the kiss, her hands moving against Reagan's back, then lower, cupping her, pulling her up hard against her again.

"Please, Reagan," she whispered against her mouth. "I'm so close."

"I know you are. I could feel you tremble when I touched you," Reagan whispered back.

"Okay...so I'm begging you."

She felt Reagan smile against her breast. She smiled too, wondering when the last time was she'd been on the verge of an orgasm and paused to have a conversation about it. But her smile vanished as Reagan's hand returned to her, her fingers sliding over her clit only briefly before once again filling her.

This time, Reagan didn't stop and Shelby lost herself in her desire, her mouth opening, taking in Reagan's tongue again, wrapping her own around it. There was no slow buildup, no wave to ride in. Her orgasm blasted through her like an explosion, seemingly shredding her body into thousands of tiny pieces. She screamed out loudly, gripping tightly around Reagan's waist to hold on, feeling as if she was falling even though she was lying down.

She felt dizzy...and embarrassed. God, she *never* screamed like that. She braced herself as Reagan's fingers withdrew from inside her, then she moaned as Regan's hand pressed hard against her clit, squeezing out the last of her orgasm.

She finally relaxed back against the bed. Her heart was still pounding, and she took several deep breaths, trying to slow her racing pulse.

"Paybacks are hell," she murmured, her eyes still closed. Reagan's quiet laugh caused her to smile. "You think I'm kidding."

Reagan lay down beside her and pulled her into her arms. Shelby buried her face against her neck, breathing in the scent of her. Her lips moved, nipping against her skin, moving up to find her mouth. It was a gentle kiss this time, slow and sensuous, making her desire flame all over again.

She rolled them over, holding Reagan down beneath her. She raised her eyebrows teasingly as she smiled.

"My turn."

CHAPTER THIRTY

"You're killing me."

Shelby left her breast and went back to her mouth. "Do you give up?"

"You're evil," she said, her mouth twitching in a smile. "Pure evil."

Shelby's tongue swirled around her nipple once again, and she raised her hips, trying to find contact, but Shelby avoided her.

"I'm dying. Please…"

"Do you give up?" Shelby whispered as her hand slipped between her legs, teasing.

"*God*…yes. I give up. You win." Reagan looked at Shelby through half-opened eyes, seeing the sensuous smile on her face. "Please…I'm dying," she said again.

Shelby leaned down, kissing her slowly on the lips. "I'm sure no one has died from foreplay."

"I don't want to be the first."

Shelby smiled against her lips. "I told you…paybacks."

"Please…I'm begging you. End this already."

Shelby's knees pushed her legs farther apart and she moaned, thinking that—finally—Shelby would stop this slow, delicious torture.

"With my mouth," Shelby said quietly. "I'll end it with my mouth."

Reagan thought she would surely melt right into the bed. She was trembling, and she couldn't stop as Shelby moved slowly down her body, her kisses leaving her skin tingling as they passed over her.

I'll end it with my mouth.

Reagan breathed deeply, fearing she would pass out. Shelby had been torturing her for what felt like hours. She had nearly climaxed four times, but each time, Shelby had pulled away at the last moment, making her wait. Apparently her wait was over as Shelby settled between her legs.

"Open."

"Oh, *God*," Reagan moaned, doing as Shelby requested.

Shelby cupped her hips, pausing only a second before lowering her head, her tongue slicing through her wetness. Reagan could feel herself throbbing, pulsing, and she squeezed her eyes shut, hoping to prolong this sweet, sweet pleasure. But Shelby's mouth closed over her clit, taking it inside, suckling it like she'd done her nipple earlier. It was simply too much. Her hips rose off the bed almost violently as her world spun, pulling a scream from her as she held on to Shelby, squeezing her tightly as Shelby continued, her tongue now raking back and forth against her clit. To Reagan's amazement—and disbelief— she felt another orgasm build. She let go, letting Shelby have her way. When Shelby's tongue went inside her, in and out so quickly, Reagan hardly had time to thrust against her. But she didn't need time. Her second orgasm came slow and sweet, and Shelby drew it out, so long that Reagan was nearly reduced to tears. Her hands fell limply to the bed, and she lay there, gasping for breath as Shelby left quiet kisses along her thighs, her stomach, her hips.

She couldn't speak. She wanted to. She wanted to tell Shelby how wonderful it all was, how she'd never—ever—had two orgasms back-to-back before. She wanted to tell her that she was an amazing lover. She wanted to tell her all that and more... but she couldn't speak. She couldn't even open her eyes.

She felt Shelby move, felt her crawl up beside her, felt her cover them with the sheet and blanket, felt Shelby snuggle up next to her.

"Sleep now," Shelby whispered.

"Mmm" was all she could manage to say.

* * *

Sunlight streamed in through the east-facing window, and Reagan turned away from it. She reached out for Shelby, but the bed was empty. She sat up, disappointed to find herself alone. Her phone was on the bedside table, she picked it up and her eyes widened. It was nearly ten. No wonder she was alone.

She didn't remember waking during the night but knew that she had. She had visions of Shelby in her arms, visions of Shelby's arms around her, visions of their legs tangled as they slept.

Visions of their lovemaking came back to her as well. She had simply passed out, falling into a blissful sleep...no dreams, no nightmares...no emptiness.

She tossed the covers off and swung her legs over the side of the bed, conscious of her nakedness. Her clothes were on a chair and she went to pick them up, finding a neatly folded note on them with her name scribbled across it.

She paused a second before grabbing it. In her experience, morning-after notes were never a good thing. She took a deep breath then flipped it open.

Feel free to use my shower if you like. I've gone to my parents' suite. Another crisis to tend to. BTW...last night was fabulous. Will I see you again tonight? Please?

She grinned as she reread the note. "Yeah," she said out loud, still smiling. "I could go for that."

And another crisis? She hoped it wasn't still about the damn bridesmaid dress.

She took a peek into the bathroom, finding it twice the size of her own. The shower was still damp, and she wondered how long ago Shelby had used it. She turned on the hot water, then adjusted it to warm as she stood under the spray. It was a nice, large shower, plenty big enough for two, she thought as she grabbed the soap. Her breasts still felt tender, and she remembered Shelby's mouth on them, time and again, as she teased her with foreplay. God, it had been glorious. A slow torture, but still glorious. And she'd do it all over again.

Like maybe tonight.

CHAPTER THIRTY-ONE

"So how's the head?" she asked Stephanie, who was lying on the sofa in their parents' suite, her eyes covered by an arm.

"Must you talk so loud?"

Shelby laughed. "Champagne headaches are the worst." She nudged Stephanie's legs out of the way and sat down. "So what's up with Mother now?"

"Same."

"The dress again?"

"Well, she's relented, apparently. She's agreed to let Reagan wear a tux as long as Bernie can 'dress it up'…her words, not mine."

"So after seeing Reagan in a tuxedo last night, she realized it wouldn't be so bad after all?"

Stephanie lowered her arm. "You guys were so cute dancing together."

"So you've said."

"I think you should make a play for her."

Shelby stared at her blankly. "A *play*? You said she wasn't my type," she reminded her.

"I didn't think she was at first. But seeing the two of you together…perfect."

Shelby hoped she wasn't blushing. She hadn't really had time to process everything that had happened. She'd slept in, finding herself still in Reagan's arms. But an urgent call from her mother had roused her from the bed. She'd showered and dressed, but Reagan was still sound asleep. Instead of waking her, she'd left a short note. And now Stephanie wanted her to make a play for her. She didn't know why, but she was hesitant to let Stephanie know that they were way past that point already.

"Well, we've become friends. I think that's enough, don't you?"

"I think you're afraid of her."

Thankfully, her mother, with Bernie in tow, interrupted their conversation. Her mother looked at her questioningly.

"Have you not called Reagan?"

Shelby frowned. "Was I supposed to?"

Her mother blew out an exasperated breath. "Must I do everything?"

Shelby stood up. "Must you make such a big deal out of this? It's a tux. The one she had on last night looked very nice. Why does Bernie have to change it?"

"Well, it has to match your dress, for one thing," she said. "We can't have her dressed like the groomsmen, now can we?"

"I can use the same color and material for her vest as I did your dress," Bernie said. "It's a bright, Christmas blue. I thought we could do a white tuxedo instead of black."

"With her dark hair, that would be pretty," Stephanie chimed in.

Shelby held up her hands. "Why are you all trying to sell this to me? I'm not the one who has to wear it."

"So call Reagan and ask her to come over," Stephanie said.

"Actually, I don't know her cell number. I don't even know her room number," she said truthfully.

"I'll get her cell number from Josh," Stephanie said as she picked up her phone. "And why don't you have it?"

Shelby shrugged.

"I saw you dancing with Doug last night," her mother said. "And their cousin Duke. He's a nice boy too."

Shelby stared at her. "Did you also see me dance with Reagan?"

The disapproval on her mother's face was clear. "It was brought to my attention, yes. Must you be so obvious?"

"Obvious? You mean obvious that I'm gay?" She nodded. "Yes. Because you seem to have forgotten."

Her mother walked across the room to the window and looked out upon Estes Park. "I don't know what it would hurt for you to get to know Doug better. You never know. You might find that you like him, Shelby. He's such a nice man."

"I'm sure he is, Mother. But despite your hope that I might change…that I *could* change if I wanted to…it's not going to happen."

"You won't even try. I don't understand you sometimes."

"Mother, we've been over this countless times. I'm a lesbian. I'm not interested in men. That's not going to change."

"I simply wish you would—"

Stephanie stood between them. "Mother, can you try to convert her *after* the wedding? I've got enough stress to deal with."

Shelby smiled her thanks, then glanced at Bernie, who had been fidgeting with cloth samples, pretending that he wasn't listening. She didn't know why. He'd heard this same conversation many times before.

"I've got her number. Do you want to call her or should I?"

Shelby had a moment of panic. What if Reagan was still in bed? *Her* bed. Well, it wasn't as if Stephanie would know whose bed she was in by a phone call.

"You can call her," she said nonchalantly. Then, "But I will take her number. You know, in case I need it."

Stephanie winked. "Sure," she said before turning her attention to the phone. "Good morning, Reagan, it's Stephanie. Josh gave me your number, I hope you don't mind." Stephanie smiled and nodded at something Reagan said before turning her back to them. "Can you come over to my parents' suite?"

Shelby watched her mother and Bernie who were trying to listen. Stephanie lowered her voice enough that they could no longer make out the conversation. When she turned back around, she nodded.

"She'll be right over. She's just gotten out of the shower."

Shelby turned away from Stephanie's gaze, wondering if it was *her* shower Reagan had used. Of course that thought brought images of that very thing. She pictured Reagan standing naked in her shower, the water glistening as it ran down her body. She blinked several times, chasing the image away. It was suddenly very hot in the room. She went into the kitchen, finding a water bottle in the fridge. She held it up to Stephanie.

"Want one? It might help your headache."

"Thank you, but the four ibuprofen I took are working their magic."

"I don't know why you girls drink so much," their mother said. "It's not ladylike."

"Stress," they said in unison.

She shook her head disapprovingly at them. "You got that from your father. I like to keep my life as stress-free as possible."

Shelby nearly choked on her water. "Mother, you are the epitome of stress."

She scoffed. "I have no idea what you mean. I don't let things get to me. I don't—"

"No. That's because you project it onto everyone else," she said. "Like this," she said, motioning to Bernie. "The whole thing with Reagan and the dress or the tux. It's driving us all crazy."

Her mother actually looked offended. "I want the wedding to be perfect, that's all." She waved her hand in the air. "I hardly think that constitutes *stress*."

"It constitutes stress for the rest of us," Stephanie said. "But can we please move on? If Reagan doesn't want a white tuxedo with the blue shirt, then fine. She can wear what she wore last night."

"But—"

"Mother…it's okay. It's not going to ruin the wedding. And I speak for all of us when I say I'm sick of the drama over the bridesmaid dress."

Shelby was impressed. It was the first time she could remember her sister actually talking back to her mother. Her mother seemed shocked as well.

"I see," she said curtly.

Shelby glanced at Stephanie. "Should have eloped," she mouthed to her.

Thankfully, a knock on the door ended this particular conversation, and her mother opened the door to Reagan. Reagan glanced around the room, her expression telling Shelby that she was very aware of the tension inside.

"Am I late?"

"No. Come in," her mother said. "We were just discussing your…tuxedo."

"Oh. And what conclusion did we come up with?"

Shelby walked over to her, meeting her gaze. She felt her pulse race as she remembered how they'd ended their night, but she pushed that away. For now.

"How do you feel about a white tux?" she asked.

"White?"

"With a blue vest to match Shelby's dress," Stephanie said. "I think it would be awesome."

"White shirt," Bernie said. "Blue tie, blue vest. No coat."

Reagan looked at her. "What do you think?"

Shelby smiled. "I think you would look…very nice."

"Why no coat, Bernie?" her mother asked.

"You don't want a white coat to cover up the blue. Shelby will be in blue so you want Reagan to be as well."

Reagan finally shrugged. "Okay. I'm game."

Stephanie clapped. "Yay! Thank you!"

Reagan shoved her hands in her jeans pockets and Shelby recognized her nervousness. She made an effort to include everyone, but her question was really directed at Reagan.

"I missed breakfast and I'm starving. Anyone up for an early lunch?"

"You and Stephanie have a lunch date with my bridge club at noon," her mother reminded her.

Shelby met Reagan's eyes and silently groaned. Just what she wanted to do...visit with her mother's friends.

"I forgot," she said as she turned toward her mother. "Can't wait."

"Oh, and Reagan," her mother said, "dinner tonight is Italian fare. Please remind your parents."

"Of course. I'll be sure to mention it."

"We might not make it back in time though," Shelby said, hoping Reagan would play along with her.

"Oh, that's right," Reagan said. "You were going to...show me..."

"Tour of the park," she said with a smile. She then glanced at her mother. "I promised Reagan we would do a drive in the park this afternoon." She shrugged. "Since the weather is good and all."

Her mother—and Stephanie—eyed her suspiciously.

"Dinner is at seven. Surely you can make it."

"Of course I'll try, Mother," she said. She turned again to Reagan. "I'll call you after lunch and we'll set up a time. Will that work for you?"

"Sure." Reagan motioned to the door. "I guess I'm going to try to find Josh and see if he wants to do lunch." Her lips twitched in a smile. "I'm starving," she whispered.

Shelby smiled too and gave her a slight nod. "Have fun. See you this afternoon."

As soon as she left, Stephanie walked over to her, eyebrows raised expectantly.

"What?" Shelby asked innocently.

"Didn't you already do a tour of the park?"

"Not really," she said. "We did a hike around Bear Lake one day and then the other evening, we went looking for elk."

"Uh-huh."

Shelby shrugged. "We've become friends. I thought that's what you wanted."

"Being friends with her is one thing," her mother said. "Dancing is quite another."

Shelby sighed. "Are we back on that again?"

"You've got to admit, Mother, they looked quite cute together last night," Stephanie said.

Her mother scoffed. "Two women dancing. I'd hardly call that cute."

Shelby held her hands up, signaling an end to the conversation. "I'm going to my room to change."

Her mother nodded. "Good. I was hoping that wasn't what you planned to wear to lunch. These ladies are—"

"I know who they are," she said. "And I'll dress appropriately."

CHAPTER THIRTY-TWO

Reagan moved back up Shelby's body slowly, taking her time. Shelby's hand was running lazily through her hair, indecipherable sounds coming from her as Reagan nibbled her skin.

"If I were a cat, I'd be purring," Shelby murmured.

"If you were a cat, you could have done that to yourself."

Shelby laughed. "But it wouldn't have been nearly as much fun."

Reagan lay down on her side, watching Shelby. Her eyes were still closed, and a soft smile lingered on her face. She looked content and quite satisfied. Which, in turn, pleased Reagan. But she couldn't stop touching. Her hand moved to Shelby's breasts, her fingers teasing her nipples alternately.

"Your breasts are very sensitive," she said.

"Yes." Shelby rolled her head to the side, her eyes opening finally. "You're an excellent lover."

Reagan smiled quickly. "Excellent, huh? I'm a little out of practice."

"Trust me, you're not," Shelby said. Her hand rested on Reagan's hip, moving in tiny circles, lightly caressing. "I'm starving, by the way."

"Oh, yeah? Your fancy lunch wasn't enough for you?"

"A quiche with steamed veggies, no, and that was *hours* ago," she said.

"If we hurry, we can still make your mother's dinner," she said. "Of course, we'd have to shower first."

A slow, sexy smile appeared on Shelby's face. "If we shower together, we'll *never* make dinner."

"What do you suggest?"

Shelby pushed her over and climbed on top, kneeling between her legs. "I vote for a shower," she said. "I happen to have connections with the kitchen staff. I'm fairly certain I could get them to bring the leftover lasagna up here." She wiggled her eyebrows. "What do you say?"

"Tempting."

Shelby leaned down, kissing her slowly, thoroughly. "Tempting?" she murmured against her lips. "Is that a yes?"

"Yes."

* * *

Reagan lifted the lid on the serving tray, her eyes widening. "Wow. Are we having company?"

"I told you I was starving," she said, watching as Reagan stole a meatball from the tray.

"Are we going to get into trouble?"

"Because we missed dinner? Or because we lied about going to the park?"

"Either."

"They'll never know about the park, and yes, my mother will be annoyed that we missed dinner." She took a plate and scooped out a section of lasagna, then added some of the pasta that was smothered in a pesto sauce. "And right now, I don't care."

Reagan took a plate and put a large helping of lasagna on it, then paused. "Have you told Stephanie about us?"

Shelby shook her head. "No. Did you say anything to Josh?"

"No."

"I think Stephanie suspects something is going on, but I told her we were just friends," she said. She met Reagan's gaze. "I don't know why, but I kinda want to keep this private."

Reagan nodded. "Yeah. It's their wedding."

"Not to mention, the teasing would be merciless," she said with a smile.

"And I'm sure your mother wouldn't approve. I am just a lowly farm girl, after all."

Shelby nudged her with her shoulder. "Oh, Reagan, you're not a farm girl. And even if you were, that's not the issue my mother would have."

"I'm a woman."

"Yes. I'm afraid she still has her sights set on Doug." She laughed. "She even mentioned Duke as a possible candidate."

"Wow. She must really be desperate for you to find a man," Reagan teased.

Instead of sitting at the bar in the small kitchen, Shelby went to the sofa. Reagan followed and sat down beside her.

"My mother thinks it's a game we play," Shelby explained as she took a bite of the lasagna. "Oh, this is really, really good."

"Mmm," Reagan agreed as she chewed.

"Every so often, she pretends she doesn't know I'm gay and will try to set me up with sons of some of her friends," she said.

"Like the ladies you went to lunch with?"

Shelby nodded. "Two of them have sons about my age."

"Was it brought up today?"

"No, thankfully. It was mostly all wedding talk." She sighed. "I love Stephanie to death, but honestly, I'm so ready for this to be over with."

"Well, we only have a few more days," Reagan said as she twirled pasta on her fork.

"I didn't mean I was ready for *this* to be over with," she said with a smile. "But real life is right around the corner, isn't it?"

"I know. I need to figure out what I'm going to do with my life now."

Shelby met her gaze and was surprised to see some of that old sadness return. For the last several days, there had been no hint of the haunted look that had shadowed Reagan's eyes the first week. She reached over and touched her hand, rubbing against it lightly.

"Let's enjoy the next couple of days and not worry about real life just yet, huh?"

Reagan smiled. "If we enjoy it too much, we're going to get caught."

"Yeah. I suppose we should participate in the group outings." She leaned over and kissed her lightly. "But tonight…will you stay with me?"

"I'd love to."

CHAPTER THIRTY-THREE

"You look beautiful, sis."

Stephanie turned from the mirror, her white gown flowing around her. She looked radiant, and Shelby felt a tiny stab of jealousy. This was something she would never have.

"Thank you. But I'm nervous," Stephanie admitted.

"Are you?"

"It's…it's a big step. I mean—"

"Good Lord, you're not having doubts, are you?"

Stephanie shook her head. "No. I don't think so. Josh is—"

"Perfect for you."

"He is, isn't he?"

Shelby smiled and walked closer, giving her a hug. "He is. And soon it'll be over with and he'll whisk you away to Hawaii. All this *madness* will end."

Stephanie nodded. "Yes. It's been too long—this celebration. I think it's taken its toll on Mother too. She was more stressed than I was at the rehearsal last night."

"I think we're all ready to call an end to this," she said. "It's been fun. Certainly different, that's for sure."

"Yes. At least you and Reagan seem to have hit it off. Do you think you'll keep in touch after this?"

Shelby shrugged. "I don't know."

And really, she didn't. While they'd spent a lot of time together the last few days—and nights—they hadn't really talked about seeing each other. Reagan still didn't know what she was going to do or where she was going to go. Shelby suspected Reagan still had some things to work through on her own... namely, whether she could ever pick up a camera again.

"Girls? Are you ready?"

Their mother's shrill voice called from the other room, and Shelby took a deep breath, offering a smile to Stephanie. "It'll be over soon," she said again.

Stephanie surprised her by her tight hug. "I love you. I don't think I would have made it had you not been here."

"I love you too."

When the door opened to the bedroom, it wasn't their mother who came in, rather their father. He stopped in his tracks, his gaze traveling over both of them.

"My God, but don't you two look lovely." He came forward, kissing Shelby affectionately on the cheek, then turning to Stephanie. "You make a beautiful bride." He leaned forward, kissing her as well. "I couldn't be prouder."

"Dad, don't make me cry," Stephanie said. "I just got my makeup done."

"You look pretty handsome yourself," Shelby said, noting his black tuxedo.

"Thank you. And if you're ready, I'll escort you down."

"What about Mother?"

"She went ahead of us. She wanted to make sure everything was in place."

"I thought she did that a couple of hours ago," Shelby said.

"Yes, so did I." He stuck his elbows out to them. "Shall we?"

Stephanie nodded. "I guess I'm ready."

* * *

"Why are you nervous? You're not the one getting married," Josh said as he straightened Reagan's tie. "You look beautiful."

"You don't think it's too much?"

Her mother came and stood between, all three of them looking at their reflections in the mirror.

"You look lovely, Reagan," she said. "And Josh…how could Frank and I have produced such beautiful kids? You get more handsome every year."

Reagan smiled as Josh blushed.

"Well, don't tell Dad, but I think we got your genes and not his."

Their mother laughed, then linked arms with them both. "What a special day. I'm so thankful to have you both here. I feel so blessed."

Reagan and Josh exchanged smiles in the mirror.

"What's so funny?" their father asked as he joined them.

"Oh, just last-minute visiting," their mother said. "Is it time?"

"Just about. You ready?"

"Yes. Why don't you and Josh head down? We'll be there in a minute."

Reagan raised her eyebrows questioningly. "Something wrong?" she asked when the door closed.

Her mother shook her head. "No. I haven't seen you in a couple of days though. The hotel isn't *that* big, is it?"

Reagan felt a blush light her face, but she managed not to turn away from her mother's curious gaze.

"I've been…around," she said evasively.

Her mother laughed. "Thirty-two years old and you still blush. It's very endearing."

"Mom…"

Her mother waved her protest away. "So? I assume you've been with Shelby? I've been by your room a few times."

Reagan tilted her head. "You could have called."

"Is that a yes?"

She sighed. "Yes."

Her mother smiled, but there was no sign of teasing. "Shelby is good for you, I think. You look almost back to normal."

Reagan shook her head. "Almost. But yes, she's been good for me. She's taken my mind off...well, what happened over there, it's not forefront in my mind anymore. At least, not at the moment." She shrugged. "When I leave here, who knows?"

"Are you ready to tell me what happened?"

She took a deep breath. She didn't really want to go into it all again. If she talked about it, she was afraid it would no longer stay at the back of her mind. But her mother was looking at her expectantly, and she didn't want to shut her out.

"There was a bomb," she said quietly. "I was...shooting, like always. Our team leader—my friend—Richard tried to protect us, I guess. He ran toward the bomber, shielded us." She looked away, picturing Little George's face etched in terror, seeing the blur of Richard as he ran into her frame. "I did nothing to help," she said quietly. "I just continued clicking away with my camera, as if nothing out of the ordinary was going on." She looked back at her. "There was a little boy. The bomber had him." She swallowed. "Richard took action. I did nothing but capture it all with my camera. Right up until the bomb went off."

Her mother stared at her, questions in her eyes.

"Were you in...danger?" she asked.

Reagan nodded. "If Richard hadn't...well, if he hadn't..." she sighed. "Yes. I might have been killed."

Her mother stepped closer, cupping her cheek with one hand. "Oh, my sweet Reagan. You grieve for your friend, yet you're eaten up with guilt." She dropped her hand. "And here I am being thankful for your friend. Selfish, I know, but I'm glad he took action and you did not."

Reagan tried to blink her tears away. "I feel like a coward."

"Why? Because you were spared?"

"No. It all happened so fast. But in retrospect, I wouldn't have done anything different. I wouldn't have run toward the bomber. If anything, I would have run away."

"That doesn't make you a coward, Reagan."

"No? Richard didn't run."

"So that's it? You're either a hero or a coward? Nothing in between?" Her mother took her hand and squeezed. "It's not all black and white, Reagan. It's not either-or."

She blew out her breath. "It's just something I need to work through, Mom, that's all."

"So where will you go? Everyone is leaving tomorrow or Sunday. Will you come back to the farm with us?" She paused. "Or do you have another assignment?"

Reagan shook her head. "I haven't…I haven't been able to pick up a camera, so no. I don't have an assignment."

"You know you're welcome to come home. We would love to have you there for as long as you need."

Reagan smiled. "Thanks. But I remember how cold January can be out at the farm."

Her mother nodded. "Well, just know you're welcome." She paused. "Or maybe you have plans with Shelby?"

Reagan leaned over and kissed her mother's cheek. "No, Mom. I may go to San Diego, hang out at the beach and chill out for a while, try to wrap my head around all this. I have a friend there."

"Okay. Whatever you need. Just don't disappear on us."

"I won't."

Her mother nodded. "Well, I suppose we should head down. We don't want to keep them waiting."

Reagan glanced back in the mirror. "Do I really look okay? It's a really bright blue, isn't it?" she asked as she tugged on her vest.

"You look very nice, Reagan. And I imagine this color will look beautiful on Shelby too."

CHAPTER THIRTY-FOUR

Shelby took a moment to look around. Bruce and the staff had done a wonderful job of transforming the ballroom into a wedding chapel. Most of the Christmas decorations remained, including all of the trees that had been brought in and decorated for the dance. The colorful Christmas lights, though, had been replaced with white and blue to tie in with Stephanie's color scheme. As the music started, the guests turned, watching her. She was surprised at the number of people who had stayed over for the ceremony. She took a deep breath, nodding slightly as Doug held his elbow out, waiting for her to link arms with him.

She looked down the aisle slowly, seeing Josh and Reagan walk to the front and stand on either side of the minister. Next to Josh stood Geoff, his friend from law school. She tried not to stare, but her eyes were drawn back to Reagan. She looked nearly pristine in her white tuxedo pants and shirt, the blue vest an exact match to her own dress. Reagan locked eyes with her, and Shelby nearly faltered in her step. The look in her eyes said Reagan was remembering how they'd spent the morning. Who knew making love in the shower could be so much fun?

She smiled slightly, acknowledging Reagan, then turned her gaze to Josh, who was nearly beaming, not showing any signs of nervousness. As they approached the front, she separated from Doug and went to stand beside Reagan. Doug took his place next to Geoff.

The music changed, and everyone's gaze again turned to the back where Stephanie stood between their parents. Stephanie looked radiant...and nervous. Shelby smiled reassuringly at her and gave a short nod.

As her parents escorted Stephanie down the aisle, Shelby became aware of Reagan's shoulder brushing her own. She moved closer to her, relishing the contact.

"You look beautiful."

The words were whispered so quietly she barely heard them. She chanced a quick glance at Reagan, seeing the fire in her eyes. She hoped everyone's attention was on Stephanie and not her as she briefly touched hands with Reagan.

She would have liked to have said the ceremony was beautiful and touching, but the truth was, her mind wasn't on it and she listened to very little of it. Instead, she was conscious only of Reagan beside her. She closed her eyes briefly, picturing Reagan as she'd been that morning, dripping wet as she'd held Shelby against the shower wall—her mouth at her breast, her hand between her thighs.

And now here it was...Christmas Day. Or rather, evening. The lengthy wedding celebration was nearing its end, which meant her affair with Reagan was as well. Cocktails and cheese, champagne and cake would follow the ceremony, then Stephanie and Josh would make their escape. Their father was flying them to Denver bright and early tomorrow to catch a flight to Hawaii. She assumed most of the guests would be leaving tomorrow too, although the rooms were paid for through Sunday.

She and Reagan had not really finalized anything. She had planned on heading back to Denver tomorrow too. She had laundry to do, and she needed a day to recoup before going back to work on Monday. She knew Reagan's parents were leaving as well. She glanced over at Reagan. Would she stay another day? Would she ask Shelby to join her?

"You may kiss the bride."

Clapping ensued, and Shelby brought her attention back to the happy couple as Stephanie and Josh exchanged a rather intimate kiss before turning to their guests with big smiles. They linked arms and headed down the aisle. Shelby placed her hand in the crook of Doug's elbow, letting him escort her as they followed Stephanie and Josh. Reagan and Geoff followed them.

And just like that...it was over with. Nothing disastrous happened because Reagan wore a tux. Nothing scandalous happened, and there were no mishaps for her mother to bemoan. The service went off without a hitch. She almost felt sorry for her mother. What would she focus on now? The wedding planning had been at the center of her world for the last year. Where would she turn her attention to now?

"You look amazing. That color is stunning on you."

She turned to Doug. "Thank you. You look very nice too."

He tilted his head. "I'm going to stay on until Sunday. What are your plans?"

She smiled quickly. "Sorry. Leaving tomorrow. But it was very nice to meet you. Have a safe trip back," she said dismissively and turned away, finding Reagan watching. She smiled at her and headed in her direction.

"Short and sweet," Reagan said. "My kind of wedding."

Shelby let her gaze travel over Reagan. "That tuxedo is perfect for you."

"Oh, yeah?" She smiled wickedly. "I'll let you take it off of me later if you'd like."

Shelby met her eyes. "I'm fairly certain I'll need help with my dress too."

Reagan's mother came over, holding her phone up. "You two stand together. I want to take your picture."

"Mom..."

Shelby laughed and grabbed Reagan's arm, slipping her hand around her elbow. "She looks dashing, doesn't she?"

Margie nodded. "She is most beautiful, yes." She smiled sweetly. "The two of you together are simply stunning."

"Mom..." Reagan groaned again.

"Well, it's the truth," she said as she pointed her phone's camera at them. "Smile!"

* * *

Reagan set the champagne glass down after having taken only a sip...just enough to participate in the toast. She'd never seen her brother looking as happy as he did tonight, and she'd hugged him tightly before he and Stephanie had slipped away. She was a bit envious. Not necessarily for their honeymoon, but spending a few weeks on a beach in Hawaii sounded like fun. And it was a very long way from Afghanistan.

But so was San Diego. She hadn't been there in years, and she hadn't seen Gillian since she'd run into her at a party in LA almost two years ago now. She'd first met Gillian in college when she had been a guest speaker in one of her classes. Gillian was probably thirty years older than she was, but they'd become friends. If there was anyone she would call her mentor, it would be her. But it was hard to maintain friendships—relationships of any kind—as she bounced around the globe, going from conflict to conflict, slowing down just enough to catch her breath before heading out again.

When she'd last seen Gillian, she'd extended an invitation to visit, to relax on the beach, to chill out for a while. That was right after Reagan had returned from Serbia. She should have taken her up on it then. Serbia had been a rough assignment and she couldn't wait to get out of there. But she was about to head to Colombia and the drug wars and she couldn't spare a week to "chill out."

She hoped Gillian would be receptive to a visit now. An extended visit. Reagan had to decide what the hell she was going to do with the rest of her life. Maybe Shelby was right. Maybe she was chasing the wrong things. Maybe instead of conflicts and war, she could turn to politics. Maybe follow presidential candidates around as they gave speeches and stumped for votes. She silently groaned at that thought.

"Just shoot me," she murmured.

No, she'd rather chase anything but politicians.

She felt someone walk up behind her, and she turned, finding Shelby there. She let her gaze roam over her, the strapless dress showing just enough cleavage to be enticing.

"I'm very tired," Shelby said with a subtle smile. "Are you?"

"Yes. Very, very tired. In fact, I think I should be in bed within fifteen minutes."

Shelby laughed. "Do you think anyone would miss us?"

"No." She looked around. "It's winding down anyway, isn't it?"

Shelby nodded. "Meet you up in my suite?"

Reagan gave her a slow smile. "Fifteen minutes?"

Shelby returned her smile. "Fifteen minutes."

CHAPTER THIRTY-FIVE

Shelby leaned back against the pillow, the sheet pulled only to her waist. Reagan was on her side, leaning on an elbow, her hand lazily moving in circles under Shelby's breasts.

"You could come to Denver with me," Shelby offered.

Reagan's ministrations paused for only a moment before resuming their endless brush against her skin. "And do what?"

"You could stay with me until you decide what you're going to do."

Reagan sighed. "Tempting." She looked up. "Very tempting. But I've got to get my life back in order." Her hand stopped its movements altogether, and she rolled onto her back. "I need to sort out everything, decide what I want to do. I'm good with a camera," she said. "But I don't want to chase wars anymore."

Shelby rolled to her side, reversing their positions as she now leaned on her elbow, her hand reaching out to touch Reagan. Her voice had a bit of the old sadness in it, and she wondered if she'd simply been suppressing it this last week or if it really had disappeared for a while. Now that the wedding was over, real life was about to roll around again...bringing real life issues to the forefront once more.

"Where will you go?"

"I'm going to San Diego, I think," Reagan said. "I have a friend there I can stay with, someone I can talk to. She was in the profession too."

Shelby was surprised by the hint of jealousy she felt. "An old lover?"

Reagan smiled. "No. Gillian's quite a bit older than me. A mentor, if anything." She took Shelby's hand and brought it to her lips, kissing the back gently. "I need to thank you...for rescuing me."

Shelby smiled. "Is that what you call this?"

"I was in a dark place. You could have left me there," Reagan said. "I know at first I wasn't very good company."

"Maybe I should thank you for rescuing *me*," she countered. "I would never tell Stephanie this, but the prospect of spending nearly two weeks up here celebrating a wedding was not at the top of my fun list. But you made it fun, Reagan."

Reagan again kissed her hand. "I'm going to miss you, Shelby."

Shelby nodded. "I'll miss you too." She paused. "Will I ever see you again?"

"I hope so." Reagan squeezed her hand tightly. "I just need some time to...to get *me* back," she said.

Shelby understood. Of course she did. Reagan had suffered a personal loss, had witnessed something traumatic...something awful. She didn't expect her to have dismissed it simply because they were lovers. Reagan had obviously managed to ignore it for a while, had put it at the back of her mind. But now...now it was time to put this affair aside and get back to reality.

And the reality was that Shelby had a life in Denver to get back to. She had projects at work that needed her attention. She was actually looking forward to getting back. She was not, however, looking forward to returning to her empty apartment. Sharing living space with Reagan these last four days had made her realize how lonely her apartment really was. Maybe it made her realize how lonely her *life* really was.

Shelby met her eyes, trying to read them. "You're leaving in the morning?"

Reagan nodded. "You?"

"I suppose. It's not that long a drive for me but I do have things to tend to before work on Monday," she said. She tilted her head. "You're not driving all the way to San Diego, are you?"

"Actually, I thought I might. Head south into New Mexico, then cut across the desert. Been a long time since I've had a road trip."

Shelby tilted her head, a slight smile on her face. It did sound like fun. She almost wished Reagan would ask her to go along. Would she go? No, of course not. She had a job to get back to. She had her life to get back to.

"What?"

Shelby met her eyes. "I'm going to miss you."

"Yeah. Me too."

Shelby rolled onto her back and tugged Reagan with her. "We have several hours until dawn. I'm not ready to say goodbye just yet."

Reagan settled between her legs, pressing hard against her, but her kiss was soft, gentle. Shelby wanted to melt right there as Reagan's lips nibbled at her own.

"And I'm going to miss making love with you," Reagan whispered. "It's been the best."

Shelby moaned as Reagan's mouth found her breast. "Yes... the best."

CHAPTER THIRTY-SIX

Shelby stood at the window of her office, watching the snowflakes swirl against the glass. To say she was in a blue mood would be an understatement. She couldn't seem to get back into the swing of things, even after four days. A quiet knock at her door brought her attention from the snowy scene outside.

"Come in."

Rachel, from the marketing team, opened the door about halfway and peeked inside, eyebrows raised.

Shelby returned her questioning gaze.

"Spring break? The new prices at Steamboat? Did you get a chance to look it over?"

"Oh. Yes. Sorry," Shelby said as she moved to her desk. She pulled up the comparison chart she'd created that morning. "I think we need to come down on the prices a little. We're still above what everyone else is offering."

Rachel walked fully into the office. "If we're going to put together a package deal for lift tickets and shuttle, then we're pretty much at our limit."

"Let's shoot for one hundred percent occupancy," she said. "Last year during the spring break period we were at eighty-eight percent. Come down on the prices a little and get to one hundred percent, and we'll easily beat the numbers."

"Okay. I'll rework it." Rachel paused before leaving. "Is everything okay? You seem a little distracted."

Shelby smiled and waved her question away. "I'm fine."

But she sighed heavily when the door closed, and instead of sitting at her desk, she returned to the window. Maybe it was only Stephanie's text of a picture of her and Josh on a warm, sunny beach that had her feeling blue. Maybe it had absolutely *nothing* to do with Reagan Bryant.

She'd known the woman two weeks. Twelve days, to be exact. Yes, they'd become friends. And yes, they'd become lovers. But still, it was all of twelve days. You don't really—truly—get to know someone in only twelve days.

She laughed lightly. The twelve days of Christmas. But Christmas had come and gone. The wedding had come and gone. And Reagan had come and gone too.

Was she already in San Diego? Was she lying on the beach, soaking up rays? Had she picked up her camera? She glanced at her phone. She could always call her. But she didn't want to intrude, didn't want to take away from the time that Reagan said she needed. Of course, Reagan could always call her too.

She finally turned from the window with another sigh. They'd had a brief affair, nothing more. It wasn't like it was anything deeper than that. It wasn't like she was on the verge of falling in love with her or anything.

"Of course not," she murmured. No, not her. She didn't fall in love. Not now. Not ever.

So with that thought firmly in her mind, she sat down at her desk and pushed Reagan Bryant from her mind.

* * *

"You ever been shot at?"

Gillian nodded, the corners of her eyes wrinkling up as she grinned. "Hell, yeah. Been shot at more times than I can remember," she said in her gravelly smoker's voice. She pulled her shirt up, exposing her belly. "Took a hit to my side one time during a street fight in Mexico City."

The scar was long healed, but Reagan stared at it, wondering if she'd have been able to go back out on the streets if she'd been shot. Gillian must have read her mind.

"Took me a while to get my groove back," she said. "Don't mind sayin', I haven't been to Mexico City in twenty-eight years." She filled up the small tumbler with tequila and slid it toward Reagan. "When I was your age, I was all over the damn place."

"Chasing wars?"

Gillian nodded. "Yeah. That's where the action is." She leaned forward. "But we sacrifice so much, don't we? Hell, I never even fell in love. Lovers here and there, that's about it."

"I thought you were seeing some newspaper guy."

"Sex. Not the same as being in love." She tossed back her shot of tequila and slammed the glass on the table. "Now when are you going to tell me what the hell you're doing here? You show up on my doorstep out of the blue, looking like a lost puppy. What's going on?"

Reagan swirled the liquid in her glass, watching as it circled the rim without spilling. She finally brought it to her mouth, drinking it down in one swallow.

"You hear about Richard?"

"Richard? Oh, yeah. A bomb. It's awful."

Reagan nodded. "I was there."

Gillian's eyes widened. "You were working with him? I thought the last time we talked, you said you were never going back to Afghanistan."

"I know. But I owed him a favor." She slid the empty glass toward Gillian, nodding as she refilled it. "I was shooting when the bomb went off. I got it all," she said quietly. "Right up to the end."

"Damn, kid. You put any of them out there?"

Reagan shook her head. "No." She met her gaze. "I haven't even looked at them. Hell, I haven't even picked up the damn camera since that day."

Gillian's eyes softened. "Is that what this is all about?"

"Yeah." She drank the tequila quickly, feeling it burn her throat. "I should have been killed too."

"Oh, Reagan. In our profession, the places we go, hell, we put ourselves in danger all the time. You knew that going in."

"I know. And I've been in the line of fire before. But this... this was different. Richard was a good friend. No matter how hard I try to remember the good times, the fun times...all I see is the bomb going off. All I see is Richard being torn apart."

"Were you injured, Reagan?"

She shook her head. "A few scratches, bruises, nothing more."

"What about the rest in your group?"

"Yeah. We lost three. Another badly injured." She ran a hand through her hair. "I haven't touched my camera since then."

Gillian nodded. "Been there, done that," she said as she filled yet another tumbler with tequila. "Why do you think I got out of the business?"

Reagan shrugged. "Don't really know. I guess I thought you got tired of the travel, tired of the constant movement."

"That too," she said. "I told myself I was getting too damn old for it. Told myself to let the young ones do it. Like you." She lit a cigarette and took a deep drag, blowing out the smoke slowly. "But you reach a breaking point, Reagan. We choose the type of stories to cover...we choose to chase wars. You see enough death, you start to get numb to it. You start to expect it. Hell, sometimes you hope for it just to get a better shot." She drank down the tequila. "That's when I knew I had to get out."

"You think that's where I am? That I need to get out?"

"Only you can know that, Reagan. But you're what? Early thirties?"

She nodded. "Been doing this ten years now." She leaned back in her chair, feeling mellow from the tequila. "A friend suggested that I was chasing the wrong things. She said instead of wars I needed to chase smiles and happiness." She smiled, remembering Shelby's words. "Switch gears. Shoot weddings and birthday parties."

Gillian laughed. "That's switching gears all right." She stubbed her cigarette out. "You tired of the news altogether? Tired of current events?"

"I'm just tired, period," she said. "Tired of the travel, for sure."

"Then settle down somewhere," Gillian said. "There are lots of opportunities to make a living with your camera. I'll warn you, though, after living the life you have, it's easy to get bored with a tamer subject. You might be shooting a wedding and hope the bride and groom get into a fight at the altar," she said with a laugh.

"What did you do?"

"Besides lecturing to college students? I still do that, by the way. I make the profession sound all glamorous and exciting," Gillian said.

"I remember. What else did you do?"

"Oh, I made a little money shooting beach scenes for a calendar one year. Bored me to tears," she said. "I still freelance some. Wildfires and such." She lit another cigarette. "Truth is, I don't pick up my camera much these days."

Reagan nodded. Even when she'd first met Gillian, back in college, she couldn't recall a time where she had a camera at hand. Unlike Reagan who practically slept with hers. That is, until recently. Is this how she would end up? Drinking tequila in the middle of the afternoon and not giving her camera another thought?

Well, right now, she was just mellow enough not to care. Gillian's tiny bungalow was only two blocks from the beach. So she stretched her legs out and enjoyed the sunshine on this last day of the year. Gillian had said she could bunk on her couch for as long as she wanted. Maybe staying a couple of weeks wouldn't hurt. Who knows? Maybe she might find something that would give her the itch to pull her camera out again. A beach sunset might do the trick.

She closed her eyes for a moment, surprised that an image of Shelby's face popped into her mind as easily as it did. She'd be lying if she said she didn't miss her. She missed sharing a bed with her, sure. But she also missed their conversations, their teasing…their playfulness.

She missed the mountains, the blue, blue sky, the crisp air. She missed Shelby's laugh, missed her touch…missed looking into her eyes, watching them change color when Shelby was aroused.

Yeah, she missed her. She should probably call, let her know she'd made it safely.

Maybe tomorrow.

CHAPTER THIRTY-SEVEN

"So you're not going to press charges?"

Her father shook his head. "Not yet. Let's wait and see what we find with the other audit. Mark swears Aspen was the only hotel that he touched."

"And he's agreed to make restitution?"

"Yes. And I'll give him this...he didn't just blow the money he embezzled. At least he invested it wisely."

Shelby sat down across from her father's desk. "So he gets nothing more than a slap on the wrist. Amazing."

"Bringing it all out in the open, Shelby...I didn't see the point. He's going to repay, that's the important thing. And, of course, he'll never work for us again." Her father leaned forward and rested his elbows on his desk. "As far as I'm concerned, it's over and done with. The attorneys are dealing with the repayment issue, and he's already been removed from his office."

"I'm sure rumors are swirling at the hotel. Is William going to let everyone know what happened?"

"I haven't decided. What is your opinion on it?" he asked.

"I would make it perfectly clear why Mark lost his job," she said. "Let everyone know that we don't tolerate dishonest employees, regardless of position." She crossed one leg over her knee. "And I do think we should audit housekeeping. Aspen has the worst numbers, by far."

"Well, if you wouldn't insist on providing such nice, thick towels and robes, maybe so many wouldn't go missing," he teased.

"The types of guests we have in Aspen aren't the ones to steal towels and robes, and you know it."

He sighed. "I know. And that's really what I wanted to talk to you about," he said.

She frowned. "Auditing housekeeping?"

"No. Running a tighter ship at each hotel. Having a presence there." He paused. "Us."

She stared at him. "What are you saying?"

"I want to relocate to Aspen."

"Aspen?" She tried to keep the surprise from showing on her face. "Well, I know Mother has suggested it in the past. And you do spend an awful lot of time there."

He looked away from her, and she noticed that he was tapping his index fingers together, something he never did. So she leaned closer to his desk, waiting until he met her gaze.

"When you say relocate to Aspen, do you mean the corporate office or your place of residence?"

He folded his hands together, stilling his fingers' nervous movements. "Is there really a need to have the corporate office here in Denver? With the technology today, is there really a need for us to all be in the same place?"

She drew her brows together, trying to read between the lines to understand what he was saying. She decided it was serving neither of them to talk around the issue.

"What's going on, Dad?"

He paused for a long moment, then got up and stood by the window. It was a sunny day but bitterly cold. Frost still clung to the glass. She looked past him out into the blue sky, having a sudden urge for springtime, still several months away.

"I'm getting older," he said. He turned to her, smiling slightly. "I had this all rehearsed but I can't seem to remember it now."

She felt her heart catch. Was he ill? Is that what he was trying to say? But she said nothing, waiting for him to continue.

"I need some…some happiness in my life," he said. "I need to make some changes. Changes that are years past due."

She stood up and walked closer to him. "Are you having an affair?" she asked him bluntly. He didn't shy away from her gaze.

"I've met someone, yes."

"God, please say she's not some twenty-something-year-old gold digger," she pleaded.

He laughed lightly. "She's sixty-two. A widow. Her husband died two years ago." He held his hand up. "And no, we're not sleeping together."

"She lives in Aspen, I assume? That's why you've been spending so much time there?"

He nodded. "I met her in a coffee bar last summer. A place I never go into," he said. "An afternoon thunderstorm had just passed through, and it was cold. I wanted to get out of the hotel so I walked the street. Went in for coffee on a whim. She was doing a crossword puzzle."

She decided to be honest with him. "Stephanie and I have wondered for years if you were having an affair. Your relationship with Mother is not quite conventional."

He shook his head. "I've never cheated on your mother. That's not to say I didn't have the opportunity. Your mother and I…well, we've not been happy in many years. I didn't want to make a change though," he said. "I care about her. She's the mother of my kids…I have obligations to her, to you and Stephanie."

She held her hand up. "No. If you're not happy, don't lay that blame on us. We're all grown up now, Dad."

"I know. I'm sorry. I didn't mean to imply that I stayed with her only because of you." He sat back down at his desk and she, too, returned to her seat. "Your mother and I have not shared a bedroom in more years than I can recall," he said. "She's content with the way things are, and I suppose I was too. I was busy with the hotels. I didn't really miss having love in my life."

"Oh, Dad, that's so sad," she said.

"Yes. It is. Your mother has her friends, her clubs, her charities. She has you and Stephanie. That's been enough for her. It's still enough for her. It's no longer enough for me," he said. "When I met Beth, I realized how much I was missing out on."

"But you're not…*involved?*"

"She won't have an affair with me. She knows I'm married."

"That's admirable of her, I suppose," she said.

He smiled. "She's four years older than I am, yet I can't keep up with her. She bikes all over Aspen. She skis nearly every day during the season. She's very active."

"Retired?"

He nodded. "She and her husband owned a business there. When he got sick, they sold it. So, no, she's not a gold digger, as you suggested."

She stood, pacing slowly across the floor, trying to wrap her mind around this. "So what are your plans? I mean, with Mother."

"I'm going to file for divorce," he said. "She'll be devastated."

"Yes. I imagine she will."

"Beth makes me happy, Shelby. Life is so short. One day you wake up and you're fifty-eight years old, and you feel like life has passed you by."

"I'm not judging you, Dad. I know how Mother is. I just spent nearly two weeks with her, remember?"

His expression softened. "She wasn't always that way, you know. She used to be fun and spontaneous."

"Spontaneous? Mother?"

"Hard to believe, I know. Now, everything has to be planned out, right down to the final detail." He paused. "But me and your mother…that's not all I wanted to talk to you about. That issue is something I have to deal with, not you. But there's something else I needed to talk to you about."

"Moving the office to Aspen?"

"Yes. But I want a presence at Estes Park and Steamboat too. I know you have a fondness for Estes Park."

Her eyes lit up. "You want me to work from there full time?"

"Yes."

"What about my staff here? What about Rachel and Toby and Stephanie?"

"I know you rely on Rachel and Toby. We'll have to decide if we'll ask them to relocate or keep an office here in Denver for them. And then there's my staff too."

"And what about Stephanie?"

"Well, you keep telling me she needs something to do in her field. I know she's not happy here, and I know she doesn't contribute like you do, Shelby. I know all that. I also know she and Josh…well, they're just getting started," he said. "We'll find something for her to do."

She sat back down, trying to process it all. "You want me to move to Estes Park," she said, more of a statement than a question.

"Are you in favor of it or does it not interest you at all? I know it's asking a lot. You'd be essentially responsible for the operation there. You and Bruce. You don't have to live at the hotel, of course, although I'd like for you to."

She nodded. "I'm interested. I love it there. And my suite at the hotel…it'll need some renovations if I'm going to live there full time," she said. "It's something Stephanie could do—design and oversee the renovation." She leaned forward, resting her elbows on her thighs. "What about Steamboat?"

"A quick flight from Aspen for me," he said. "I can divide my time for now. But it's something I've been thinking about for the last few months. This thing with Mark just pushed it along." He got up and went to his corner credenza, taking out two glasses. Without asking, he poured scotch into both and handed her a glass. "I know it's a lot to take in, Shelby. It's not something we're going to rush into. But I'd like us to be moved by late spring, early summer," he said.

"What about Mother?"

"That can't wait. I'll talk to her soon."

She tilted her head. "Can you at least wait until Stephanie gets back from Hawaii? I don't want to be the only one Mother has to turn to."

"I know the two of you never saw eye-to-eye, even when you were younger. You were much too independent for her liking," he said.

Shelby nodded as she sipped from her drink. "She and Stephanie get along much better."

He smiled. "I don't know if it's so much that or that Stephanie doesn't talk back to her."

She smiled too. "Well, there's that. Also my disdain for clothes shopping and having no fashion sense plays a part."

He leaned back. "You know, since I've met Beth, I've come to appreciate simpler things," he said. "She is the complete opposite of your mother. Well, opposite of what she is now. I told you before how much she changed after we married."

"You blame yourself for that," she stated.

"Yes. I think, at first, I was trying to impress her with all the things money can buy. Little by little, she changed from the innocent girl I'd married into a full-fledged socialite. She embraced her new lifestyle and never looked back." He sighed. "And along the way, she changed into a completely different person."

"A person you were no longer in love with," she finished for him.

He met her gaze, and she was surprised by the sadness she saw there. "I loved your mother very much once. But I suppose we've both changed."

She nodded. "Everyone changes over time, I guess."

He looked at her expectantly. "And what about you?"

"Me?"

"We haven't visited much since the wedding. You spent a lot of time with Josh's sister." He smiled. "Any news there?"

She laughed. "Are you fishing for gossip?"

"Maybe."

Her smile faded. "Well, there isn't any. I've not talked to her." She raised an eyebrow. "Why? Were you hoping something would come of it?"

"My youngest daughter just got married and she seems very happy. My oldest daughter, however, seems…well, a little more distant than usual."

She shook her head. "I'm okay."

And she was, she told herself. Even though she'd barely made it through the weekend without calling Reagan. She thought it would be a friendly gesture to check on her. But in the end, she'd talked herself out of it. Reagan had her number too.

Thankfully, Stephanie would be back in the office tomorrow. Their flight had gotten in late last night and today was her "recoup" day, as Stephanie had said. Tomorrow they would look at pictures of sun, sand and surf. She hoped it would push her winter blues away for a while.

Because winter blues is what she had. She'd spent a lonely New Year's Eve longing for company. Oh, she hadn't been alone. She'd had her pick of parties to go to. But even surrounded by people, she felt alone…and so very lonely.

With Stephanie coming back, things would get back to normal. And now she had planning to do…a move to make. Was she ready to relocate to Estes Park permanently? Would she be happy there? Or would her loneliness only compound itself?

Who would have thought that such a brief affair with Reagan Bryant could cause all this unrest in her life? She'd always prided herself on being emotionally calm, cool…collected. She had no turmoil in her life, no personal relationships that caused undue stress—not unless she counted her mother. She was happy with her job, happy with her friends, happy with her life.

Until Reagan Bryant walked into it.

And then walked right back out.

Who would have thought she'd miss her so?

CHAPTER THIRTY-EIGHT

Reagan walked along the beach, her eyes scanning the water, absently watching the surfers that were scattered about. It was another gloriously sunny day, and even on a Thursday, the beach was alive with people.

Two weeks had turned into nearly six and she found she loved the funky vibe of Ocean Beach. There was a diverse and eclectic group of people who lived there and most of them embraced their inner hippie. People-watching had become a new favorite pastime and she had to admit, there were several occasions where she'd reached for her camera, wanting to capture the moment.

Like now, for instance. The young girl in the tie-dyed T-shirt with bright red shorts to match, dancing with no less than four hula hoops as the waves lapped at her ankles. Or the pier itself, which stretched far out into the ocean, low tide making it appear much larger than it was. It would be crawling with people soon as sunset approached. She let her gaze follow the length of it, imagining the scene as the sun fell into the ocean. Yes, she nearly itched to hold her camera.

Like she had yesterday when she and Gillian had walked over to Newport Avenue in the early evening for the local farmers market. It was an overload to her senses with all the fresh, colorful produce, but it seemed more like a festival than a farmers market. Vendors were selling arts and crafts, T-shirts and tie-dyed hats, crystals, jellies and jams, and there were more food booths than she could count. The place was rocking, including a live band that entertained the crowd. They ended up getting fish tacos and tamales from one of the food stands and eating while they listened to the music. By the time they got home, Reagan was feeling energized and, surprisingly, more like her old self.

Of course, she knew simply being here in Ocean Beach wasn't the sole reason for the change in her. Gillian had convinced her to see a therapist. Twice a week for the last four, she'd slowly gone from being detached and evasive with Dr. Reynolds to finally opening up and sharing the still-vivid images in her mind with her. Dr. Reynolds never once suggested she view the actual images on her camera though. Quite the opposite. She didn't think it would serve any purpose to see them, she'd said. For that, Reagan was thankful.

So now, as she walked the beach alone, she knew it was time to pick up her camera again. It was time to put the past behind her. She'd tossed around a few ideas of what she could do, but she hadn't settled on one. She did know, however, what she would *not* do. And that was going back to what she had been doing. Ten years was a little early for burnout, as Gillian had suggested, but she knew she was done with it. Being away from it for over two months now, she realized how depressing her life had been. She no longer wanted to see death and destruction. She wanted to see beautiful things...like the sunset off the pier in Ocean Beach. Like a snowcapped mountain peak surrounded by blue. Like a rainbow over the forest after a summer rain. She wanted to see bright colors...greens and reds and blues. For so long, her colors had been brown and gray, black and white. Even the clothes she wore...drab and colorless, anything to blend in and not bring attention to herself. That was her job. Fade into the background where no one would notice her...that's how you got the best shots. That's how you got the *real* shots.

Yeah, she'd faded into the background so much, she almost forgot she was there. Like when Richard was killed. It was almost like she wasn't really there.

But she was. And she didn't ever want to be there again.

CHAPTER THIRTY-NINE

"Okay, so you're in a mood."

Shelby rolled her eyes. "Just because I don't like the kitchen design, I'm in a mood?"

"I told you, there is limited space to work with."

"I know that."

Stephanie threw up her hands. "You want me to cram twelve hundred square feet into a space that is seven hundred. Make up your mind already."

"Now who's in a mood?"

"Look, let's just take the room next to your suite and be done with it."

"I don't need anything that big," she said.

"If you're going to live there full-time, why be cramped? That way you can have a full-sized kitchen and an extra-large bathroom. And a dedicated office."

Shelby sighed and sank down in her office chair. At first, she'd been excited about redoing her suite. Stephanie's enthusiasm over getting to design it had been infectious. But she'd balked at tearing down the wall between her suite and the next room, even if it did make sense. Her father had said to do whatever she wanted. But somewhere in the last few weeks she'd lost her drive. Maybe it was the stress over the whole thing. Even though her mother knew nothing of the plan to dissolve the corporate office here in Denver, she did know of the impending divorce. That, as expected, had been a disaster. She had been distraught and inconsolable. And then she got angry. When she realized he had no intention of backing down, she resorted to acting like a lovesick teenager trying to make him stay. It was pathetic to watch. Had she not known that her parents hadn't shared a bedroom in years, she might have felt sorry for her mother. As it was, it was simply pitiful to see her act that way.

"Well?"

She glanced over at Stephanie, who was watching her. Even though Stephanie had shouldered the brunt of their mother's angst, she still had that newlywed glow about her. She smiled quickly.

"Okay. Take the wall out."

Stephanie did a fist pump. "Yes!"

"But remember…my taste and your taste are not the same," she said.

"Oh, I know. You're boring. I'll tone it down for you," she teased.

"And I want the island in the kitchen."

"I know, I know. But if I were you, I'd take advantage of the restaurant and do room service every night."

"Cooking relaxes me," she said.

"Speaking of that…you've been a little testy lately. What's going on?"

"Testy? Oh, gee, I don't know. Our parents are getting a divorce and I'm moving to Estes Park."

"I still can't believe it," Stephanie said.

"The divorce? Or my move?"

"Both. I'm going to miss seeing you every day."

"I know. It'll be a change."

"For us too. But I'm happy that Dad is trusting me to find new office space here," Stephanie said as she sat down across from her. "I'm still shocked about Dad's mistress."

"Why? We both suspected he was having an affair. And he did tell me they weren't sleeping together."

"And she's sixty-two?" Stephanie shook her head. "I would have thought he'd go for a younger woman," Stephanie said.

"I had visions of her being in her twenties," she said with a laugh. But her smile faded. "Does Mother know about her yet?"

"She hasn't said anything to me. But Shelby, I really feel sorry for her. She's devastated."

"She'll still have her big house, she'll still have her money. She'll still have her bridge club and friends," she said. "I mean, what's really going to change for her? He spent so much time in Aspen as it was, she had to have seen this coming."

"I know."

"And it's not like she's the first one in her group of friends to get divorced," she reminded her.

"I think she's worried that they're all gossiping about her."

"You mean like she did when Barbara House got divorced?"

Stephanie laughed. "Yeah, like that." She paused. "So what's been going on with you?"

Shelby frowned. "What do you mean?"

"You've been a little...I don't know...quiet." She shrugged. "Everything okay?"

"Yes. Fine."

Stephanie leaned forward. "Have you talked to Reagan lately?"

Shelby shook her head. "No...not since the wedding."

"Really? I thought maybe you guys hit it off. You certainly looked like you did with all that dancing," she teased.

"We...we became friends," she said cautiously. "But I've not spoken to her. She had some things to work through."

"Oh, God...I know. The bomb! Can you believe that?"

"She told Josh?"

Stephanie shook her head. "No. Told her mother. Then she took off for San Diego. As far as I know, no one's talked to her since. That's why I thought maybe you had."

Shelby stood up quickly and frowned. "No one's talked to her in over two months? Aren't they worried about her?" She tried to keep emotion out of her voice but feared she failed. God, why hadn't she just called her already?

"I think they're used to her being away," Stephanie said as she watched her. "So why haven't you called her?"

Shelby sat down again. "I don't know, really. She...she needed some time, like I said. I assumed she would call me if she wanted to talk," she said. Which was the truth. But when Reagan didn't call...well, each day that passed made it seem like a lifetime ago that they had been lovers.

Stephanie raised an eyebrow. "Just how involved were you two?"

Shelby kept her expression even. "Not involved. I told you, we became friends."

"And?"

"And what?"

Stephanie threw up her hands. "God, you're so difficult," she said. "Why must it be a big secret?"

Shelby stared at her. Yes, why was she keeping it a secret? She sighed. "Okay, so maybe we...we bonded a little," she said evasively.

"Bonded?"

She rolled her eyes. "Okay...so we slept together. Is that what you want to hear?"

Stephanie laughed. "Was that so hard to say? And I already knew that."

"How did you know?"

"Josh and his mother both went to her room very early on two occasions and she was not there."

"That hardly implies that she was in *my* room."

"Plus you were both acting strange."

Shelby waved a hand in the air. "Doesn't matter anyway. I've not heard from her."

"So again...why haven't you called her?"

"I told you, I was trying to give her some space." She ran her fingers through her hair. "Honestly, Steph, after the wedding, I invited her here. I told her she could stay with me for a while until she figured out what she was going to do."

Stephanie pointed her finger at her. "I *knew* you liked her."

"We're not in high school, you know. I was just giving her an option because she didn't know what she was going to do," she said, knowing it was a lie. Truth was, she knew she would miss Reagan and had hoped to spend more time with her. She met Stephanie's gaze. "She turned me down."

The smile left Stephanie's face. "I'm sorry. But maybe she really did need to get away. I mean, her mother said she was shouldering some of the blame for her friend's death."

Shelby nodded. "She was."

"So call her. See if she's okay."

"It's too late. Too many weeks have passed," she said. "It would be weird to call now. And if she wanted to keep in touch with me, she would have called." That was the truth and she knew it. Which meant that Reagan didn't want to keep in touch. They'd had a brief affair, that's all. That was evident by Reagan's silence. Of course, couldn't the same be said of her? She'd not reached out to Reagan. Was Reagan thinking the same thing of her?

"You're being stubborn. You never let anyone get close to you, Shelby. I think Reagan would be good for you. And I think you'd be good for Reagan."

She stared at her. "What is it that you're expecting from this?"

Stephanie's expression turned serious. "I'd hoped that you'd fallen in love."

"In *love*? Stephanie, I knew her for all of twelve days. And I'll remind you again, you told me she wasn't my type."

"And you told me that I had no idea what your type was." She leaned closer. "Shelby, I saw the two of you together. When you looked at each other, there was something there."

"Don't be ridiculous," she scoffed. "We became friends, we enjoyed each other's company, that's it." When Stephanie would have commented, she held her hand up. "Enough about Reagan. Don't you have contractors to line up for this remodeling of my suite?"

Stephanie stood up with a sigh. "Yes, I do." She paused. "If you need to talk…"

Shelby smiled quickly. "I think we just did."

CHAPTER FORTY

Reagan had to admit that it was beautiful...and she also had to admit that she knew nothing about shooting a waterfall. Oh, she had some shots. Thirty or forty, maybe fifty. All amateurish at best.

Perhaps Gillian had been right. After ten years of people being her subjects, moving to nature and landscape photography would not be seamless. She was also twelve years removed from the last photography class she'd taken.

She moved away from the tripod and glanced up into the sky. The sun was trying to peek through the clouds even though the forecast had promised an overcast day with misty rain. Photography class or not, she knew water and bright light did not mix well. It was a chilly Wednesday morning in early March and she had the waterfall all to herself, even though it was an easy drive from Portland.

Gillian had hooked her up with an assignment—a calendar featuring the waterfalls of the Colombia River Gorge in Oregon. Gillian had also given her some pointers for aperture settings and shutter speeds. It seemed simple enough at the time. But once she'd gotten out here—and had been overwhelmed by the lush greenness of it all—she realized just how far out of her element she was. She was used to capturing people's faces, their expressions. She was used to capturing the rubble of collapsed buildings as people sifted through it, looking for possessions… or worse, loved ones. She was used to the ugliness of war…and all that it entailed.

Not this. Not this nearly pristine scene of deep green swallowing up a raging waterfall. She stepped away from her camera, taking in the sights around her. Wet moss clung to rocks and water seemed to be seeping out from everywhere. There were so many different shades of green it nearly made her dizzy. But her eyes were drawn to the waterfall—Horsetail Falls—where the water plunged a hundred and seventy-five feet. Her plan had been to shoot here, then take the trail up— and behind—the upper falls. The trail to this point had been steep in places and very wet. She imagined it only got worse the higher up it went.

Sunlight flittered through the trees, and she looked up, finding a patch of deep blue as the clouds parted. She stared at the sky, unable to pull away, even after the clouds closed up again, hiding it.

An involuntary smile lit her face. It was the color of Shelby's eyes. She would forever associate the deep blue sky with Shelby, she realized. As she'd told her that last night…she'd been in a dark place. Shelby had brought her out into the light, had chased away some of her demons—at least for a little while.

And she missed her.

She wished she'd called her back in December when she'd first gotten to San Diego. But she kept putting it off, telling herself that Shelby had probably already forgotten about her. She was back in Denver, back in her life. And anyway, as she'd told her mother, Shelby was out of her league. Oh, they'd had fun. And sure, Shelby had invited her to Denver. But she had a nagging feeling that the offer was only made in passing.

Her eyes moved back to the waterfall, following the endless flow absently, her thoughts still on Shelby. She would call her after all, she decided. If nothing else, just to let her know that she'd picked up her camera again. She hadn't looked at any of her last shots, taking her therapist's advice. Gillian had offered to go through them, but Reagan had said no. She simply downloaded them to a file and stored it away. Maybe someday she'd take a look at them. Not now. Not anytime soon. But she thought Shelby would want to know that, at least.

She took a deep breath, then let out a long sigh. She suddenly felt very lonely. She didn't know a soul in Oregon. She didn't know what the hell she was trying to do by shooting waterfalls either. She reached for her camera and quickly removed it from the tripod. That, at least, felt natural. She was folding up the tripod when she heard a sound behind her. She turned, smiling as two squirrels scuffled under a tree not far from her. Instinct brought her camera up and she was shooting away without thinking.

This...this was normal. Capturing movement, capturing expressions. Not of people, no. She laughed as the squirrels scurried away. Not people, no. Squirrels, of all things.

The clouds parted again and again she caught a glimpse of blue. Words Shelby had said to her once popped into her mind.

"If I were a photographer, wildlife would be my subject."

She glanced to where the squirrels had been, then back to the waterfall. It was beautiful. It was powerful. But it wasn't calling to her. She knew right then and there that taking this assignment had been a mistake.

"So maybe I'll chase after some wildlife," she murmured with a half smile.

CHAPTER FORTY-ONE

"So...you like it?"

Shelby stared at what once was her modest suite. Even though Stephanie had kept her updated on the progress and had shown her pictures of the remodel, she still wasn't prepared for the change. The full-size kitchen had everything she wanted.

"Well?" Stephanie asked again.

Shelby turned to her. "It's...huge." She smiled. "But I love it. You did a great job."

Stephanie's face lit up. "Thanks." She grabbed her hand. "Let me show you the bedroom. Oh, but first, your office. You're going to love it."

Shelby stopped in the doorway of her new office. The back wall was all windows, facing west. The view of the mountains was breathtaking. She glanced over at Stephanie. "How do you expect me to get any work done?"

"I take it you like the view?"

She walked fully into the room, pausing to run her hand across the smooth surface of the desk before moving closer to the windows. Snow still clung to the upper peaks, but the mountains were splashed with sunshine this time of day. The aspens had budded out, their yellowish-green a nice contrast with the darker colors of the spruce, fir and pine trees on the mountainside. Spring was right outside her windows, making her anxious to get out there.

She turned around. "When will it be ready?"

"We can move the rest of your furniture this week," she said. "There are just a few odds and ends to do. Ceiling fan in the bedroom, for instance." She motioned down the hall. "Come take a look."

The bedroom was much larger than her old one, and it, too, faced west. She walked inside, trying to picture where the bed would go.

"It's bigger than you wanted, I know," Stephanie said. "But if we made the bathroom any bigger, it would be obscene, especially with the Jacuzzi tub—which is fabulous, by the way."

She walked toward the master bathroom. "What about a larger closet?"

Stephanie looked at her skeptically. "It's already huge. And I've seen your wardrobe. You won't fill half of it."

That much was true, she admitted. And without having a corporate office to go into every day, she doubted her business suits would get much wear. As she went into the bathroom, her eyes widened.

"Oh, my God! It *is* obscene," she said.

Stephanie brushed past her. "TV in the mirror. I love that part." She turned a circle, motioning in both directions. "Kind of a hers and hers design," she said. "Two toilets, two separate vanities."

Shelby raised her eyebrows. "Was that really necessary?"

"Just planning for the future," Stephanie said with a wink. "Because we had the room, I made the walk-in shower bigger than you requested," she said, motioning to the shower. "You can fit six people in there easily."

"Great. That'll come in handy for all those orgies I have," she said dryly.

Stephanie ignored her as she walked over to the corner and the Jacuzzi tub. "I know the window is not that big, but it's all the wall space I could spare."

The tub had been an afterthought. She was mainly a shower person, always had been. But ever since the spa day with Reagan, she'd looked at Jacuzzi tubs differently. She stared at it now, picturing herself using it, relaxing after a long day—a glass of wine, a view of the mountains. She looked at the opposite end, imagining Reagan joining her. She turned away quickly. More than four months had passed since the wedding. Why would she think it would be Reagan she'd share a bath with?

"What's wrong? You don't like it?"

Shelby forced a smile to her face. "No. I love it. Really."

Stephanie's face dropped. "It's too much, isn't it? I just thought—"

Shelby held her hand up, stopping Stephanie's apology. "No. I really do love it." She widened her smile. "I'll probably spend all of my time in here taking bubble baths."

"Well, I hope you'll spend most of your time in the kitchen since you were so adamant about that," Stephanie said.

"Yes, I'm going to love the kitchen. Thank you," she said as they left the bedroom.

"Better you than me," Stephanie said. "I've never enjoyed cooking. I'm glad Josh does or we'd starve to death," she said with a laugh.

"You've spent a lot of time up here. Has he been okay with that?"

She grinned. "Absence makes for great sex."

Shelby held her hand up. "Please. I do *not* need to hear about your love life."

Stephanie linked arms with her as they went back into the living area. "Married life is really, really nice," she said. "I hope you get to experience it someday."

"Well, if I ever meet my Princess Charming, I'll snatch her up," she said good-naturedly. "Until then, I'll take your word for it."

"Yeah, but I think you have to actually date in order to meet her. You, my beautiful sister, have done none of that." Stephanie looked at her with raised eyebrows. "The last date you've been on was before my wedding."

"Keeping tabs, are you?"

"Yes. It's going on five months. What's going on?"

She shook her head. "Nothing. I've been busy, as you know."

Stephanie's expression softened. "Why don't you call her?"

Shelby didn't pretend not to know who she was talking about. "Has Josh heard from her?"

She nodded. "Yes. She was evasive though. Told him she had a long road trip planned and not to worry about her."

Shelby frowned. "What does that mean?"

Stephanie shrugged. "Don't know. But he said she sounded like her old self."

"Good. Maybe time away was what she needed."

"But you still have no intention of calling her?"

"What for? Like you said, it's going on five months." She walked away from her, trying to sound as nonchalant as she could. "We had a little fling, Steph, that's it. Don't start thinking it's some fairy tale or something. It's not."

"But you were so cute together. Have you seen the wedding pictures?"

"I have," she said, although she'd purposely skipped over the ones with her and Reagan in them. "And we were cute because we were wearing matching colors."

Stephanie stared at her. "I think you both fell a little bit in love."

Shelby laughed, although it sounded forced to her ears. "Don't be ridiculous. You don't fall in love in twelve days. In lust, maybe, but not love."

"So the sex was good?" Stephanie asked, her voice dropping to a near whisper.

"I don't want to hear about your sex life...you don't get to hear about mine," she said.

Stephanie's laughter rang out. "If she's anything like Josh... ooh, la la."

Shelby laughed too. "Enough. Back to all this," she said, waving her hand at the room. "Can I be in by next weekend?"

"Yes. I'll line up the movers."

She took another look around at what was soon to become her new home. Bigger than even her current apartment, it no longer resembled the small suite she'd called her own for the last few years. She was suddenly very anxious to move here. Spring was in the air and summer would be right behind it. She had a wonderful view out of her office and bedroom windows. She was only a short drive from the national park. She would have endless biking and hiking trails at her disposal. It would be perfect. And in time, she'd meet more of the locals and make new friends. It would be a good move. She was feeling stagnant in Denver as it was.

Yes, it would be a good move. She needed a change, she decided. Maybe that would chase her blue mood away...a blue mood that had followed her since Christmas.

CHAPTER FORTY-TWO

The place was a mess, but she didn't care. Boxes were stacked in the kitchen and those were the third ones she tackled. Her bedroom was set up and her bathroom boxes were unpacked enough for her to manage a shower, at least, but the boxes in the kitchen had to go. She refused to order room service for a second night. Of course, unpacking boxes wouldn't fill her fridge and pantry.

She should have taken Stephanie up on her offer to help her unpack. But it was Friday, and she knew Stephanie hadn't been home much this week. She'd waved her offer away and told her to go home to Josh and enjoy the weekend.

Which is what she planned to do. The weather was perfect for late May and she wanted to get out to Bear Lake and take in a hike in the morning. Most of the elk had probably already moved up to the higher elevations, following the snow melt, but maybe she'd find a herd still milling around.

She opened up a large box, pulling out her old cast-iron wok. It was well seasoned, but she couldn't recall the last time she'd used it. She made a mental note to plan a stir-fry for dinner next week as she tucked it into a drawer. She unpacked the boxes methodically, putting her most used items within easy reach. However, she lost interest in her task with four boxes done and three more still to go.

She leaned against the island, surveying the mess around her. It suddenly became too daunting of a task to finish.

"Nothing wrong with room service," she murmured with a sigh.

With that, she grabbed her key and wallet and headed to the door. Maybe a trip to the grocery store would restore her good mood. She'd never minded grocery shopping. In fact, she found it relaxing.

But once she got downstairs, she glanced toward the bar, seeing Zach behind the counter, stacking shot glasses. She glanced at her watch. It was nearly five. Perhaps the grocery store could wait.

Zach gave her a smile as she sat down at the bar. "Hey, Shelby. I heard you were moving in this weekend."

"Yes. I'm in the process of unpacking. It couldn't hold my interest any longer though," she said.

He nodded in understanding. "You want a beer or something?"

She tapped the bar top with her fingers. "Gin and tonic," she said finally.

He raised an eyebrow. "That rough of a day? You haven't ordered one of those since the wedding," he said as he filled a glass with ice.

"I don't know. I'm just feeling kinda…well, I don't know," she said with a forced smile. "I'm hoping to get out into the park tomorrow for a hike. I hope that'll brighten my mood."

He glanced behind her as a group of four guys came in. She watched them in the reflection of the mirror behind the bar, thinking they barely looked old enough to drink. Zach must have read her mind.

"Don't worry. I'll card them," he said as he placed her drink in front of her.

When he went over to their table, she wondered if he would start treating her more like a boss rather than in the friendly, teasing manner he usually did. She hoped not. She liked Zach, and she hoped he continued to view only Bruce as the manager. As much as her father wanted her to take the reins, for the time being, she'd let Bruce run things as he'd been doing. He was even-keeled and his employees liked him. She didn't want to rock the boat.

She took a sip of her gin and tonic, then looked up as she saw movement in the mirror. She nearly dropped her drink. Was she seeing a ghost? As their eyes held in the mirror, she knew that this was no ghost. Reagan looked the same. Except for her eyes. There was not even a trace of the sad, haunted look that she remembered.

"Is this seat taken?"

Shelby turned, noting the smile playing around Reagan's mouth. She raised an eyebrow. "You look familiar. Don't I know you from somewhere?"

A half smile lifted one corner of Reagan's mouth. "Yeah. You know, it was Christmas, there was a wedding. I think you attacked me in a supply closet."

Shelby returned her smile. "Was that *you*?"

Reagan nodded. "I remember it like it was yesterday."

"Do you now?"

Reagan leaned closer. "Should I refresh your memory?"

"Well, it's kinda coming back to me now."

Zach walked over to them, a grin on his face. "Hey, Reagan. You want your usual?"

"Damn, Zach. It's been over six months. You still remember?"

"What can I say? I keep up with my regulars."

Reagan laughed. "Well, I think I'll just have a beer."

"Sure thing."

Reagan glanced at her drink. "Are you stressed? I believe gin and tonic was your cure for that, if I recall."

Shelby shrugged. "Well, yeah, been a little stressed. Moving does that."

Reagan nodded. "Yeah. I heard a rumor you'd moved up here."

"No rumor. True." She paused. "You spoke to Josh, I imagine."

"I asked him not to tell Stephanie."

"Why?"

It was Reagan's turn to shrug. "I thought maybe you might run and hide from me if you knew I was coming." She smiled as her beer was placed in front of her. "Thanks, Zach." Reagan took a swallow of her beer. "I'm sorry I never called you, Shelby."

"I didn't call you either."

Their eyes held. "I…I wanted to call you," Reagan said. "It was just…every day that passed, well, I thought you probably didn't…well, I doubted I even crossed your mind at all." She pulled her eyes away. "So I didn't call." She looked back at her quickly. "I thought about you a lot."

Shelby nodded. "I thought about you too." She finally gave in, moving her hand to touch Reagan's arm, letting her fingers reacquaint themselves with Reagan's skin. "You were never far from my mind, Reagan." After a gentle squeeze, she pulled her hand away. "How are you?"

"I'm good. Really good, actually."

"So San Diego was the right thing to do, I guess."

"It was just what I needed. I spent two months there, got a lot sorted out." Reagan laughed quietly. "Drank a lot of tequila," she said. "Gillian drinks it like water."

Shelby smiled at that. "And your camera?"

Reagan nodded. "Yeah. I made friends with my camera again."

"That's great." She paused. "So what are you chasing now?"

"Well, I had an assignment in Oregon, but that didn't work out."

"How so?"

"Waterfalls. I learned that I wasn't really into waterfalls," Reagan said. "I did meet a couple of squirrels that talked to me though."

"Squirrels?"

"Yeah. A friend told me once that she would shoot wildlife if she were a photographer. I thought I'd give it a try."

Shelby nodded, her face relaxing into a smile. She remembered that conversation well. "So you started with squirrels, huh?"

"Actually, I was staring at this waterfall, trying to find some inspiration and realizing that it wasn't for me. These two little guys came up behind me and were rolling around at the base of this tree. I just started shooting them. They're not people, which is what I'm used to, but they have expressions and personalities too, and I got a couple of good shots."

"That's wonderful. I'm so glad you're not going back to what you were doing."

"Me too. I'm just not sure I can make a living doing this though, but we'll see. I may have to do weddings and birthday parties on the side too," she said with a laugh.

"Glad you remembered all my advice."

"I did." Reagan paused for a moment, then turned to look at her. "So...are you dating anyone?"

Should she tell her that she'd declined every offer of a date, blind or otherwise? Should she tell her that in the back of her mind she'd been holding out hope that Reagan would pop back into her life again? Or should she play it safe and just...

"No, I'm not dating anyone," she said. "You?"

Reagan shook her head. "No. Gillian tried to set me up with someone but...well, she wasn't my type."

"That's a pity."

"Yeah. Besides, when I picture someone naked, it's always you."

Shelby laughed. "You do?"

"Of course." Reagan leaned closer. "Don't you?"

"A naked version of you may have crossed my mind a time or two," she admitted.

"That's nice to know."

Shelby smiled slightly. "So? Feel like an early dinner? Or maybe take a drive to the park?"

"Yeah. Anything," Reagan said.

"Anything?" She raised her eyebrows playfully. "Does that mean...*anything*?"

Reagan leaned closer again, her voice low. "If you're referring to how we last saw each other—I believe we were naked—then, yeah, *anything*."

She laughed delightedly. "I see you still just dive right in. No foreplay, huh?" Reagan's smile was contagious and Shelby found herself returning it.

"Don't mention foreplay," Reagan said. "You almost killed me."

Shelby let her smile fade slowly. "You know, we can go up to my room. Order room service or a pizza or something," she suggested. "You can tell me what you've been up to these last few months."

"I probably need to find someplace to stay first. Rooms here are out of my budget, I'm afraid."

Their eyes met again, and Shelby heard the unspoken question hanging between them.

"You can stay with me tonight," she said quietly.

The look in Reagan's eyes was one she knew well. She was surprised at how quickly—and easily—nearly six months faded away. It could have been just last week that they'd seen each other.

Reagan finally nodded. "Okay. I'd love to."

When Shelby smiled again, she realized it was with relief. She'd been afraid that Reagan would say no. But then, why would she say no? She still remembered the last words Reagan said to her when she'd left her suite all those months ago.

I had a good time.

Yeah…it had been a good time. In fact…the *best* time.

So why had Reagan hesitated?

CHAPTER FORTY-THREE

"So you had a close encounter with a bison?"

"A *herd* of bison," Reagan corrected as she bit into the slice of pizza. Instead of room service, they'd ordered a pizza, which had just been delivered. As soon as she opened the lid on the box, her stomach rumbled, reminding her that she'd missed lunch. She'd been in too much of a hurry to get to Estes Park—and to Shelby—to take the time for a lunch break. They were sitting on barstools at the island instead of using the small table that was shoved against one wall. "This hardly looks like the same place," she said, motioning to the kitchen.

"I know. I didn't envision it being this large, but Stephanie talked me into incorporating the unit next door. That allowed me to have a full-sized kitchen and an office," Shelby said. "Not to mention, a huge bathroom." She raised her eyebrows teasingly. "With a Jacuzzi tub."

"I think I love those. I'm fairly certain I do."

"Do you? The last time we were in one, you were rather shy, if I recall."

She reached over and stole a pepperoni off Shelby's pizza. "I was afraid of you, what can I say?"

Shelby nodded. "Yes, I think you were," she said. "So before Yellowstone, what? Canada?"

"After I left Portland—after I decided that waterfalls weren't for me—I went up to Seattle for a few days."

"Do anything fun?"

"Did a few touristy things, yeah. I've been all over the damn world, and that was my first time in Seattle. Then I headed east, into Idaho. Caught some nice weather along the Snake River, so I hung out there for about a week."

"Camping?"

"Yeah. I picked up some gear at a consignment shop. Nothing fancy and bare minimum," she said. "And I froze my ass off a couple of nights."

"I can definitely see you camping," Shelby said with a nod. "I've never been. As much as I enjoy hiking and the outdoors, it's usually done around here and I have the hotel to go back to. I never really saw the point of staying out and camping when I have a nice bed and a real bathroom right here."

"I'll have to agree with you," she said. "And I got tired of eating cold food out of cans."

"Bare minimum, meaning no cookware?"

"I had a Swiss army knife and a spoon," she said.

"Sounds adventurous."

Reagan laughed. "Not so much. But I saw some beautiful country. I think I'd like to go back in late summer, early fall. There was still snow in a lot of places."

"I know. Even though summer is right around the corner, they're still getting snow up on Timberline Road," Shelby said.

Reagan took another slice of pizza from the box. "You been to Bear Lake?"

"Not yet. I usually came up here with Stephanie to check out the progress on the suite so I didn't really get a chance to get out." She raised her eyebrows. "You game?"

Reagan nodded. "Yeah. I'd like to hike with you. Maybe we can catch some elk."

"Will you take your camera?"

Reagan grinned. "Yeah. I'd like to capture some elk. I'd like to shoot you too."

"Really?"

Reagan leaned closer. "I'd like to do a lot of things with you."

A slow smiled formed on Shelby's face. "Do any of them involve being naked in a Jacuzzi tub?"

Reagan looked into her eyes, seeing the beautiful blue that she remembered, watching as the color darkened a bit. That, too, she remembered. She leaned closer, touching Shelby's lips with her own in a brief kiss. When she pulled back, Shelby's eyes had changed yet again.

"You're going to stay with me tonight, right?"

The question was whispered quietly, and it echoed again in Reagan's mind. Should it be this easy? Could they fall back together like this as if no time had passed at all? If she stayed the night, would she ever want to leave again?

"You're hesitating," Shelby said as their fingers entwined. "Why?"

"Honestly? I'm a little afraid."

Shelby raised her eyebrows. "Of me? Still?"

Reagan met her gaze and held it. She wanted Shelby to understand what she was really afraid of. The only way to do that was to tell her. "I'm afraid if we're together...I'm afraid I'm going to fall in love with you and you're going to break my heart."

Shelby squeezed her fingers, still holding tight to her gaze. "That's funny. I was kinda thinking the same thing," she said. "Although Stephanie thinks I'm already in love with you."

"Really?" She lifted a corner of her mouth in a smile of relief. "Is that what Stephanie thinks?"

Shelby tilted her head. "So you'll stay?" she asked again.

Reagan nodded. "I think I'd love a Jacuzzi bath."

* * *

Shelby moaned as Reagan's mouth and tongue teased her nipples, first one then the other. After the Jacuzzi bath—in which Reagan wasn't shy in the least—Shelby was so sated, she was certain she'd fall into a deep sleep as soon as they got in the bed. However, Reagan had other ideas.

"You're going to be begging me," Reagan predicted as her tongue flicked lazily at her nipple.

"No doubt," she murmured. "But remember...paybacks are hell."

"I remember well," Reagan said. She pulled her mouth away from her breast. "In fact, I think you almost—"

"Quit talking already," she said.

Reagan laughed quietly, then covered her mouth with her own in a leisurely kiss. "You know what I want?"

"I hope it involves an orgasm. Mine."

"Yes, it does," Reagan said as her lips again moved to her breasts. "Roll over onto your stomach," she whispered.

Shelby moaned in anticipation and did as Reagan requested...gladly.

* * *

Reagan leaned back against the pillows and pulled Shelby into her arms. She let out a contented breath as Shelby's fingers played idly against her skin.

"Will you stay with me a while?"

"A while...tonight?" she asked.

"No." Shelby raised her head, her blue eyes still shimmering in arousal. "I mean, a while. Tomorrow...next week. A while."

Reagan let a slow smile form. "I think I could be persuaded."

Shelby sat up and rested on her elbow. Their eyes met for a moment, then Shelby leaned over and kissed her lightly on the mouth.

"I should warn you," Shelby said. "I'm going to fall in love with you. I may never let you leave."

Reagan felt her heart hammer in her chest. She nodded slightly. "I think that'd be kinda nice. I don't think anyone's been in love with me before."

"No?"

"No. Pretty sure not." She held Shelby's gaze. "I've never been in love before either."

Shelby's smile was sweet and it nearly melted Reagan's heart. "Oh, yeah? Never before?"

Reagan shook her head. "No. But it's a pretty nice feeling. You know, in a scary sort of way."

Shelby laughed quietly. "There's nothing scary about it, Reagan. Well, maybe it is. But if it is, it's scary for both of us." She paused. "I've never been in love before either."

CHAPTER FORTY-FOUR

"A Christmas wedding? You're not serious?"

"Why not? You guys did it."

Stephanie and Reagan were sitting on barstools in her kitchen, and Shelby walked up behind Reagan, looping her arms over her shoulders affectionately.

"Yeah...what's wrong with a Christmas wedding?" she asked.

Stephanie looked up at her. "Have you *forgotten* the stress of it all? You should take the advice you gave me—elope!"

"It's not like your mother will be involved," Reagan said. "She hardly speaks to me as it is."

Shelby reached for the bottle of wine that was nearly empty. "She would never plan anything extravagant for me anyway. Not unless it was a man I was marrying," she said.

Stephanie laughed. "Oh, my God! She's just waiting for something like this. You're insane to even consider it."

"Probably. But Mother won't be a problem. The last time I saw her, she said that if I had a fondness for a Bryant, perhaps I should reconsider Doug...since he's such a nice man and all."

She walked around the island to the wine rack and pulled out another bottle. "She still says stuff like that just to annoy me."

"She's mellowed quite a bit since the divorce," Stephanie said. "At least, I think she has. She's no longer wishing ill will for Beth."

Shelby shook her head. "I don't know that I'd say she's mellowed," she said as she topped off the three wineglasses.

"Well, I can't believe you two are getting married. I never thought this day would come," Stephanie said. "I'm so happy for you. When did you decide?"

Reagan laughed. "I think it was when she accosted me in the supply closet at the dance."

Stephanie laughed too. "Shelby accosted *you*? In a closet?"

"She did. She snatched me off the dance floor."

"It's because you were threatening to kiss me while we were dancing," Shelby reminded her.

"Yeah. Maybe it was when we were dancing that I decided I wanted to marry you." Reagan took her hand and let their fingers entwine. "Or maybe it was when you kissed me that first time in the car."

Shelby leaned down and kissed her now. "And maybe it was when we first met and you propositioned me in the bar."

Stephanie laughed. "I forgot that you hit on her," she said. "You didn't know who she was."

"I knew who she was," Reagan said seriously. "I knew she was the most beautiful woman in the world and I started to fall in love with her that very instant."

Shelby held her gaze for a long moment, then bent down and kissed her again. "I should have said yes."

"You two are so cute," Stephanie said. "I take full responsibility for this, you know. If I hadn't insisted that Shelby make friends with you, this wouldn't have happened."

Shelby smiled. "Yes, you can take the credit. But back to the wedding...all we want is a simple ceremony with you and Josh and our parents. No one else."

"Gee...that sounds like how my wedding plan started out," Stephanie said.

"Oh...and we want to get married in the park," Reagan said. "And it'd be really nice if there was an elk or two around."

Stephanie stared at her blankly. "An outdoor wedding? In Colorado? At Christmas? With an elk?" She shook her head slowly. "Who *does* that?"

Reagan smiled up at Shelby. "Crazy fools in love."

Bella Books, Inc.

Women. Books. Even Better Together.

P.O. Box 10543
Tallahassee, FL 32302

Phone: 800-729-4992
www.bellabooks.com

Printed in the USA
CPSIA information can be obtained
at www.ICGtesting.com
JSHW020834141123
52050JS00001B/3